THUNDER ON
THE RIGHT

MARY STEWART

MARY STEWART

THUNDER ON
THE RIGHT

HODDER AND STOUGHTON

First Published August 1957
Hodder Paperback edition 1960
Second impression 1964
Third impression 1964
Fourth impression 1966

Printed in Great Britain
for Hodder and Stoughton Ltd.,
St. Paul's House, Warwick Lane, London, E.C.4,
by Richard Clay (The Chaucer Press), Ltd.,
Bungay, Suffolk

CONTENTS

To

My Parents-in-law

FREDERICK and HESTER STEWART

CHAPTER I

ACADEMIC OVERTURE

THE Hôtel du Pimené, Gavarnie, takes its name from the great peak of the High Pyrenees in whose shadow, at early morning, it lies. Beyond the palisade of trees shading its front courtyard runs the road from Lourdes; behind the hotel and below it, in a gorge of the rock on which it is built, roars and tumbles the River Gave-de-Pau, on its way from the high corrie of the Cirque to the slow winding courses of the Low Pyrenees. The dining-room windows give on to this little gorge, so that anyone sitting at table may look straight down on to the damp slabs of the bridge that leads to the skirts of the Pic du Pimené.

At one of these windows, on a blazing fifth of July, sat Miss Jennifer Silver, aged twenty-two, eating an excellent lunch. This was not her first visit to France, and she was savouring that heady sense of rediscovery which that country wakes perpetually in her lovers. And the little dining-room, with its chattering cosmopolitan crowd, its exotic smell of good food and wine, and the staggering view from its windows, presented a cry quite astonishingly far from Oxford, which was Jennifer's home. . . . Perhaps, however, not such a very far cry after all; for, from the next table, where sat two middle-aged women, tweeded and brogued in defiance of the lovely Southern morning, came snatches of a conversation which smacked decidedly of the newer alchemy.

"My dear Miss Moon"—a morsel of *truite maison*, exquisitely cooked, waved in admonition on the end of a fork—"gravity separation of light and heavy constituents, as you know, is believed to be essential to the production of

7

such banding. That shown by these particular rocks appears to be of the rhythmic type, the small-scale rhythmic type."

"I quite agree with you, Miss Shell-Pratt." Miss Moon dug into her trout with the dogged efficiency and artistic appreciation of a bull-dozer. "Indeed, as Steinbascher and Blitzstein have it in their admirable *Einführung in die Ursprünge der Magmatiten durch Differenziationen*, the troctolites . . ."

But here the waitress, a pretty dark-haired Bordelaise without a word of English, brought the *croquettes de ris de veau à la Parmentier*, the *pommes de terre sautées*, and the *petits pois en beurre*, and Jennifer, not unnaturally, missed the remainder of this fascinating exchange. She was making again the wonderful discovery that simple greed is one of the purest of human pleasures. The food on the journey had been pleasant and adequate, but little more; this, she thought, helping down the sweetbreads with a mouthful of topaz-coloured wine, was a sufficiently promising start to a holiday somewhat oddly conceived. . . . She remembered Gillian's letter in her pocket, and the slightest of frowns crossed her face. That could wait: she had resolutely refused to worry during the three days' journey from Oxford, and she was not going to begin now that she would soon be seeing Gillian herself.

But, all the same, as the *meringue Chantilly* succeeded the sweetbreads at her table, and the hypersthene gabbros succeeded the troctolites at the next, her mind began, in spite of herself, to turn over the events which had led up to her arrival this morning in the little Pyrenean hotel.

Jennifer, whose father was the Bullen Professor of Music at Oxford (his *Sixty-eight Variations on the Fifth of the Thirty-three Variations by Beethoven on a Waltz by Diabelli* was, you will remember, the sensation of the Edinburgh Festival of 1954), had lived most of her life at Cherry Close, the lovely old house whose high-walled garden backs on to

St. Aldate's, right under the bells of Christ Church. She was an only child, but any loneliness she might have felt came to an end when she was seven, for then her half-French cousin Gillian, who lived in Northumberland, came, on the sudden death of her parents in one of the first air raids of the war, to live with the Silvers. She was with them for almost six years, a welcome answer to Mrs. Silver's problem of finding what she would have called "a suitable companion" for Jennifer. At the end of the war Gillian married one Jacques Lamartine, who had been stationed with the Free French near Oxford, and soon after left England behind for the headier climate of Bordeaux, her husband's home.

So Jennifer at thirteen was once more alone at Cherry Close. She attended, daily, a small expensive private school near her home, and was sent for a final year to an even more expensive finishing-school in Switzerland. This latter adventure beyond the walls was the only one which Mrs. Silver, with her unswerving devotion to the standards of a fading age, would have tolerated. One was "finished", one came home, one was brought out, one was suitably married . . . this had always happened in Mrs. Silver's world and she had never thought beyond it. If Jennifer herself had any ideas about her own future she never mentioned them. She had always been a quiet child, with a poised reserve that her mother mistook for shyness, and a habit of accepting life as it came, happily and with a characteristic serenity that Mrs. Silver (herself voluble and highly strung) found insipid. Mother and daughter got on very well indeed, with a deep affection founded on almost complete misunderstanding.

Professor Silver knew his daughter rather better. It was he who at length insisted (emerging briefly from a Bartokian abstraction to do so) that since she was coming home to live in Oxford she might as well pursue some form of study.

Mrs. Silver, abandoning her delightful—and, she knew, impossible—dreams of Drawing-rooms, was brought finally to agree, finding some consolation in the fact that Jennifer chose to study Art rather than one of the more unwomanly of the sciences.

So Jennifer came home again to attend Art School and live at Cherry Close. It was not to be supposed that those high walls would be left long unstormed, for Jennifer at eighteen was growing very lovely indeed. She had been a plainish child, with the promise of beauty in the fine bones of the face, and the silken texture of the straight, pale-gold hair. Now the promise had been fulfilled, and Mrs. Silver anxiously girded herself for battle against the impecunious and ineligible hordes of students with whom Professor Silver thoughtlessly filled the house. But she need not have worried. Jennifer was as unconscious of—or indifferent to—their admiration as even her mother could have wished.

That is, until she met Stephen Masefield.

He had come up a little late, having already done his National Service, and having had the ill fortune to do part of it in Korea, where he had been wounded. It was a full year after his return to an English hospital before he was reckoned fit to take up the life so brutally interrupted. He was twenty-one, and full of a bitter sense of time wasted, and power perhaps atrophied with the laming of his body. He flung himself at his music as if it were a beloved enemy, and over his spasmodic, almost savage brilliance, Professor Silver alternately nodded and swore.

From the first Stephen monopolized Jennifer. There seemed to be nothing remotely lover-like about the relationship that Mrs. Silver watched with an anxious eye; Stephen seemed to have neither the time nor the energy to waste in love-making, and the idea did not appear to have entered Jennifer's head. What none of them realized was that the serenity of Cherry Close, and the unruffled sweetness that

was Jennifer's main characteristic, were both acting on
Stephen like powerful drugs. He himself, immersed in his
all-other-excluding music, was only dimly conscious of his
need for her; Mrs. Silver, her fears allayed both by her
daughter's silence and Stephen's preoccupation, dreamed
of a more eligible future and stopped worrying.

Until the night of the last Commem. Ball, when Mrs.
Silver, hurrying down at the sound of the taxi—it would
never have occurred to her to give Jennifer a key—opened
the door upon a tableau that sent her heart down into her
fur-trimmed slippers.

There was Jennifer, a lovely ghost in silver-white, with
one foot on the bottom step, and her head turned back
towards Stephen, whose hand was on her arm, detaining
her. Mrs. Silver could not see Jennifer's face, but she
could see Stephen's, and what she saw there made her open
the door wide and gather her daughter with a pretty show
of ceremony into the lighted safety of the hallway. Stephen,
declining with rather less ceremony her invitation to come
in and drink coffee à trois, turned on his heel and walked
away down the dark street.

Next day he was gone—gone with a brilliant First in his
pocket, off to Vienna for a further two years' study, while
Mrs. Silver hurriedly re-planted the briars round her sleeping princess, and Cherry Close, emptied of Stephen's
disturbing presence, gradually sank back into its old bell-
haunted peace. Two years ago. . . .

Jennifer was brought sharply back to the present as the
waitress whisked away her empty plate. At the next table,
she could hear, the hypersthene gabbros had given way to
the olivine gabbros, the orthopyroxene to olivine and clino-
pyroxene; at her own, the *meringue Chantilly* was replaced
by grapes, peaches, and five kinds of cheese. Jennifer
sighed, shook her head in genuine regret, and asked for
coffee.

"Have it with me," suggested a voice.

She looked up in surprise. A man who, from his table in a corner remote from hers, had been steadily watching her throughout the meal, had now risen and approached.

He was perhaps some twenty-six years old, tall and brown-haired, with a thin face and sensitive mouth. His eyes were of a vivid, long-lashed hazel. There was about his movements an odd loose-jointed abruptness that seemed to hint at some intense nervous drive within, but for all that he moved well, with a certain grace that his slight limp did nothing to mar. He was a singularly attractive young man; more than that, he looked like a man who would some day matter. There was nothing of success-hunting ruthlessness in his face; the impression was due to some expression in the brllliant hazel eyes which belied the gentleness of the mouth.

Jennifer's eyes lifted, and widened on him, while a wave of colour ran up into her cheeks, and then receded, leaving her marble-pale.

She said, on a note of unbelief: "Stephen!"

He smiled down at her, and pulled out a chair. "Jenny . . . may I?" He held out his cigarette-case and if it was a trifle unsteady she was in no condition to notice.

"But—*Stephen*! What in the wide world are you doing here?"

"Holidaying. I've been here for a few days already."

"But—*here*?"

He misunderstood her deliberately. "Oh, not at this hotel. In Garvarnie. I'm lodging rather more humbly than this at the Épée de Roland, but I sometimes eat here."

She took a cigarette almost dazedly. "Stephen, what an extraordinary coincidence!"

"Isn't it?" His tone was so smooth that she glanced at him warily, to see him watching her with amusement—and something else—in his eyes.

She said uncertainly: "Well, isn't it?"

"Of course it's not. I thought it was time I saw you again, that's all. I've come straight from Oxford."

"Did Mother—did they know you were coming here?"

A smile touched his mouth. "I made it fairly clear, I think."

She said irrelevantly: "You've changed."

The smile deepened. "You mean I'm not so easily frightened away as I was?"

Colour stained her cheeks again. "No, of course not! How silly! But——"

He prompted her gently. "But?"

"I did think you might have called to say good-bye that time," she said, not looking at him.

"I did."

Her eyes lifted. "*Did* you? When?"

"Fairly early, on the morning after the ball. Your mother said you were still in bed so I had to go without seeing you. I sent you good-bye. Weren't you told?"

She shook her head without speaking, and at the bleak look that touched her face he felt anger lick through him again as it had done that morning two years ago, when he had gone impulsively back to Cherry Close, hoping for he didn't quite know what. Perhaps a short half-hour with Jennifer before his train left. . . .

But it was Mrs. Silver who came to him in the big music room, and proceeded to explain exactly why it was undesirable for him to see Jennifer that morning—or, in fact, ever again. She did it unanswerably, charmingly, cruelly . . . she dealt in the kindest possible way with his lack of means, uncertain prospects and, finally, with the undoubted instability of the musical temperament. . . . Stephen was too unhappy and too angry to appreciate the delicacy with which this last was touched on by the Professor's wife, with one hand resting gracefully on her husband's big Steinway grand, and one eye, figuratively speaking, on his study door. . . .

There was no fighting back. There was too much truth in what she was saying, and besides, Stephen was not himself fully aware of what it was he wanted. He only knew that last night the realization that he would not see Jennifer again for two years had overwhelmed him like the wave of a bitter sea. The promised years in Vienna, till then a golden dream, presented themselves all at once as years of exile, years of drifting alone on the tossing waters of uncertainty, away from the still and quiet centre of his life. Jennifer. . . . But if he was only just aware of his own feeling in the matter, he was miserably unsure of Jennifer's. The revelation last night should have been a beginning; it had come, instead, at the end. . . . So, because he had to—and because he had a train to catch—Stephen accepted the plain, killing common sense of what she said to him, went to Vienna, and wrote once a week to Jennifer—long, sprawling, conversational letters, mostly about his work—letters that an elder brother might have written, and that Mrs. Silver certainly might have read. . . .

By the end of the two years' exile there was no doubt whatsoever in Stephen's mind as to what he wanted—had to have, if he was ever to be whole and at peace again. It would have taken a dozen mother-dragons far better armed than Mrs. Silver to keep him from seeing Jennifer and making the beginning denied him two years before. But he did not even have to do battle; that had already been done by Professor Silver, to whom his wife, agitated by the news of Stephen's coming, had appealed. Stephen, once again facing a parent in the big music room, found himself dazedly listening to Professor Silver talking about his prospects in an entirely different manner. . . . There would be, it appeared, a vacancy which Professor Silver was pretty sure Stephen could fill . . . would see, in fact, that he *did* fill. . . .

Stephen came to with a jerk, and said warily: "Here, sir?"

"Undoubtedly." Professor Silver's eyes glinted. "The other place," he added, "would not be at all the kind of thing that Jennifer is used to."

And Stephen, still in a daze, had eventually found himself out in the street, with the Gavarnie address in his pocket, and the Professor's final injunctions ringing in his ears: "You need a holiday, don't you? What's against going up there? Have you enough money? Good; well, good luck. She's in London just now, with an aunt, but if I were you I'd get straight to Gavarnie and meet her there. You'll both of you stand a much better chance off the home pitch, as it were. But—go carefully, my boy. I don't think she's quite the fragile little blossom her mother thinks she is, but don't rush your fences."

So here he was, sitting in silence, watching her averted profile, and painfully conscious of the two-years' gap that must be bridged, of all the things that must be said and that he must school himself not to say—yet. And Jennifer, carefully studying the end of her cigarette, felt the silence drawing out between them, not the easy silence of companionship that used to be theirs, but a pause charged with some new and disturbing element that she did not understand. What had happened? Why had he looked angry? And—why had he come? Her heart began to beat lightly and fast, but her face was shuttered, and she gave no sign. How could she, until he spoke more clearly? And Stephen, watching her, sensing some uncertainty in her, shut down even harder on his own hopes and desires.

Impasse. . . .

Then through the silence tramped the capably shod feet of Miss Shell-Pratt and Miss Moon, as they left their table and proceeded, still talking busily, towards the lounge.

"How were they bedded?" Miss Moon's eager query rang out almost directly above Stephen's head as they passed his chair. "Horizontally or vertically?"

Miss Shell-Pratt was brusque. "Vertically, Moon, vertically. And the bedding was much disturbed. . . ."

The dining-room door clashed behind them. Stephen had swung round and was staring after them, with a bemused expression that made Jennifer begin to laugh.

"What in the wide world was *that* about?"

"Geology, Stephen, just geology! I've been listening to it the whole of lunch-time. You can have no idea of the excitements of geology!"

"So it would appear." He got to his feet. "It sounds an extraordinary science. I suppose they do it at Cambridge. Come on, Jenny, let's get out of here; I want to stand you a liqueur."

CHAPTER II

PRELUDE

THE lounge was crowded, but they found two chairs in a cool corner, and Stephen ordered drinks. Around them the conversation surged in an exciting hubbub of languages and accents. Three Frenchmen just beside them were absorbed in a passionate discussion of a recent bank robbery in Bordeaux, a party which had visited the Cirque that morning was showing off to a party which was to visit it that afternoon, two Swiss climbers were comparing experiences with a French boy, while, still at Jennifer's elbow, the troctolites were having it all their own way.

". . . Not been up to the Cirque yet? Then *don't* hire a mule from the man with——"

"—A colourless amphibole——"

"—Who murdered the bank clerk. It was the Dupré gang all right. They got Marcel Dupré, but the woman—his sister, wasn't it?—she got away——"

". . . I tell you the wretched mule tried to *trot*——"

"—Up a sheer face of four thousand feet——"

"—With a red-spotted troctolite——"

"—But they'll catch her, you mark my words . . . unless she's over the frontier already . . ."

"Thank God," said Stephen at last. "Here come the drinks."

The waiter, with a tray laden with drinks, was weaving his practised way between the tables, managing with the *expertise* of the French professional to waste no time whatever and yet appear to take a vital interest in the subjects dear to his clients' hearts. He threaded his way swiftly through the conversation, shedding the drinks as he went,

17

with a technique that bespoke much practice in this kind of inverted potato-race. . . . Pernod, messieurs? Yes, it was a disgrace, that robbery. The papers said one of the criminals had hanged himself in his cell. *Tant mieux* . . . Madame? Cinzano? Indeed yes, Paul Lescaut should keep his mule under better control. It was the grandmother of the devil, that one. . . . Messieurs? Your Dubonnet—a guide? The best was Pierre Bussac, but he was not often in the village; in fact, he had not been down with his mule since—let me see, yes, it was the night of the bad storm, three weeks ago; but if monsieur wished to arrange for a guide there was Robert Vrillac. . . . Mesdames? Vichy water . . . ah, yes, there *were* rocks hereabouts, no doubt; he had certainly been told so. . . .

He escaped with some relief to Stephen's table, and set down the benedictines with the air of one who had brought the good news to Aix against considerable opposition. Benedictine, monsieur . . . *merci*, monsieur . . . and he hoped the pictures were going well? With an air of subdued triumph he slid away.

"How in the world did he know that?" demanded Stephen.

"What did he mean?"

"Only that I mess about with water-colours as a hobby. It's rest and recruitment of the spirit, and what you'd probably call comic relief."

"I wouldn't! I might even admire them. I know all the right things to say. I never knew you sketched, Stephen!"

"I've never dared to tell you, my dear. Well, I'll await your expert judgment. . . . And meanwhile, I gather, you've come to see your cousin?"

She nodded, but a shadow touched her face, so that he said quickly: "What is it, Jenny? Is there something wrong?"

"N-no. That is, yes, Stephen. I'm worried about her."

"Would you like to tell me?"

"Yes. You never met Gillian, did you? She married Jacques the year the war was over. He had something to do with the wine trade; they had a nice house in Bordeaux—I once stayed with them there—and they were very happy. Then a few years ago Jacques died, and as there were no children and Gil was on her own in Bordeaux we rather hoped she'd come back and make her home in England. She hadn't been left very well off, either. But she wouldn't come. She seemed to have some silly ideas about being a burden to us, or something. Later we heard she'd taken a job teaching English in a local convent school. Then, last spring, she was ill—oh, not seriously; I gathered it was a kind of 'flu, not dangerous, but weakening and depressing. At any rate, she seemed to take a long time to get better. We wrote again and tried to persuade her to come to England—she'd had to give up her job—but she finally said she was coming up here, into the Pyrenees, to try and recuperate."

"Here? In Gavarnie?"

"Not exactly. She's staying at a convent in the next valley. It's called the Convent of Notre-Dame-des-Orages, and it's also an orphanage."

"I've seen it. It's in a wild little valley a few miles from here."

"Well, that's where she's staying. She wrote to tell me all about this last month, and suggested that I might come up here for a holiday. I said I would, and then I got another letter from her."

He was watching her. "And just what was wrong with that other letter?"

She said slowly: "She told me she was glad I was coming because she very much wanted to talk to me, to discuss . . ." Her voice tailed off, and she looked up at him, her eyes shadowed. "Stephen, Gillian says she's thinking of becoming a nun."

She stared at him with a sort of horror, and in spite of himself, Stephen laughed. It was apparent that to Jennifer, aged twenty-two, a convent was about as normal a habitat as the palace of the Dalai Lama.

"What a hidebound Protestant conscience!" he said. "Why shouldn't she?"

Jennifer laughed too, a little ruefully. "I know. It's silly of me. But, Stephen, that's not all that I'm unhappy about. I'm beginning to think she must have been taken ill again, up at the convent. I told you she wrote to me again. It was the night before she left for Gavarnie. Look, here's the letter. . . ."

She groped in her handbag and gave it to him.

It was dated June 12th. . . . "I'm awfully glad you're coming. I want very much to see you, and talk to you about this thing. By the time you get this I shall be at Notre-Dame-des-Orages, and, I hope, feeling a good deal better. I hope that up there I'll come a bit nearer to finding the answer . . . you know what I mean. I haven't time now, and anyway I'm not clear enough in my own mind yet, but I'll try and write more to you about it when I get up to the convent. I'm beginning to look forward to the drive up. The old car's still going strong, and we've arranged to start early tomorrow. . . . Try the Hôtel du Pimené; I believe they do you very well there, and it's reasonable. But I'll see if it's at all possible for you to stay at the convent—these places usually take guests, and it'll be pleasanter, as it's some way from Gavarnie (and much cheaper too, I expect!). I'll let you know when I write. . . ."

Stephen looked up to find Jennifer's eyes fixed on him with the same shade of anxiety in them.

"But she didn't write to me again," she said. "That's three weeks ago, and I haven't heard another word. I didn't write back, because I was waiting to hear from her by every post. I don't even know if she's arrived."

"Well," said Stephen reasonably, "I should stop worrying. Now you're here, there's an easy way of finding out."

Jennifer finished her drink and got to her feet. "I know. I'm going up to see her now."

She spoke with such determination that he looked at her quizzically. "To prise her loose?"

"Of course, if I can." She met his look, and laughed. "Why not?"

"You versus the Holy Roman Church? Why not indeed? What d'you suppose the College of Cardinals would say?"

"They can say what they like," said Jennifer calmly, picking up her handbag and making for the door. "I'm thinking of Gillian."

Stephen, with a fleeting memory of Mrs. Silver, grinned and followed her.

*   *   *

They made their way through the little village and began to climb the hillside road that winds through the valley of the Gave d'Ossoue. Behind them the houses seemed to sink and dwindle into the sunny hollow, till the coloured roofs and the church spire and the little curved bridge appeared as a huddle of small bright toys at the end of a white ribbon of road.

It was a golden afternoon. The road lifted its length before them along the hillside, the valley unfolding itself in curve after curve. The road was, to begin with, narrowly enclosed, with steep green meadows falling sharply to the stream-bed on the right, to rise again beyond the water in sheer pastures where cattle grazed with slowly-tolling bells. The valley twisted towards the south, and before them the great barrier of dim-green peaks which barred it had, miraculously, parted, and now valley and road were cupped between pine-clothed slopes soaring, rich in sunlight, towards still more distant crests of blue that brushed the sky. And these, faint with distance, etched in with snow and shadow against the long fingers of cloud that clung to them were, unbelievably, but the first ridges of the greater barriers beyond.

It did not seem so very far to the Valley of the Storms. This ran from the south, a narrow green cleft springing from the Spanish range, and its icy rush of water, the Petit Gave, tumbled into the Gave d'Ossoue some three miles above Gavarnie.

"There you are. That's the Vallée des Orages," said Stephen. "You'll see the convent as soon as you pass that bluff." He looked down at her. "Would you rather go on by yourself now?"

"Yes, please. And thank you, Stephen."

"The pleasure was mine," he said formally, and smiled. "See you tonight."

She turned off the road into the track—it was little more —that climbed the smaller valley. She walked steadily, and soon, as she rounded a curve of the track, she saw, some distance ahead of her, set back against the mountain-side to the left, the high white walls of the convent. A small square tower jutted up to catch the sunlight, vividly white against a rampart of pines beyond, and, even as Jennifer glimpsed it and guessed its nature, she heard, floating out on the thyme-laden wind, the silver sound of a bell.

She tilted her head to listen, smiling, her whole being pierced, rinsed through, tingling with a keen delight. But presently the very beauty of that pure passionless note, insisting beat by beat upon the strangeness of the place, took her with a new sensation, part pleasure and part fear, and wholly dream-like. To her, suddenly, in that high haunt of bells and tumbling waters, the mission on which she was bound seemed to lose reality. With the remote white walls of the convent, backed against that single sharp wedge of pine-wood, Gillian could have no connection. Even to think of Gillian living in Bordeaux, a French-woman among the French, had been fantastic, while to imagine her here—slim, blonde Gillian, with the Northumberland sky in her grey eyes—to imagine her here, quiet and cloistered among the Sisters of Our Lady of the Storms, was just not possible. Gillian, shut away in this lonely valley, perhaps for ever. . . .

Her steps faltered, and stopped. She found herself staring up at the distant convent walls as if they were a prison, an enchanted fortress to be stormed—the Dark Tower itself, circled by its watching hills. And she had come alone to storm it, a stranger, a resented intruder . . . alone. Alone. The very word, in this wild valley, sounded colder, thinner, more forlorn.

A little shiver touched her, and was gone like the fleeting shadow of a bird's wing. She found herself glancing round quickly, even apprehensively, an involuntary reaction that annoyed her even as she made it. The hills waited. The sun beat down steadily on the empty valley. There was no movement but the rush of the white water; no sound but the distant chiming of the bell and the thud of her own heart. . . .

The sound that had been steadily gaining on her senses through the rushing of the water was not, after all, the beating of her heart. It was a swift beat, *accelerando*, that thudded behind her, up the turf of the valley-track, bringing with it that faint crawling sense of excitement, that slow apprehensive prickling of the skin that is our inheritance from countless long-dead men to whom the sudden sound of galloping hoofs spelled danger.

The thudding grew, swelled, and burst into the open valley, as the three horses swept round the bend and came on at a gallop, manes flying, chestnut necks outstretched.

Jennifer stepped quickly off the path, but her care was unnecessary for, before the cavalcade reached the point where she had been, the leading horse, checked by his rider, swerved sharply and plunged from the track, down the steep meadow towards the stream. The two following horses, riderless, swung after him. She caught a flying glimpse of the rider, a youth of perhaps eighteen, with a supple, wiry young body, and a dark, Spanish-looking face. He sat easily in the saddle, the effortless response of his body to the horse's movement conveying a sort of fierce pleasure in the great brute's plunge down the slope. Near the bank she could see him take hold of its head to steady it, seeming, as he did so, almost to grow down into the body of the horse; the wild gallop checked, steadied, and the beast gathered itself at the stream's edge and leaped the wide rush of water. The loose horses, saddleless, and with reins knotted high on their necks, took the jump after him, and the sunlight flowed and glanced from their bodies as they flew.

Boy and horses—they were so beautiful that they made the eyes sting and the throat ache. It was like watching a faultless flight of shining arrows going into the gold. . . .

Then, with a heave of quarters and a scramble of hoofs and a rattle of stones, they were gone round a far bluff of the bare mountain.

The bell had stopped. The dust swirled and fanned and began to settle.

A peasant lad had taken his horses home from the village hiring; that was all.

Jennifer shrugged off the mountain magic, and quickened her pace up the valley.

CHAPTER III

DEMANDE ET RÉPONSE

THE convent gate, set in the high, blind white wall, was of dark wood, with an arched top and heavy wrought hinges. Jennifer, having pulled the old-fashioned bell-pull, waited in the hot silence. A grasshopper, leaping across her shadow, spread parasol wings of palest powder-blue, and the tiny lizard that flicked across the baked stone seemed part of the same enchantment that hung around her in the stillness. The smell of the pine-woods beyond the far wall of the buildings was dark and aromatic, spell-binding too in the drifts of memory it cast across the clear air.

But the rosy-cheeked girl who at length opened the gate dispelled the last wisps of magic. She was, presumably, one of the orphans housed by the good sisters; she was very young, not more than fourteen, and her solid sturdy body was clad in a dusty-blue cotton smock. Her face shone round and country-fresh as an apple, and her bare legs were brown as a nut. She grinned shyly at Jennifer, her round blue eyes curious.

Jennifer spoke in French.

"My name is Silver. Jennifer Silver. I believe I am expected: I have come to visit my cousin who is staying here —Madame Lamartine."

The effect of this simple gambit was unexpected. The smile vanished from the cheery apple-face as quickly as a shadow wipes a high-light from a pippin's cheek. The child said nothing, but hugged herself a little nearer to the edge of the gate, very much as if she would have liked to shut it there and then.

"I hope," went on Jennifer politely, "that I haven't

come at an inconvenient time? Am I allowed to come in?"

The girl, still staring round-eyed, opened her mouth as if to speak, then shut it again, and shuffled her rope-soled slippers in the dust.

Jennifer, a little taken aback, began again. "If it's convenient"—then a thought struck her, and she asked—"you are French, aren't you, not Spanish?"

The girl nodded, hovering now, it appeared, on the edge of a nervous giggle.

"Then have the goodness," said Jennifer firmly, unable to imagine why a tongue-tied child should be appointed door-keeper, "to take me to someone in authority. Take me to the Mother Superior, please."

At this, to her relief, the girl stood back and pulled the gate wider. But her eyes, still staring as if fascinated, held in them some element of uneasiness that Jennifer by no means liked. Under that childish china-blue brightness it was as if dismay lurked—yes, and some obscure horror. Something, at any rate, that was not just mere shyness and fear of strangers; something that was beginning to communicate itself to Jennifer in the faintest premonitory prickling of the spine. Something, Jennifer told herself sharply, that was being dredged up out of the depths of the subconscious, where half a hundred romantic tales had contributed to feed the secular mind with a superstitious fear of the enclosing convent walls. This, she added with some asperity, as she stepped past the staring orphan into a tiny courtyard, was not a story in the Radcliffe vein, where monastic cells and midnight terrors followed one another as the night the day, this was not a Transylvanian gorge in the dead hour of darkness. It was a small and peaceful institution, run on medieval lines perhaps, but nevertheless basking quietly in the warm sunshine of a civilized afternoon.

Nor, indeed, was the courtyard across which the orphan

now began to lead her even remotely suggestive of flagellations, of nuns walled up alive, or of the other commonplaces of fictional convent life. Heat and light beat back in tangible waves from the beaten dust of the floor, and from the white walls where hanging creepers, partly masking the glare, drooped heavily round the arched windows. The yard was unbelievably still and hot, a little well of stillness where you almost had to push through the palpable heat of the air, and, at its centre, like a symbol, the well itself stood ankle-deep in parched grass, the bucket hanging motionless, bone-dry, from the rope.

The two wings of the convent building formed the south and east walls of the courtyard, and at their junction stood the chapel, with its square tower jutting up above the roofs. The girl led the way diagonally across the yard towards this corner, where an archway gave on to a stone passage, a kind of tunnel which skirted the end of the chapel, and led straight through the south block of the building into the gardens beyond.

Inside the tunnel it was dim, and beautifully cool. Jennifer paused a moment, gratefully, as the chill of the stone poured over her like a cold breeze. To her left a shallow flight of steps led upwards into a flagged hallway; further along the tunnel a heavy door, with a bell-rope looped up beside it, suggested an entrance to the chapel. Opposite the chapel door was another which, she found later, gave on to the refectory and kitchens, with the dormitories of the orphans and lay sisters above.

Her young guide led the way quickly up the steps into the hall, which was apparently the centre of the main offices of the building. Here the sunlight met them again, but this time mitigated by the lovely traceries of stained glass, which laid its peacock train of gold and green and amethyst along the flags, to where the treads of an imposing staircase barred them.

"I suppose," began Jennifer, as her guide started in a great hurry for the stairs, "I suppose——"

But the girl, with one wide apprehensive glance at her, plunged ahead, her bare legs twinkling rapidly through the jewelled light; vermilion, amber, emerald. . . . Stop, Caution, Go, thought Jennifer wildly, thrusting Mrs. Radcliffe back into the limbo from which she was irresistibly peering once more. She hurried after her guide, the variegated light flickering over her dress, and swimming into shadow on the panelled wall of the staircase, where saint after saint peered dimly from the brown varnish of small and undoubtedly mediocre canvases. St. Sebastian, of course, abundantly transfixed by arrows; St. Teresa on a cloud, miraculously suspended; a third and dimmer figure, withdrawn into the darkness of the varnish, but still indubitably surrounded by a flock of pigeons, geese, storks, bullfinches, and what looked remarkably like a cockatoo. . . . St. Francis and his friends slid back and down the shaft of the staircase as Jennifer, chasing after her guide, emerged into a long upper corridor, abundantly lit by the afternoon glare which struck now through plain windows against a white wall and a row of light-wood doors. And here, in niches between the windows, stood the saints again, triumphantly emergent from the obscurity of their canvases, little statues brave in the brightness of red and blue and gilt, with the varied gaiety of flowers round their feet.

Mrs. Radcliffe, defeated, dwindled and faded in the superfluity of light, and Jennifer spoke with a decision that brought the scurrying orphan to a halt half-way along the corridor.

"Tell me, please"—the girl turned and faced her—"shall I be able to see my cousin today?"

But here the orphan, to Jennifer's amazement and growing exasperation, suddenly clapped her hand to her open mouth, not quite in time to stifle a shrill nervous giggle.

Over her hand the blue eyes stared with the same fixed and disconcerting look. She gulped and said nothing.

"Now look," began Jennifer. Then, as the uneasiness of the girl's demeanour communicated itself to her yet again, she said in a voice sharpening with apprehension: "Is anything wrong? Is my cousin ill? She *is* here, isn't she—Madame Lamartine?"

Then, to her embarrassment and dismay she saw that, though the child still gulped nervously into her hand, there were tears of real distress in the round blue eyes. But as Jennifer moved towards her the orphan ducked back and, turning, scoured away down the corridor as fast as she could. Her steps slithered and rattled down the staircase, receded rapidly across the flagged hall below, and were gone.

Jennifer, thus marooned in the empty corridor, stared after the child for a moment in amazement mingled with uneasiness, then, with a mental shrug, began to look about her.

The doors on her right were all closed; the saints on her left remained uniformly silent; but at the very end of the corridor's bright avenue she saw facing her another door whose carved lintel and elaborate scrolls of ironwork held a suggestion of importance. This, surely, must be the Mother Superior's room, towards which she had charged the orphan to lead her? Jennifer hesitated for a little, further oppressed now by the silence round her; it became, momently, less and less possible to walk up that length of corridor and knock boldly upon a door. The out-of-the-worldness of the place pressed heavily upon her, and she remembered all at once that from first to last the orphan had said no word. Perhaps, thought Jennifer, hovering miserably in mid-corridor, this was the sort of convent where nobody ever spoke? Trappist, that was the word. Or were Trappists always men? And could one teach——?

And here, like a hair-prickling draught on the back of the neck, came the feeling that she was being silently watched. From behind.

She turned her head over her shoulder, to meet the bright brown stare of St. Anthony, smiling down at her from his niche with its immortelles and its nest of dead candles; St. Anthony, who found that which was lost . . . there was nothing in that fixed and plaster smile which could have caused the little *frisson* of goose-flesh a moment ago. She turned further, and met the gaze of a still, black figure standing, like yet another statue, in an open doorway. But the door had been shut when she passed it a moment ago. And the eyes of this statue were alive.

So effectively had the silence and the strangeness of the place done their work that, for half a moment, Jennifer's mind failed to register the simple fact; that here at last was one of the inmates of the place who could tell her what she wanted to know. Instead, at the sudden sight of the black-robed nun standing behind her, she experienced a sharp sense of shock; that sickening contraction of the stomach muscles, the swift chilly emptying of the blood from the heart that momentarily cancels normality of reason and action. Here, in the sun-glaring corridor of the convent, one might surely expect to meet a nun, robed as this one was robed? But such had been the magic of the high valleys, the charged strangeness of the silence, and the inexplicable demeanour of the girl at the gate, that Jennifer stared at the black-habited figure before her with all the horror and apprehension that she might have accorded to a supernatural being fresh from the medieval mysteries of the Inquisition.

Then the figure spoke, and moved from its doorway, shedding as it did so its ghostly anonymity, and becoming instead a tall woman with a coolly authoritative voice.

"*Buenos dias, señorita.* The Reverend Mother is at present occupied, but perhaps you can discuss your business just as well with me? Will you please come in?"

*   *   *

The room into which Jennifer followed her bore the same evidence of poverty as did the rest of the convent. It was small and square and, beyond the scanty furnishing provided by the flat bed, single chair, chest-of-drawers, and prie-dieu, it held nothing. The floor, of scrubbed white boards, was innocent of polish, and the plain uncarved prie-dieu was placed, deliberately it seemed, so that the kneeler's gaze was turned away from the sun-drenched prospect of meadow and mountain, and directed towards a crudely carved crucifix—an effigy that made it only too plain that the cross was an instrument of torture. The odour of sanctity here, thought Jennifer, as she passed into the sterile sunlessness of the room, was too clearly the odour of sackcloth. If this was the rule that directed the Sisterhood of Our Lady of the Storms, then less and less could it be the place for Gillian.

The owner of the room closed the door softly, and turned.

Seen here, in the clear unshadowed light from the small window, her appearance seemed as Spanish as her first words had suggested. Somewhere, a score of times, Jennifer had seen those high-bred, fine-boned features, on faces gazing proudly from ruffed and jewelled canvases. The longish nose and arched nostrils, the clean angles of cheek and jawbone, the thin line of a once-passionate mouth—here was the breeding and arrogance of old Spain, starved, as it were, into submission. Only the eyes, large and dark, spoke still of what fire had been there once, and they were hooded hawk-wise, under lids no longer smooth, but crinkled and bistred like fading poppy-petals. Their once deep lustre had shallowed and flattened, so that they showed as unreadable, as expressionless, as the obsidian gaze of a sphinx.

She remained standing just inside the door, with her hands folded and hidden, traditional fashion, in the long sleeves of her robe. Robe and headdress were alike of black, unrelieved by any delicate contrast of white frill or wimple to frame the face. Over the heavy floor-length robe she wore a species of tunic reaching to the hips and girdled at the waist with a knotted cord. This medieval-looking garment (here Jennifer was reminded sharply of a seventeenth-century Spanish canvas) had a hood which completely concealed the hair and was fastened close under the chin, framing the face. Over it was a fine light veil which fell below the shoulders. All that relieved the sombre black was the small cross on her breast and the rosary hanging from her waist.

With a slight inclination of the head she indicated the single chair to Jennifer. She herself remained standing near the door.

Jennifer sat down. To her own surprise, the illogical feeling of discomfort persisted. Faced now as she was with one of the inmates of the convent, this woman who stood quietly in traditional medieval garb against the austere simplicity of white wall and unvarnished deal, she should surely have been able to dismiss her earlier tremors as absurd. Why, then, should the appearance of the woman realize rather than quell the senseless unease of the past few minutes?

Then the Spaniard's hand moved from her sleeve and came up to touch the cross at her breast, and Jennifer understood, if only with a deepening puzzlement. On one of the long white fingers glowed a big ring, an amethyst, its colour blandly feminine against the black tunic. As Jennifer's eyes, faintly shocked, followed the movement of the ring, she saw, too, that the tunic and robe gleamed with the unmistakable heavy sheen of silk. The veil was of silk, too, as fine as lawn.

. . . Now the long fingers were playing with the pectoral cross. There, too, Jennifer caught the wink of a jewel; the male glitter of a ruby answering the softer amethyst. . . . The effect was one of sombre richness, and—against that simple white background—curiously unpleasant.

"And how can I help you?" came the cool, precise voice.

Jennifer banished what must after all be only a momentary and slightly nerve-ridden impression, and introduced herself and her mission without delay.

"My name is Silver, and I'm the cousin of Madame Lamartine, who is, I understand, staying here with you. . . ."

She paused, not quite knowing why she did so. The black eyes watching her showed no expression, but the ruby on the woman's breast sparked and then dulled again. She said nothing.

Jennifer found herself going on, a little hurriedly:

"She wrote to ask me to come and see her, so I've taken a room in Gavarnie for a fortnight. I arrived this morning, and have come straight up, hoping to see her today. Is it possible, or have I come at an inconvenient time?"

She paused expectantly. For a moment the woman did not reply. Then she repeated, slowly: "You are Madame Lamartine's cousin?"

"Yes."

"She told you that you could come here and see her?"

"Yes," said Jennifer again, trying to keep the edge of impatience out of her voice.

"But you are English."

"So is she. She married a Frenchman, and her mother was French, but she's English."

"But——" The woman began to speak, then stopped short, and the heavy lids came down over her eyes, but not in time to conceal a flicker of puzzlement, and something else that Jennifer could not read. She was silent.

"Does it matter?" asked Jennifer. "Surely she mentioned the fact that I'd be coming to see her? Naturally, I assumed that I could, or she'd have written to put me off."

The other did not raise her eyes. She said slowly, almost absently: "No. No, she did not mention it. We were not aware that she had any . . . connections."

There was something so queer about the tone of the last sentence that once again Jennifer felt that curious stir of uneasiness. She said, keeping her voice pleasant and unworried: "I see. I'm sorry to have taken you unawares. But I'd be very glad to see her now that I have come. Will you take me to her, please, Sister?"

But the woman in black still stood there without response, and suddenly Jennifer's impatience and earlier uneasiness gathered and broke in a jet of apprehension. All at once it became urgent, immediate, that she should see Gillian: it was both wrong and absurd that this should be made so difficult; a convent was not a prison, and, in any case, Gillian could not possibly have taken any vows yet, so the convent rules could not bind her. Why, then, should these impalpable barriers be erected between them at every turn? Ridiculous as the suspicion appeared, she began to see, in the silence of the girl at the gate, and in the unresponsiveness of this woman, evidence of a mysteriously motivated effort to keep her away from Gillian.

She said levelly: "I know that my cousin has been ill; she wrote and told me so. If she is ill at present, I should be glad if you will tell me the truth about it. In any case, well or ill, I should like to see her. At once, please."

This, at any rate, elicited some response. The heavy lids lifted, and the expressionless eyes met hers.

"I am afraid that is not possible."

"You mean I *can't*?" Jennifer moved sharply. "Why not? She's here still, isn't she?"

Something flickered again behind the dark Spanish eyes, and, quite suddenly, Jennifer felt once more, deep inside her, the cold twist of fear.

"*Isn't* she?"

"Oh, yes," said the cool voice, "she is here. She died two weeks ago, *senorita*, and was buried in our churchyard. Shall I take you to her now?"

CHAPTER IV

THE WALK TO THE
PARADISE GARDEN

IT was in a state of merciful numbness, as yet unthawed into grief, that Jennifer, following her new guide, retraced her recent steps. Down the corridor, between the blind doors and the glaring windows, where the saints waited, dumb in their shadowed niches . . . *I have found that which was lost* . . . St. Anthony's changeless smile passed over her unheeding head; nor did she lift her eyes as she went softly down the broad staircase between yet other ranks of watchers . . . St. Francis, St. Teresa, St. Sebastian . . . whatever of consolation lay in those dim canvases went unsought; she gave them never a glance. The hall, rich still in swimming light that swarmed gold-dusty with motes of blue and scarlet and topaz, the tunnel's cool echoing passage, the chapel door . . . these flowed by like a dream, forgotten even as it passes.

And then they had left the building, and over them broke the brilliance of the blazing garden.

If poverty had been the keynote of the convent buildings, its garden was redolent of wealth. There was, even here, certain evidence of monastic austerity, in that no flowers grew for the sake of their beauty alone, but the formal beds beneath the peach trees were rich with thyme and lavender and purple rosemary, while the feet of the pear and apple trees espaliered on the surrounding walls stood deep in a silver drift of sage. A row of apricot trees lent support to a disciplined riot of vines; below it, in careful ranks, fading stems were weighted with the fabulous red of tomatoes. There was even a pair of orange trees, standing sentinel at

the end of a box-bordered path, looking, with their sym-
metrical heads hung with glossy green fruit, for all the
world like guardians of some fantastic gateway to fairy-
tale, or to the herb-garden pictured on some faded medieval
page . . . basil, vervain, borage; saffron, hyssop, juniper;
violet for heart's-ease, and blue clary and the little lemon
thyme. . . . Over all hung the scent of spices and warm
earth, and the resinous smell of the near pine-woods
mingled sleepily with the fragrance of lavender. Not a bird
sang, but the air was loud with bees.

Of none of this was Jennifer even remotely aware;
neither, it appeared, was her black-robed guide, who, for
some doubtless cogent reason of her own, passed swiftly
between the orange trees with downcast eyes, and led the
way along a path whose borders held back a tide of balsam
and drowsy poppies, towards an iron gate set in the east
wall of the garden. But before she reached it, something—
whether it was the sudden high drone of a bee passing too
near her cheek, or the flash of a lizard across the path, or the
muted plop of a ripe apricot falling among the herbs—some
small jerk at her senses recalled Jennifer to herself.

She checked her pace, and spoke. "Sister, please."

The woman turned. The white hands were hidden again,
but the ruby sparked as the sun caught it. The shadow of a
peach-tree, making patterns with the sun upon her black
habit, cast a veil across the upper part of her face.

"Please," said Jennifer, holding her with a little gesture,
"just one moment. Please tell me a—a little more about it.
It's been a bit of a shock, you see. I'd be glad if you'd tell
me—how it happened."

"What do you want to know?"

Under the circumstances, the question was sufficiently surprising, but the cool voice, no less than the woman's whole
indifferent demeanour, made it an outrage. A healthy prick
of anger stabbed through the numbness of Jennifer's grief.

She said, hotly: "Somewhat naturally, I want to know everything about it! I come here, expecting to see my cousin; I've heard nothing from her since she wrote three weeks ago asking me to come; I have the greatest difficulty in finding out anything about her—and now you tell me that she's dead, and expect that to be enough! Don't you think I have a right to know how she died, and why none of her relatives has been informed of her death?"

Throughout this outburst the other did not move, but stood listening with bent head, a humble attitude that somehow completely failed to suggest humility; Jennifer found herself, indeed, with the odd impression that the Spaniard was indulging in a species of swift and unpleasant calculation. However this was, it appeared to result in a change of attitude, for when Jennifer stopped speaking the other seemed ready enough to volunteer the information she sought; indeed, she was almost concerned to give an account so full that there would be nothing left to ask.

"She died of pneumonia, following a car accident which occurred on her way here from Bordeaux, on June the thirteenth. She drove herself up on a bad day, after a period of heavy rain. It was evening, and very stormy, when she came up the valley from Luz, and she was a little way below Gavarnie when the accident happened. It's thought that some boulders and clay above the road had been loosened by the rain; at any rate, an avalanche of stones and small rocks apparently swept the car off the road into the gorge. She——"

"One moment." Jennifer interrupted the even narrative. "What do you mean by 'it is thought', and 'it appeared'? Don't you *know* how the accident happened? If Gil—if Madame Lamartine died of pneumonia *following* the accident, surely she was able to give some account of it herself?"

"But no." The answer was emphatic. "She gave no account of it. I have said that it was a wild night; well, when the car went into the gorge, madame was bruised and shaken, but luckily escaped worse injury. There, the gorge is not deep. Nobody saw the accident. She managed to get up here, without help, but it is a long way, and in that terrible storm——" Inside the black sleeves the hands sketched a tiny gesture. "When she reached our gate she was exhausted, completely exhausted. We took her in and put her to bed, but the shock had made her ill, and by the next day she was delirious. After that, it did not take long. She died eight days later, on the Tuesday. We did what we could."

"But I don't understand—*where* did you say this happened?"

"About six kilometres below Gavarnie."

"Then why," asked Jennifer, "didn't she go to Gavarnie for help? Why did she struggle all the way up here? Didn't she go through the village? And didn't anybody see her?"

Anxiety and shock had, unconsciously, sharpened Jennifer's voice, so that the rapid questions sounded almost like an accusation, but if the other resented the tone she made no sign, keeping her eyes on the ground and her voice smooth.

"There I cannot answer you, *señorita*. Why she acted as she did I do not know. The fact remains that she did *not* go to the village for help, but came on up here, alone. It may be that the accident had dazed her, so that she could only remember enough to struggle to the place she knew she was making for; it is certain that when she reached our gates she was in the far stages of exhaustion. She was wet through, and fainting. The damage was done from which she died."

"I—see. You had the doctor from the village, of course?"

"Of course." The black eyes came up at last to meet Jennifer's, and in them, unmistakably, was anger, but she went on evenly enough: "Rest assured that we did what we could, *señorita*; we have some skill in these matters. M. le

Médecin was good enough to say that she could not have been in better hands." She paused, and then added: "Father Anselm was with her at the end. He will tell you that she died at peace."

Round them, in the quiet garden, rose the thousand healing scents of leaf and flower. Jennifer, her anger fading, felt herself touched with a sense of shame. She said, impulsively: "I'm sorry, Sister, I didn't mean to imply that you didn't look after my cousin; I'm sure everything was done that could be. You must forgive me—this has been a shock, you see; even yet, I can't really take it in. It seems impossible that Gillian——" She stopped.

A smile touched the corners of the thin mouth, and was gone. When she answered, her voice had lost its coldness, and was gentle enough. "I understand, *señorita*: believe me, I understand. This has not been easy for you. Perhaps I told you too directly; here, you see, we grow to accept the fact of death, and we do not regard it as a tragedy. It's hard for us to remember that, to you, death is only grief."

"You're perfectly right, of course," said Jennifer, "and I would have understood that if the news hadn't come so suddenly. But you see, I've come a long way, with all the excitement of expecting to see my cousin at the end of the journey. We've been so many years apart, and there's— there was so much to say. That's partly why it was—well, so shattering. If only we'd been told about it before——"

"But that was impossible. I told you she was ill, delirious. She could tell us nothing about herself or her people. If we had known there were relations we should of course have let you know, but she mentioned no one."

"Yes, of course. You said so. It was only," said Jennifer, half-apologetically, "that I thought there ought to have been some mention among her papers, my own letter, perhaps——"

"There was nothing."

The Spaniard's voice was smooth and her face had showed no change of expression, but the finality of the little sentence was as palpable as a blow. "*Nothing*," she repeated, in that flat voice that still gave the impression of over-emphasis. Almost of warning, thought Jennifer. *Keep off: keep out.* And again behind the veiled eyes came the gleam of what, this time, was discernibly calculation. The certainty that her instinct had been right—that here was something, if not wrong, at least not fully explained, assailed Jennifer with a rush. She said nothing more, but watched the shuttered face, waiting for the explanation that would wipe away the uneasiness that the interview had awaked in her. But the Spaniard made no attempt to explain anything. She smiled again, and Jennifer wondered how she could ever have seen any warmth in that arid twisting of the lips.

She turned away with cool decision towards the tall wrought-iron gate in the wall. "And now, if you would like to see your cousin's grave . . ."

Without another word, Jennifer followed her out of the garden.

CHAPTER V

MARCHE FUNÈBRE: dolente

THE graveyard was small, bounded on three sides by the same high walls, and on the fourth by the chapel, whose transept door gave directly on to the smooth turf. In the wall opposite to this another door led apparently straight out on to the mountain side, but this, unlike the entrance to the chapel, was shut, and half-hidden under a cascade of crimson rambling roses. This green close was in its own way as lovely as the garden: here, at any rate, the austere monastic hand had been withheld. Somebody had shorn the grass, it is true, and the few graves were neat and orderly, but where the wind had blown the seeds of mountain flowers across the wall they had been allowed to lie in their drifts upon the turf—crocuses, starred saxifrage, and strange tiny bells of white and yellow and germander-blue.

The silk robe swished across the grass as the Spanish woman led Jennifer towards a grave by the far wall, where morning-glories, showering their trumpets almost to the ground, served half to conceal the newly cut turf that gaped its sharp reminder of recent burial. Beside this mound, a crouched black shape was kneeling; a nun, trowel in hand. To Jennifer's raw nerves, it appeared as though she was engaged in the macabre pursuit of digging little holes in the new grave—and such was her state of mind that she would have found such an occupation hardly surprising. But even as the now familiar little worm of horror wriggled in her vitals, she saw that the nun was merely setting plants, pressing the roots firmly down, with thick capable fingers, into the holes she had made. As she heard the steps approaching her across the grass she looked up and smiled, and the sight of her pleasant old face, with its healthy red cheeks, and the blue eyes rayed round with laughter-lines, did much to restore Jennifer's balance.

Her guide said in her precise, Spanish-accented French: "This is Sister Maria Louisa. She looks after our garden for us."

The gardener sat back on her heels, shaking back the long sleeves from her sturdy forearms, and wiping her brow with the back of her hand in a frankly peasant gesture. Beside the Spaniard she looked like a stocky farm-woman, and her voice, like her gestures, pointed the contrast between them. She nodded—a gesture curiously lacking in respect—towards the speaker, grinned widely at Jennifer, and spoke with a thick Midi twang: "Bless you, child," was all she said, but it occurred to Jennifer that she meant it literally.

"Sister Maria Louisa," went on the Spaniard—and this time the patrician note in her voice sounded unmistakably—"looks after the things of the earth."

If there was a sting in this remark, Sister Louisa did not appear to notice it. She chuckled richly, and spread out her strong grubby hands as if in evidence.

"Aye, I'm the gardener. It's me that feeds their vile bodies." She twinkled at Jennifer, and added comfortably: "It's a full belly makes a blessed soul, as often as not, and there's over-much room for the devil to rattle round in when you're empty. So I till the good Lord's garden for Him, and tend His living souls—and the dead as well. . . ." Her hand patted the turfed mound.

The cool Spanish voice was quite expressionless: "Our Sister Lamartine was the cousin of mademoiselle here. Mademoiselle has come to see her grave."

The old nun looked up sharply, her eyes puckered against the sun, and for the first time appeared to notice Jennifer's face. The smile abruptly faded from her eyes, and, reaching up an earth-stained hand, she softly touched the girl's wrist.

"My poor child." At the warm compassion in her voice Jennifer suddenly felt her eyes fill with tears, and she could only stand dumbly, while the green and gold and blue of the graveyard close swam together in a haze. She saw, dimly through tears, that the Spanish woman had moved away, going silently towards the chapel entrance. Jennifer was surprised at the intensity of the relief she felt as the tall black figure vanished into the interior of the chapel.

Sister Louisa, still kneeling by the grave, put out a hand again. "Sit here by me, child," she said gently. Jennifer obeyed her without a word, and for a short time there was silence, while the nun went placidly back to her work of setting plants.

"You didn't know of her death till now?" asked the old nun at length.

Jennifer shook her head.

"I suppose you wouldn't, at that. We none of us knew she had relations; she never spoke of them. I don't know why, but we never thought she had any people." The short strong fingers touched the turf again like a caress. "This is her grave, you know."

Jennifer nodded again without speaking. The feeling of the warm springy grass beneath her was comforting, and before her eyes the small starry flowers were swimming now into focus. She put up a hand and brushed away her tears.

"You cry if you want to," said Sister Louisa. "I'm old and more than a bit silly myself, and I get a bit confused when I think about things that aren't what her ladyship calls 'of the earth', but I know what's a comfort at such times and what isn't, and it's not the least use telling you just yet that your cousin's better off where she's gone to, because you're just not going to listen, and very natural too." She pushed a small plant into place with a decisive gesture. "So you go ahead and cry. When you've finished being unhappy for yourself, then's the time you can begin to think about how lucky *she* is."

"Lucky?"

The old nun's eyes lifted for a moment. "Yes," she said. Then she picked up another plant, and began lovingly to straighten out its roots.

"They told you how it happened, child?" She jerked her head, peasant-like, towards the silent buildings.

"Yes." Jennifer found that her voice was steady enough. "She—the Sister who brought me out here—she told me."

Sister Louisa sat back on her heels. "*She* told you? Where was the Reverend Mother when you came?"

"I understood she was busy. The Sister saw me instead."

"Sister nothing," said the old nun roundly, and in tones that could only be called worldly in the extreme. "*She's* not a member of our Order—no, nor won't be either, as long as the Reverend Mother's got any say in the matter, and that's flat."

She met Jennifer's surprised look, and grinned like a slightly shamefaced elderly gnome. "Maybe I do set overmuch store by the things of the earth, at that. I'll do penance for this, but I'm naught but human, and her ladyship tries the patience, that she does. 'Sister Maria Louisa'"
—the mimicry, in the sturdy Midi accent, was irresistible, and in spite of herself Jennifer began to smile—" 'looks after the things of the earth . . .!' Holy Virgin, what does *she* do, with her silk gowns and mantillas and rings on her fingers?" She seized a plant and clapped it smartly into place. "She'd no business to see you and upset you like that. There's ways and ways of telling people bad news, and it's easy to see she's not the one to do it. I'll not deny she runs the place well—second to none—but she shouldn't try and do the Reverend Mother's job for her as well as everything else! I've said it before and I'll say it again!" She gave the plant a sharp monitory prod and then slanted

a blue eye at Jennifer. "Ah, I've made you smile, child. Much'll be forgiven me for that."

It was obvious now that it had been pointed out: the Spaniard's richly solemn black had been given the conventual air only by its setting, and by the accessories of cross and rosary. No wonder it had looked wrong, thought Jennifer, looking now at Sister Louisa's rough serge habit and cotton veil and at the wimple framing the cheerful old face with its lovely white. The cross on Sister Louisa's breast was of silver, and on her earth-grimed hand was the plain gold ring of her spiritual marriage. Her habit, as she knelt, was rucked up to reveal thick black stockings and rather appalling old shoes.

She was rattling happily on. "Yes, Doña Francisca's our bursar, and a very good one she is, with a head on her shoulders and a way with her . . . if she'd only mind her own business and——" But here Sister Louisa rather belatedly recollected herself. She went on, with the cheery malice now expunged from her voice: "She came over here in the Spanish troubles—many years ago now. Her family were something big, old as the hills and very rich, sort of near-royalty, I always understood. . . . She has a name as long as your arm, *de* something *el* something *y* something else—you know the kind of rigmarole? Well, they ran into trouble and lost everything . . . I never heard the rights of it because she's not the one to talk to such as me, but anyway she got out of Spain in some sort of after-dark way, and came to us. The Reverend Mother had known her folks, years before, and I think I heard tell that Doña Francisca's family had endowed our Order heavily a long time ago. Maybe that's why the Mother let her stay, though she'd never let her take her vows, and I heard tell she's been mad keen to do that ever since she came."

Jennifer, interested in spite of herself, asked: "And in all that time she's not—what's the phrase?—taken Orders?"

"Professed." Sister Louisa gave her singularly un-monastic chortle. "No, she hasn't. It's a queer thing, that, and of course I don't know the rights of it, but everybody says"—again that twinkling gossip's glance sideways—"everybody says the Reverend Mother won't hear of it, for all she lets her run our business affairs. No vocation. At least *that*," added Sister Louisa, punching another plant into place, "is what they *say*."

Jennifer, recalling the impression of smouldering personality that she had glimpsed behind that still patrician mask and hooded eyes, thought she could understand the obviously deliberate usurping of the Reverend Mother's position in such matters as her own interview this afternoon. And the contrived effect of the Spanish woman's costume—that was surely deliberate too? What was perhaps surprising was that such a woman should be content to stay in such a tiny and isolated place, but possibly her family connections explained that. . . . Jennifer found herself remembering suddenly that she had several times called Doña Francisca "Sister", and had not been corrected.

Sister Louisa was watching her with a shrewd blue eye. "You'll be thinking I'm a wicked old gossip, and perhaps I am. But if my chatter takes your mind off your troubles it'll do more good than harm. Are you feeling better, child?"

"Yes, thank you, Sister. I—I honestly don't think I've really taken it in yet. I don't find it awfully easy to believe that Gillian . . . I mean," said Jennifer not very coherently, "it's different when you *see* it happen yourself, isn't it?"

"I know. Doña Francisca would tell you all about it, though, didn't she?"

"As a matter of fact she told me very little—or perhaps I wasn't in a fit state to grasp everything. I know that there was an accident, and that my cousin came here in a bad storm, and fell ill and died here."

"Eh, dear, yes." The grubby hand made a quick gesture

towards the silver cross. "It was a terrible storm we had that Monday night. It's not for nothing that we call this the Valley of the Storms." She cocked an inquiring eye at Jennifer. "You're English?"

"Yes."

"With a French cousin?"

"She was English, too."

The nun turned a surprised face to her. "English? But she spoke——"

"Oh, yes." Jennifer made the explanation again. "She spoke like a Frenchwoman. Her mother was French, you see, and she herself married a Frenchman. But her father was English, and she came from the North of England."

"I see." The old nun nodded. "But it's still strange that she didn't speak of these things—not even of her husband."

"He died a while ago."

"Ah, I see. But you—did she know you were coming here?"

"Yes, indeed. She wrote herself to ask me to come. She recommended a hotel in Gavarnie, and said she would see if I could be housed for a little while here, at the convent."

"Then surely," said Sister Louisa, with another of her bright glances, "surely it's more strange still that she didn't speak of you to anyone?"

"I thought so at first," said Jennifer, "but, of course, if she was delirious with fever, she would hardly remember——"

"Well, yes, of course. But there were many times when she was lucid, too. That's why it seems so odd——"

Jennifer sat back abruptly on her heels and stared at Sister Louisa.

"You mean—she *wasn't* feverish all the time?"

"Of course not. You know how these things go; there is delirium, followed often by a period when the patient's mind is quite clear—very weak, you understand, but quite sensible. She did have times like that, so I believe."

"But," said Jennifer, "Doña Francisca gave me to understand that Gillian—my cousin—was delirious all the time, and had no chance to remember me!"

Sister Louisa's shoulders lifted in a remarkably unmonastic shrug. "As to that, I can't tell you any more, child. I didn't see your cousin myself, but I had certainly understood from Celeste——"

"Celeste?"

"One of the orphans—the eldest of them, a sweet child. She and Doña Francisca nursed your cousin."

"Doña Francisca did that?"

"Indeed yes. She's skilled at it. It was she who took her in, and she insisted on looking after her herself with Celeste to help her. We're a tiny community, you know, and though Doña Francisca may have a temper and a high-nosed Spanish way with her"—she grinned suddenly—"she's a good doctor in sickness. I can speak for that myself: I get rheumatism every winter, and she's very good to me."

"And Celeste told you that my cousin had these periods of sanity?"

"I don't know whether she said so for sure, but that's what I'd understood. In fact, that's why I'm so busy here planting these things—you know what they are, child?"

"No, what?"

"Gentians. They're bonny flowers. In the spring the grass on the grave will be blue, bluer even than those morning glories."

Jennifer stared at her. "But——"

"Oh, yes, there are gentians out now, on the mountains, I know. Look, there's some here now in this bowl. But the ones I'm setting are the spring ones. I brought them in myself so that she'd have gentians for the spring. She loved the colour, you know. Celeste told me that. That's what made me understand your cousin had been able to talk sense for a bit; she told Celeste these were her favourite flowers. She'd hardly say that in delirium, would she?"

"Hardly. But——"

"Celeste used to gather them for her, and when she died, I planned to plant them on her grave. It's a small service, but one I like to do for them. . . ." She made a little gesture towards two other flower-covered mounds. "Sister Thérèse loved pansies, you see, and old Sister Marianne always said the prettiest flower of them all was the mountain daisy. And so here are gentians for your cousin. . . ."

"I—I see. It's very sweet of you." But something—some shaken and breathless undertone in Jennifer's voice—made the old nun cock an eye at her again.

"What's the matter, child?"

Jennifer did not reply for a moment. She sat looking down at her hands, gripped tightly together in her lap, while her grief-stupefied mind struggled to assess a new and sufficiently startling idea.

Sister Louisa put down her trowel with a tiny slap. "Something's up. What is it?"

Jennifer looked up then, thrusting back the soft hair from her forehead as if by that act she could comb away the tangles of her confusion. She met the anxious old eyes levelly.

"Sister Louisa, my cousin was colour-blind."

The old woman gave her a puzzled glance, then reached half-automatically for her trowel again. She picked up another plant and began to set it in its place. "Well?"

"You understand what that means?"

"Well, of course. When I was a girl I had a friend whose brother suffered the same way. They might never have known it, but he went to work on the railway, and they soon found out and dismissed him. It was the signals, you understand—the red and green lights. He couldn't read them." She thrust the earth down round the gentian's roots. "A misfortune, child, but like all misfortunes, it concealed the hand of God. He took a job as a waiter instead, and now he has his own restaurant in Menton, and six children, and his wife is dead. Which," added Sister Louisa, slapping the earth down smartly with the trowel, "you would also count as a blessing, if you had known his wife. God rest her soul."

"Quite," said Jennifer, uncertain of the response to this gambit.

Sister Louisa passed it with a momentary twinkle. "But —your cousin, you said? I always understood that it was a thing men suffered from, not women, mademoiselle. The doctor told us that, I remember."

"Yes," said Jennifer. "It's quite true that it's usually men who are colour-blind, and the commonest kind of blindness, at that, is the kind your friend's brother had, which confuses red and green. But Gillian—my cousin— was not only colour-blind, she suffered from a very rare variation of it, tritanopia."

Sister Louisa put down her trowel again, and looked at her with deepening bewilderment.

"What?"

Jennifer had used what she imagined must be the French equivalent for the word—*la tritanopie*. She plunged on this again. "Tritanopia. It's blue-and-yellow blindness."

Sister Louisa's gaze moved to the bowl of gentians, blazing blue against the grass. Then it returned, won- deringly, to Jennifer. "You're telling me that your cousin, that Madame Lamartine——?"

Jennifer nodded. "She couldn't distinguish blue from yellow at all: as far as one knows she saw them both as varying tones of grey. In other words," she finished, "she wouldn't have known a gentian if she saw one!"

The old nun looked down at the plant she had just set on

the side of the mound. "I must have been mistaken," she said humbly. "But when I got them for her I was so sure——"

Jennifer leaned forward swiftly and touched her hand. Her face was taut.

"No, Sister! How could you be mistaken about such a simple thing—you *and* Celeste as well? You told me that Celeste often picked them for her?"

"Yes, but——"

"Who gathered these?" Jennifer indicated the bowl on the grave.

"Celeste."

"And Celeste did tell you, in so many words, that Madame Lamartine had liked the gentians, and said they were her favourite flowers?"

"Oh, yes, she said that. But, my child"—the old nun's eyes were still bewildered—"I don't understand. Why should your cousin pretend——?" She broke off, and shrugged her shoulders. "But after all, it's no great matter. This—these flowers I plant—it is only a gesture, that's all, a gesture for the living. Daisies, pansies, gentians . . . they are all one to the dead." She picked up her trowel, and returned once more to her task. Her eyes lifted briefly to Jennifer's strained face. She added, gently: "What's the matter, child? It is nothing, after all. A mistake——"

"But it can't be a mistake!" cried Jennifer. "It's such nonsense, that's what worries me! As you said, why should she pretend, and over such a silly little thing, too, when all the time——" She broke off and sat biting her underlip. Her fingers tore nervously at the short grass. "At any rate, it's—queer," she finished, and, suddenly, for some reason, found herself remembering Doña Francisca's hooded and obsidian gaze. A tiny shiver touched her out of nowhere. "Queer," she added, half to herself, "*another* thing that's queer . . ."

Sister Louisa rammed the soil round another plant with thick, capable fingers, and then wiped her hands on the grass. She said, sturdily practical once more: "I think, my child, that we're making a mystery out of nothing. And it isn't even 'queer'; if you think of it, your cousin was surely only being polite. If Celeste gathered flowers for her and brought them, of course she would say she liked them: she might even, to please the child, say they were her favourite flowers. You mark my words, it's as simple as that."

"Oh, yes," said Jennifer. "Oh, yes. Only——"

"Only?"

"If she was sufficiently mistress of herself to think of courtesies like that, she was able also to send a message to me," said Jennifer flatly. "And that, after all, was rather more important."

"Yes, yes, of course. You are right. It is odd that she didn't do that."

"*If* she did not," said Jennifer.

Across the charged little silence she met the startled gaze of the old nun squarely. She said, measuring her words: "Doña Francisca certainly gave me to understand that my cousin said nothing about me and sent no message. But then Doña Francisca also gave me to understand that my cousin had never come out of her delirium. You say the last statement isn't true. Perhaps the first isn't either."

"I—my child——" The old nun faltered and stopped. The stubby hands which she twisted together were beginning to shake. It was obvious that the pleasures of slightly malicious gossip were one thing, but this direct accusation quite another. Bewilderment and distress clouded the old eyes. "All this talk—I don't understand."

"No more do I," said Jennifer, and was momentarily surprised at the hardness of her own voice. "This girl, Celeste: is she likely to be lying?"

Inevitably, the emphasis was there, laying itself faintly on the pronoun, conjuring up on the moment the image of the other "she". It was as if the long shadow of the Spanish woman lay coldly between them across the turf.

The old nun's hands were frankly unsteady now, so too was her mouth. "Celeste? Oh, yes; oh, yes. She is a dear, good girl, a dear, good girl. *She* would never lie. . . ." Again the emphasis. The shadow stirred. "And why should she? To say that Madame Lamartine liked the gentians—it's so unimportant, that, so trivial——"

"Exactly." Jennifer looked away from the old woman's patent distress. She sat back on her heels, her eyes on the lovely tracery of the gate that barred back the spendthrift green-and-gold of the apricot trees, and spoke softly. "One does not trouble to lie, Sister, about things that don't matter."

The old nun said nothing.

"Look at it," said Jennifer, "look at it both ways. If she spoke about the gentians out of mere politeness—felt, in fact, well enough to talk about trivialities, why did she send no message to me? If, on the other hand, her liking for the flowers was genuine . . ."

Sister Louisa sat quite still. "Well, child?"

"Then she had no message to send because," said Jennifer, "she had never heard of me. She spoke no English because she didn't know any. Don't you see?"

She was kneeling upright now, facing the old nun, her hands pressed down hard on her thighs. The knuckles showed bone-white.

"Don't you see what it means?" she repeated, almost in a whisper. "It means that it wasn't my cousin Gillian!"

Across the vibrant blue of the gentians the two stared at one another.

"*In either case,*" said Jenny, "*I don't believe the woman who died could have been Gillian!*"

Deep in the convent buildings, imperatively, a bell rang.

CHAPTER VI

LES PRÉSAGES

IT was as if the sharp sound of the bell recalled them both from some confused borderland of suspicion to the sane realities of the sunlit afternoon. Sister Louisa started, with a little exclamation, and began hastily to gather her tools together. Her hands still trembled slightly, and her movements were confused and age-betraying, but with the ringing of the bell she seemed to recollect, if not the complete serenity, at least some of the dignity and poise of her vocation.

She said, with a very creditable assumption of calm reproach: "You are distressed, my child; you can't know what you are saying. It isn't possible that such a mistake——" She broke off, swallowed, and said bravely: "There'd—why there'd be no earthly reason why Doña— why anyone should lie to you."

Jennifer said nothing. She, too, had been recalled to herself, to a sharp realization of her folly in speaking like this to one of the community to which Doña Francisca—in whatever capacity—belonged. And the force of Sister Louisa's last statement could by no means be denied.

"Besides," said Sister Louisa, almost querulously, "there were papers. She had papers."

Jennifer looked up quickly. "*Had* she?"

"Yes. You must see them. They'll show you—but we won't speak about it any more," said the old nun firmly, and groped uncertainly in the grass at the foot of the grave. "Now where did I put my little fork?"

"It's here, under the roses."

"Thank you, my child. That's the lot, I think. Now I

must go. That's the bell for the children's service." She began, somewhat creakily, to rise. Jennifer got to her feet, and lent her a hand. "Thank you, my child," said Sister Louisa again, and peered sideways up at her, adding with a quiver still in her voice: "And as to what we've been saying —don't think of it again. It was wrong of me to listen, but you were in such distress—believe me, I understand how grieved and shocked you are. It came too suddenly, and you were perhaps not told the news"—she paused—"as you should have been. You'll feel different tomorrow when you've had some sleep. All these—ideas; they'll sort themselves out and disappear in the morning."

"Yes."

Sister Louisa patted her on the arm, her confidence palpably increasing. "You're upset," she said, "and unhappy, and you can't make yourself accept the fact that your cousin's dead. But you will—you really will—feel better tomorrow."

"Joy," said Jennifer in a tight little voice, "cometh in the morning?"

The old nun blinked at her, disconcerted. Then Jennifer, with a swift movement, covered the old woman's hand with her own and pressed it. "I'm sorry," she said, and smiled with an effort. "You're quite right, Sister. I was upset. I was being silly. Of course all these things can be naturally explained. Tomorrow, perhaps——"

Sister Louisa seized on the word as if it were a magic formula. "Tomorrow. Yes, tomorrow. You go back to your hotel now, child, and see you get a good meal tonight— with wine, mind you, to make you sleep—and have a good night's rest. Then if you're still worried, you come and see us again. We've nothing to hide!" She managed a ghost of her old chortle at the absurdity of this idea, and Jennifer smiled with her. "It'll be quite easy to sort out all this nonsense," said the old nun. "Doña Francisca and

Celeste will be only too glad to tell you everything they can."

The smile was wiped from Jenny's lips. She said quickly: "You won't tell them what I've been saying? I—I wasn't myself. I said some very silly things: please won't you forget them, and say no more?"

"All forgotten," said Sister Louisa stoutly. "Don't worry, child, I'll not tell." She cast a shrewd and still bothered eye at Jennifer. "If you've any more worries, you know, you ought to take them where they belong—to the Reverend Mother. You ought to see her anyway."

"Of course," said Jennifer. "Of course that's what I should do. I'll certainly go and talk to her."

"You do. Everything'll be cleared up in no time. And now I must hurry, or I shall be late for chapel." She twinkled at Jennifer in almost her old manner. "You'd think I'd be a very holy woman, wouldn't you, with the amount of kneeling I do, instead of an earthy old sinner who thinks about apples and roses a good deal more than she ought? But you'll forget anything I said that I shouldn't have said?"

Jennifer smiled and echoed: "All forgotten."

"Bless you, child. Can you find your own way out?"

"I think so, thank you."

"Then I must leave you. *Au revoir, mon enfant.*"

"*Au revoir, ma sœur.*"

The old Sister vanished through the wrought-iron gateway, and Jennifer was left alone in the graveyard.

But only for a moment, for, as she paused irresolute by the gentian-covered grave, the door in the outer wall opened without a sound, and a girl slipped through. She closed the door quietly behind her, then, as she turned, she saw Jennifer and stopped dead, her lips parted, her breast rising and falling as if she had been running. She was young, dark, and very lovely; even the faded blue cotton of

her orphan's garb could not deny the eager grace of her
body. Her hair hung loosely over her shoulders, as if the
wind of her running had tossed and ruffled it out, and her
cheeks were flushed. Her hands were full of flowers.

She hesitated for a moment, looking at Jennifer, then she
crossed the grass swiftly towards her, and knelt down by
the new grave. She pulled the fading gentians out of the
bowl, and began, rather hurriedly, to arrange the fresh ones
in their place.

"Are you Celeste?"

The girl shot her a shy upward look and nodded. Jennifer
said: "I am Madame Lamartine's cousin. I came to visit
her today, and was told of her death. Sister Louisa tells
me that you helped to nurse her. I'm very grateful to
you."

Celeste had sat back on her heels and was regarding
Jennifer with wide eyes. "Her cousin?" Her look was both
puzzled and distressed. "I—I am sorry, madame. It must
have been a great shock to find—to hear—I am so very
sorry, madame. . . ."

"Yes," said Jennifer, "it was." She was watching the
girl, but the beautiful eyes held nothing but compassion,
and a growing bewilderment. "I did not know she had a
cousin," said Celeste. "If we had known, madame, that
there were relatives——"

"You would no doubt have informed them of her illness,
or at least of her death?" said Jennifer gently.

"But of course!" cried Celeste. With a quick gesture she
pushed the hair back from her face, and stared up at
Jennifer. "Is it not strange, madame, that she should not
have told us?"

Jennifer looked at her. "Yes. Very strange. That is, if
she was not too ill to tell you, Celeste."

The girl shook her head. "There were times—several
times—when she was quite herself, when she could have

told us anything. Indeed, we asked her ourselves if there was anyone we should get in touch with."

"Did you indeed?" said Jennifer softly.

"It's usual," said Celeste, and turned back to the bowl of gentians. "And now, madame, I must go. I'm a bit late already." She pushed the last flowers into place, and got to her feet, but Jennifer put out a hand. "Just one more thing . . . I should have thanked you, too, for bringing these flowers for my cousin."

"It was nothing."

"It was a great deal, that you should have nursed her and —and comforted her." Jennifer hesitated, wondering how to go on.

The girl flushed and looked at her feet. "It was nothing," she said again. "I—I liked her." She looked up at Jennifer, and the lovely eyes were swimming with tears. "I am sorry, madame, indeed I am. And that you should have found it out—in this way——" She made a little gesture, and bit her lip.

In the face of what was, patently, quite genuine distress, Jennifer hesitated again. And in that moment someone spoke from behind her.

"Celeste!"

It was Doña Francisca's voice, and at the sound the girl started and spun round, and the red ebbed from her cheeks as the foam blows from the wave. Jennifer was conscious of a slight constriction in her own breathing as she turned her head to watch the tall black figure of the bursar approaching across the grass. Annoyed at herself, she shook her uneasiness from her, and said, calmly: "I hope I haven't made Celeste late for chapel, Doña Francisca. Sister Louisa told me how she helped you nurse my cousin, and I was thanking her."

The hooded eyes met hers briefly. The Spaniard bent her head, then turned her gaze on the girl. "You should have been in your room half an hour ago, Celeste. Where have you been?"

The girl's voice was low. "Gathering flowers for our sister Lamartine's grave." She did not look at Doña Francisca. Her hands were nervously pleating the front of her dress.

There was a flash of something that might have been irritation in the woman's eyes, but she spoke smoothly enough. "A kind thought, Celeste, but it should not have made you late. You must not let even a good impulse tempt you into neglect of what is your duty."

"No, *señora*." Celeste's face was quite pale now, and she stared miserably at the ground.

"Go at once and get ready for chapel." Doña Francisca looked blandly at Jennifer across the girl's bent head. "And come and see me immediately after your meal, Celeste."

"Yes, *señora*."

"There's just one thing——" began Jennifer. Her voice was tight and a shade over-loud, but Doña Francisca's clipped patrician command cut easily across it.

"At once, Celeste."

Jennifer's cheeks flamed, but her voice held no hint of anger as she said calmly: "If you please, *señora*. . . . Wait, Celeste!" The bursar looked considerably taken aback, and the girl hesitated even as she turned to go. It could not be very often that Doña Francisca was answered back, thought Jennifer with a certain relish. She said quickly, almost humbly: "I should like to come back tomorrow, *señora*, if I may, to visit my cousin's grave again, and say good-bye. I thought I might bring her some flowers."

Doña Francisca was watching her steadily. "Of course. When you have got over the shock you have had today, you will perhaps think of more that you wish to know from us. Ask for me when you come."

Royal permission and royal command . . . yes, I'm likely

to, thought Jennifer. Aloud, she said: "Thank you, *señora*," and then, swiftly, to Celeste: "Why did you go out just now to get these gentians? I'd have thought the rambler-roses were just as——"

But the girl stepped back a pace with a small, shrinking movement. Her face, still pale, went blank, almost stupid, and in the lovely eyes flickered the unmistakable shadow of fear. She said hurriedly: "I—I'm allowed to go. Doña Francisca knows. She said I could."

The bursar had not glanced at her. She was watching Jennifer, the dark eyes unreadable and unwavering in her still face.

She said, almost under her breath, "Go, Celeste."

The girl turned and ran into the shadow of the chapel door just as, overhead, the bell in the tower began to ring for service. Jennifer turned to meet Doña Francisca's dark intent gaze.

"I'd better go too," she said. "*Au revoir, señora.*"

"*Au revoir, mademoiselle.* And you will come tomorrow?"

"Oh, yes," said Jennifer. "I'll come tomorrow."

"*C'est bien,*" said Doña Francisca expressionlessly, as she turned to make her noiseless way across the grass after the girl. She vanished into the blackness of the chapel door.

Jennifer let herself quickly out through the wrought-iron gate into the spicy air of the garden. It shut behind her with a clang. The narrow shade of the archway dropped a band of coolness across the hot afternoon, and she paused inside it, leaning back against the bars of the gate. She found she was shaking all over; wave after wave of excitement, anger, and apprehension beat upon her mind, breaking with bewildering force across the emptiness left by the first numbing shock of grief. That had been a deadening blow; this, the reaction back towards a fearful and fantastic hope was, oddly enough, more terrible. Her whole body trembled uncontrollably; her hands clung to the bars behind her, pulling her back against the gate until the iron seemed to grow into her flesh; her heart, beating high and fast, seemed to tumble and thump anyhow through her body, now choking in her throat, now knocking against her ribs, now twisting with sickening little driving motions of pain deep in her stomach. And still she clung, her hands icy on the bruising bars. Her knees felt loose. She bit her lips to stop them from shaking, and she shut her eyes and held them shut.

And presently the tumult of mind and body began to subside. She leaned more naturally against the gate, muscle by muscle relaxing under the caress of the fragrant air. She opened her eyes and immediately, in a healing wash of warmth, the colour and scent of the garden swept up to her and engulfed her—catmint and crushed thyme, and the sharp sweet smell of apricots globed among glossy leaves; the homely friendliness of lavender and sage over whose silver leaves poppies dangled their sleep-drugged scarlet heads. A cicada, hidden in a peach-tree, purred softly. Jennifer let go of the gate, straightened up slowly, rubbing her hands together, and began, reasonably enough, to think.

And her first thought was the sufficiently overwhelming one that she had been right. What had started as pre-monition, grown through uneasiness into downright sus-picion, had flowered now, unmistakably, as fact. *There was something wrong*. Whether or not her wild hope-driven guess had been right, whether or not the business of the gentians could be explained away, the demeanour of Doña Francisca at the second interview, no less than Celeste's patent fear, showed that there was, indeed, something wrong. And she must find out what it was. That the bursar had no intention of letting her interview Celeste alone was certain: what was equally certain was Jennifer's determina-tion to do that very thing.

The chapel bell had stopped. She glanced towards the

archway that gave on to the tunnel to the courtyard. The bell-rope was looped up, and still swung slightly. The tunnel was empty. Everyone would be in chapel, and, afterwards, Doña Francisca would talk to Celeste and warn her to answer no questions. It was also possible that, forewarned as she was, the Spaniard might be able to prevent Jennifer from seeing the Reverend Mother at all tomorrow.

Jennifer bit her lips again, this time in thought. Then she made her decision. For her own peace of mind, as much as for any other reason, she must make what inquiries she could today. She would stay here, hidden in the garden, until the service was over, and then, if it were possible, she would seek out the Mother Superior straight away, and question her frankly. Quite frankly—because, said Jennifer firmly to herself, I refuse flatly to believe that the whole convent can be implicated in these lies. Sister Louisa is as honest as a daisy and as simple as God, and even Celeste seemed genuine up to a point; until, in fact, I asked her about the gentians. No, the Reverend Mother can't be in it whatever it is—that *would* be pure Mrs. Radcliffe . . . I'll see her after service, and find out what she has to say. At least she can let me see the "papers" and whatever else Gillian is said to have brought with her. . . .

The chanting from the chapel had stopped now, and the organ was weaving its way through something massive and slow, which reached the garden only in a series of vibrations surging through the ranked richnesses of herb and vine. Jennifer flattened herself once more against the gate as a shuffle of footsteps in the tunnel told of the worshippers going quietly across from the chapel to the refectory. She bent her head forward to peer through a masking vine. There were the blue-clad orphans; there were the white novices and the sombre nuns, filing across the tunnel in an orderly silence. The refectory door shut on the last nun. The watcher in the garden heard the children's voices singing grace, and then the scrape of chairs or benches as the company sat down to table.

She slipped quietly back through the gate into the grave-yard, and made her way over the grass to the chapel door. If she went through the chapel she had every chance of gaining the upper corridor without being seen, and she was sure that the big door she had noticed at the end of that corridor must be that of the Superior's room. It seemed likely that the Reverend Mother would come out of the refectory first, and once Jennifer had approached her even the ubiquitous and apparently powerful bursar could hardly prevent an interview.

What exactly she hoped to gain by that interview was by no means certain, but, in her present state of bewilderment and suspicion, any sort of plan was better than none. It was with a lifting feeling of excitement that Jennifer softly opened the chapel door and passed in out of the sunlight.

CHAPTER VII

THE JEWELS OF THE MADONNA

As she plunged from the heat of the close into the dark-censed air of the chapel, she found time to wonder, half-idly, what sort of a shrine for worship the convent's characteristic austerity would have made. The door, swinging shut behind her, lopped off its shaft of light abruptly, and for a few seconds she was blinded by the dimness. Then to her dazzled gaze the nave took shape . . . a side-aisle, with its little altar . . . the tiny transepts . . . the raised chancel . . . the high altar. . . .

She stood rooted, staring.

Basically, the chapel was the same as the rest of the convent buildings; the walls were whitewashed, the arches of doors and windows simple, the stonework plain. The pillars stood sturdy and unadorned, and the Stations of the Cross lurked, dim and inoffensive, between the windows. The only statue was a small one of Our Lady on the single side-altar. But there austerity ended. Up the length of the nave, cutting the white simplicity in two with one arrogant crimson slash, a deep-red carpet ran like a river of blood, drawing the eye swiftly on towards the chancel as the stroke on a flower's petal guides the bee straight into the gold. Past the sturdy pillars, between the plain benches, up the chancel steps, into the shadowy cave of the apse where the sanctuary-lamp glimmered above the high altar. . . .

Jennifer went quickly up the aisle and mounted the chancel steps. She paused at the low rail, beautifully carved of some dark wood, and stood, again to gaze.

It was gold, sure enough, that the crimson arrow led to; the seven-branched sanctuary-lamp was of gold, and so were the heavy twin arms of the candlesticks, but it was not these that caught and held the eye. Behind and above the high altar, away from the wall, but acting as reredos and east-window at once, was a great triptych, its three paintings heavily framed in grey and blue. And here, in the towering rush of flames and wings and the ecstasies of saints even Jennifer's half-educated eye could trace the hand of a master whose work was not commonly shrined in such places as this. Those soaring visionary gestures, the angular robes, the slashing diagonals of silver and purple and acid yellow . . . who on earth, she thought confusedly, had hidden one of the world's El Grecos in this comparative oblivion? Was there not someone—here her thoughts became, if possible, vaguer yet—were there no museums, galleries, the great churches of his own Toledo, who might stop this burying of masterpieces alive?

She pressed the palms of her hands to her eyes, and then blinked up at the picture again. Masterpiece? El Greco? It was absurd, of course. This couldn't possibly be an El Greco. Not here. It was some trick of memory, no more. But the impression persisted. Surely she could not be wrong? Of all painters, El Greco was the least mistakable. And could a copy or an imitation rouse in the onlooker that queer breathless mixture of exaltation and humility with which we find ourselves studying the best things men have made with their hands? Even as she stared at the picture, Jennifer recognized this as a fallacy; to an inexperienced eye like hers a good copy would doubtless speak as loudly of beauty as the master's own handiwork. No, she had no means of telling. But whether this was a first-rate copy, or the thing itself; it was surely sufficiently surprising to find it here in a community that elsewhere seemed to underline its poverty?

She peered at the corners of the darkening paint, in the

slender hope of some closer identification, but could see no name. Then with some confused memory of painters who marked their canvases on the back, she stepped past the altar, and peered at the back of the left-hand panel, where the side of the triptych stood clear of the wall. The frame was solidly backed, and the reverse of the canvas, in consequence, hidden. Jennifer, peering in the dim light, ran a disappointed finger down the joint of the frame. It encountered something, a paper or fragment of soft wood, sticking out between frame and backing. Pressing her head closer to the wall, and exerting her eyes in the gloom, she could just see what looked like the fraying edge of a paper whose corner was escaping from its hiding-place. She plucked at it carefully with her nails, and presently, with some excitement, drew it out.

Just what she expected to see she had no idea; if she had stopped to think she would have known how remote were the chances of finding an identifying paper tucked into a frame at least three centuries younger than the canvas. But she carried the paper to the chancel steps, where the light was better, and smoothed it out with slightly unsteady fingers. It was yellowed and dirty, and tore a little along the crease as she unfolded it. It appeared to be a letter, or part of a letter, written in French:

"—*C'est alors après avoir reçu l'assurance de notre ami mutuel que j'ai osé vous approcher.* . . ."

With rapidly dwindling interest she read on:

"—So it was with the assurance of this mutual friend that I approached you. I am relieved to hear that you are willing, and suppose it inevitable in the circumstances that you should set your terms so high. This, then, finally:—I shall come as arranged on the night of the sixth September, and

I will pay you three million francs, this being the sum
agreed upon previously.

"I note your instructions about baggage. In the circumstances they are not exactly necessary.

ISAAC LENORMAND."

That was all; a modern idiom, an unmistakably modern
hand, a signature that meant nothing. Jennifer knitted her
brows over it for a moment; should she attempt to restore
it to its hiding-place? Probably in any case, she thought,
not strictly a "hiding-place"—the letter had undoubtedly
been pushed in merely to wedge the frame, which gaped a
little at that point. It could hardly matter. But perhaps . . .

A movement, a slight sound from the dim aisle of the
Lady-chapel, set her heart unaccountably scudding. She
thrust the already-forgotten scrap of paper into her pocket,
and descended the chancel steps, annoyed that the hush and
mystery of the chapel should, apparently, have brought
back all the tremors she had been trying to put aside. She
glanced into the Lady-chapel and saw that what had alarmed
her was only a girl in a blue cotton dress, who was kneeling
at the edge of the little pool of light that bathed the Virgin's
statue; it was one of the orphans, who had crept in quietly
to pray while Jennifer had been in the chancel.

She glanced curiously at the smaller altar, to see that here
too the lavish hand had been at work, for the little statue
was finely made of bronze and ivory, and tiny jewels winked
on the hilt of the sword that pierced the Virgin's heart.
Notre-Dame-de-Douleur . . . an odd choice, surely, for a
children's chapel? Jennifer turned to hurry down the nave,
chiding herself for having wasted so much time, but as she
moved away the kneeling girl crossed herself and stood up.
It was Celeste.

Jennifer, elated at the luck which had sent the girl across
her path before the bursar had had a chance to see her,

stopped at the back of the chapel and waited. Celeste genu-flected deeply in front of the statue, then came swiftly down the aisle and turned towards the north door.

She checked when she saw the other waiting there.

"Ah, Celeste," said Jennifer, gently, "I was hoping to see you again."

"But—but mademoiselle, I thought you had gone!"

"No doubt. But I am still here, as you see. If you will be so good as to answer one or two questions——"

The uneasiness was flickering again, unmistakable, in the lovely eyes. "I don't think—I must not——" began the girl nervously.

Jennifer said, roundly: "Were you telling me the truth this afternoon, Celeste, when you said that Madame Lamartine had never once mentioned her English relatives, even when you asked her?"

The girls eyes widened. "But yes, mademoiselle! Of course! If she had told us——"

"Quite. But it seems to me quite impossible that she should not have done so, if, as you say, she was conscious and lucid at all. But if she did not—it did occur to me that there might be an explanation for this."

"Mademoiselle?"

Jenny said, directly: "Supposing she had mentioned me, and asked you—you and Doña Francisca—to write, and you had neglected to do so. Supposing——"

But Celeste, flushing scarlet, interrupted her with patent indignation.

"But she did *not* tell us! I have told you, mademoiselle—she did not! What you're suggesting is wicked! Monstrous!"

"No," said Jennifer evenly, "not wicked. Merely negligent. Enough to make you as reluctant as you apparently are to answer questions. What are you frightened of, Celeste?"

"I? Frightened? That is absurd, mademoiselle!" And indeed she looked, now, not frightened so much as angry. "Why should I be afraid of you?"

"I wondered that. And you weren't at first. It was only when I asked you why you'd gone to get the gentians."

The girl's eyes fell, once again her face went blank. She said nothing.

"Was it because you knew you'd made a mistake?"

The dark eyes lifted. "Mistake? I don't understand. What sort of mistake?"

"Never mind. But why should you mind my asking you about them?"

"I don't," said Celeste, and, surprisingly, smiled.

"Very well," said Jennifer. "Then tell me this—and I think I shall know if it's the truth: why *did* you take my cousin gentians?"

Celeste stared, perplexed. "I told you. I was—I was fond of her."

"Yes, I know. But why gentians?"

"She liked them."

"Did she say so?"

Bewilderment showed still in the girl's eyes, with, behind it, a kind of relief. As if, thought Jennifer, these, at least, were easy questions to answer.

"Yes."

"What did she say?"

Celeste lifted her hands a little, helplessly.

"Mademoiselle, I do not understand."

Jennifer was patient. "When she said she liked the gentians, what did she say? Did you bring them to her, and did she just say thank you, and how pretty they were, or what? Try to remember for me, Celeste; after all, she was my cousin, and any little thing she said—I could bring gentians too, tomorrow. . . ."

Celeste, being too young and too accustomed to the symbolic trappings of everyday convent life to see the sentimental absurdity of this, gave Jennifer a still bewildered but softer glance, and knitted her brows. Jennifer waited, her throat suddenly constricted with excitement.

"No," said the girl at length, "it was not like that. I remember how I got the idea that they were her favourite flowers. It was soon after she came. I had brought in a big bunch of flowers—all sorts—and I was putting them beside her bed. She lay watching me, and then she put out her hand—oh, so slowly"—her own hand moved out in a remembered gesture—"and touched the gentians. She said, 'The blue ones, Celeste, what are they?' I said gentians. She said, 'They are so beautiful. I never saw such a blue. Put them closer where I can see them.' So after that I brought them every day."

"Thank you," said Jennifer, on a long breath, and Celeste, seeing the look in her face, drew back with some of her former alarm.

"Is that all, mademoiselle?"

"That's all," said Jennifer, and laughed, an excited, breathless little laugh. "And please forgive me for having suggested that you were lying before!"

"It is nothing. And now, mademoiselle, if you'll excuse me——"

"Of course. You have to see Doña Francisca, haven't you?" Jennifer fought hard to keep her voice even. "Would you be good enough to show me the way to the Reverend Mother's room, please?"

"I—yes, of course." And Celeste, with a return of her old nervousness, threw Jennifer a strangely wary look as she passed her to lead the way out of the chapel.

Jennifer, following her hurrying guide across the hall and up the wide staircase, tried vainly to compose her churning thoughts into some semblance of order. What she had just listened to had certainly been the truth: the story had begun to hang together, even if, in so doing, it became more deeply a mystery. The dying woman had actually asserted that she had no relatives—and the dying woman had not been colour-blind.

She had not, in sober fact, been Gillian Lamartine.

And where, thought Jennifer, jubilant and desperate at once, as Celeste led her into the light of the upper corridor—where do we go from here? Where, in God's name, do we go from here?

For the second time that day she met the bright brown gaze of St. Anthony, staring at her over his cactus-bristle of candles. A lot of candles, a lot of answered prayers. . . .

Rejoice with me, for I have found that which was lost.

She put out a hand, and lightly touched one of the wreaths of everlastings on the saint's pedestal, then turned as her guide stopped in front of the nearest door and raised a hand to knock.

"No!" said Jennifer sharply. The girl stopped, her hand still raised.

Jennifer's face was flushed and her eyes were dark with annoyance. "I asked you to take me to the Mother Superior. That's not her room, is it?"

"Why, I——"

"That's Doña Francisca's room, isn't it?"

"Yes. I only thought——"

Jennifer's eyes and voice were cold. Mrs. Silver would have had to look twice to recognize her gentle daughter. She said: "You were asked to take me to the Mother Superior. Kindly do so at once."

Celeste's hand fell to her side. With lowered eyes she sidled past Jennifer and led her to the door at the far end of the corridor.

"This is the Reverend Mother's room, mademoiselle."

"Thank you." As the girl stood aside, Jennifer knocked. There was a gentle "Come in."

As she obeyed, she had a confused impression, behind her, of Celeste whisking away, back down the corridor. The Reverend Mother's door closed behind her. Further down the corridor, like a soft echo, another door shut, too.

CHAPTER VIII

BLUES

THE first thing that met Jennifer, as she advanced into the Mother Superior's room, was the sunlight. Through the tall undraped window it poured, and beat back in tangible waves of bright heat from the cream-washed walls and ceiling and from the white boarded floor, where a single narrow rug emphasized the fact that here, too, the rule of Spartan poverty was upheld. The two straight chairs, the plain wood table, the uncarved faldstool, bare even of a kneeling-pad, bore this out. There was nothing to mitigate the shining bareness but one plaque on the wall, a plate-shaped affair in high relief depicting the Virgin and Child. Remembering the chapel, Jennifer glanced at this with interest as she entered, then with surprise; it was a crude affair of the cheapest, a Brummagem Della Robbia, bought probably in Lourdes.

"Come in." The gentle voice spoke again from the window-seat, where, full in the sun, steeping in its rays, sat a very old nun. She did not turn her head, but gestured with one soft old hand towards a chair.

Jennifer took the chair. "I am Miss Silver, Madame Lamartine's cousin. I came up to see my cousin, and was told that she had died some days ago."

This time the old nun did turn towards her. Against the brilliant light Jennifer could not see her at all clearly, but she got the impression of a round, pale old face, softly wrinkled with age like a hand that has been in soapy water. The wrinkles were not so much the lines etched by character, as a gentle blurring of the features. The forehead under its black coif was quite smooth, and it was certain that the brows had not frowned for a very long time. The expression of the faded eyes could not be seen, but the line of the mouth was sweet.

"I heard that you had come, mademoiselle. I was sorry that you had to find such news awaiting you. It was a sad affair: it is always a sad thing for the friends of one who dies so young." She smiled. "It is not easy, I know, to regard death as a beginning rather than an end."

"No."

"You have seen your cousin's grave, child?"

"Yes, *ma mère*." She paused, wondering just how to begin asking her questions, shaken in spite of herself by the tranquil normality of the old woman's demeanour. Suspicion and uneasiness seemed very far away. . . . Age lived with kindness in this bare and pleasant room.

Mistaking the reason for her silence, the old Prioress began to talk, with gentleness but without sentiment, in a way which would have brought comfort to Jennifer had she felt herself truly bereaved, but which under the circumstances made it merely more difficult to begin her inquisition.

At length she approached the subject in what she felt to be a sufficiently roundabout way.

"I talked to Doña Francisca and Sister Louisa today," she said, "and I understand that my cousin had papers . . ."

"Certainly." The Reverend Mother spoke readily. "You must take them, of course. She managed to bring them with her, in a handbag that she tied to her wrist. Doña Francisca took charge of the baggage that was brought up later from the car, but I have the papers here."

She rose and pulled open a drawer beside her, groped in it for a moment, then turned with a flat leather handbag in her hand. This she gave to Jennifer.

"This is just as she brought it, my child. Take it with you. It's yours now."

"Thank you." Jennifer sat clutching the bag, her fingers

a little unsteady on the clasp. "Do you mind if I open it, *ma mère*?"

"Of course not. Do as you wish," and the Prioress, back in her seat by the window, bent her head over a rosary she was fingering, as if to give her guest an illusion of privacy. Jennifer thrust hasty fingers into the bag, pulling out its contents and laying them one by one on her lap . . . comb, powder, mirror, a Lancôme lipstick, keys, a roll of bus-tickets, a purse stuffed full of paper money, and a thick envelope similarly full. Jennifer counted it, over a hundred thousand francs—a hundred pounds or so. She frowned at the bills. Yes, Gillian might easily have closed her banking account, and taken out what remained of her savings; she had half-intended to stay here for ever, after all.

She turned over the envelope. Across the top corner was the printed sign of a Bordeaux bank, and the envelope was addressed, in a flowing French hand, to "Madame Lamartine, 135 R. de la Pompe, Bordeaux". The little sheaf of identification papers bore the same legend.

There was nothing else in the bag.

She began, slowly, to put the things back. The Prioress had turned towards her, her fingers stilled. She said now, gently:

"There is something more, isn't there, child? It isn't only your cousin's death that is upsetting you? What else, child? Can you tell me?"

Jennifer raised her head, blinking a little into the level glare of the late-afternoon sun.

"Yes, there is something more."

"Will you tell me what it is?"

"*Ma mère*——" She took a deep breath. "What I'm going to say must seem very queer to you, but I hope you will forgive me, and listen."

"I am listening."

So Jennifer told her. Not of her suspicions that Doña

Francisca and Celeste might know more than they said, but of the difficulty she herself had in believing that the woman buried in the convent yard was Gillian; of the strange fact that, even in delirium, the dead woman had apparently never lapsed into English, nor spoken once of England or of her own family.

"But you," said Jennifer at length, "you would visit her yourself, of course. Was she conscious when you saw her? Did she really say nothing?"

"To me, nothing. When I was told that you had come this afternoon, I was shocked and grieved that you should find such news awaiting you. . . ." She hesitated, then said quietly: "I was sorry, too, that you were not brought straight to me. But——" She appeared to hesitate once more, then reject what she had been about to say. "Doña Francisca was the one who was with your cousin most of the time, after all. Yes, mademoiselle, I was shocked, but also astounded at your coming, for nothing that your cousin said gave us to understand that she had relatives. I only hope you will forgive us for a fault we could not help committing. . . ."

"Of course. Because it's as I thought! She said nothing of her relatives because she had none—this woman was *not* my cousin, of that I'm convinced!"

"Mademoiselle——"

"A moment," pleaded Jennifer. "Listen, *ma mère*. That is by no means the oddest thing about it. . . ."

And she told the Prioress about the gentians, about the blue that the dead woman had recognized and loved, and that Gillian would never even have seen.

The Mother Superior listened without moving.

"So you see," finished Jennifer, "why I'm so convinced that it was somebody else, not my cousin, who came here that night. And, if that's the case, *where on earth is my cousin?*"

There was a little silence.

"Yes," said the old nun at length. "I see. It is certainly odd. It is more than that, it is hard to believe that any mistake so serious could have been made. . . ."

"I know that. But you can see that I don't feel I can let it rest there, and just go away?"

"Yes, I see that too. But surely, mademoiselle, if you *are* right, and your cousin is alive, why does she not get into touch with you? Or with us? You say she knew you were coming here?"

"Yes, she knew. But something may have happened to her, and that's what's worrying me."

"But what can have happened to her? And why, if the dead girl was *not* Madame Lamartine, did she permit us to address her so, more, why did she carry Madame Lamartine's papers?"

"I can't imagine, but——"

"That car that crashed that night was also your cousin's car."

Jennifer said nothing.

"And if your suspicions are true," went on the Prioress, quietly, inexorably, "we must not only ask '*where now is Madame Lamartine?*' but also '*who, then, was the woman who died?*' "

Another pause.

"This affair of the gentians," said the old nun at length. "It is this that really decides you, isn't it?"

"I think so. Yes, it is."

The Mother Superior nodded. "This way you could identify your cousin beyond mistake?"

"Only negatively. I mean, if the woman who died wasn't colour-blind, she couldn't have been Gillian. But it could almost be a positive identification too; women are very rarely colour-blind, and the blue-yellow kind is very rare indeed." She broke off suddenly, her hand to her head. "What a fool I've been! Talking of positive identification, and all the time I've never tried the obvious thing! I was thinking about other things when I talked to Celeste, but I should have thought of it straight away."

"And that thing?" queried the nun gently.

"What she looked like!" cried Jennifer triumphantly. "This girl who died—*what did she look like*?"

The old nun sat for a moment, quietly, while the little smile touched her lips again. "My child, I can't tell you. I never saw her. Nobody saw her but Doña Francisca and Celeste."

Jennifer stared at her in bewilderment. "Nobody saw her? But I thought you said you visited her."

"I did."

"Then what do you mean?"

"I mean," said the Reverend Mother, "that I am blind, my child."

And, with her back to the mocking glare of the sun, she smiled again, a little wistfully.

* * *

"I—I'm sorry," said Jennifer lamely.

The old nun smiled. "There's no need. I often think others are more conscious of my blindness than I am myself." Then she sat up and her voice took on the briskness of authority. "It seems to me, child, that the least we can do is to offer you our hospitality. I am, myself, certain that an error such as you are imagining is too bizarre to be at all likely. . . . I'm sorry, for your sake, but I am sure that your cousin is dead. When we have time to examine the facts a little more calmly, we shall without doubt find a simple explanation for everything."

Jennifer said nothing. Her hands were clasped together tightly in her lap, and she hardly heard the rest of what the nun was saying. To stay actually in the convent . . . with infinite opportunities to watch, to inquire, to check with innocent bystanders the statements Doña Francisca had made . . . this was more than she had hoped for.

The Prioress was still speaking. "But you must make what inquiries you think fit, and the place you will obviously wish to start from is here. If you will come to us——"

"You're very good. But I feel that I should be abusing your hospitality if I did as you suggest."

"It's the least we can do. The convent is guilty—albeit through ignorance—of a fault, in letting you make this sad discovery in such a way. You must allow us to atone."

Jenny smiled. "You don't have to atone. But I'd like to come. Thank you."

"Then come tonight."

"So soon, *ma mère?*"

"The sooner your mind is put to rest, the better, mademoiselle. But if you feel your hotel might make difficulties——"

"I don't think they will. I made it clear that my booking was provisional. . . . My cousin had suggested I might come here, you see."

"Then we'll expect you tonight, if you can manage it. If not, tomorrow. We'll be glad to see you any time, child. Even if your inquiries only lead you back to the melancholy truth of your cousin's death, I'm sure that our quiet community here has something to offer you in the way of comfort."

It was time, Jennifer saw, to let her suspicions lapse into silence. "Thank you," she said, simply. "I'll be glad to come. This is a beautiful place, and I imagine that if one can find peace anywhere, it is here."

The Reverend Mother's face lighted. "You feel that? I am so glad."

"I came through your chapel just now," said Jennifer. "It's quite wonderful, that altar—unexpectedly so, if I may say so, for such a little community, and one so isolated."

"Ah, yes. The place is simple, of course, but the plain style of building is in harmony with these high valleys. It would have been a mistake to build a St. Bertrand de Comminges in the Vallée des Orages. Here, in this stormy valley, we build sturdy white walls, and our windows have no need of coloured glass because they frame the mountains."

"And your pictures and lamps and carvings——"

"As to that," replied the Reverend Mother tranquilly, "I can't say. As you can imagine I've been only too glad in recent years to put all our business affairs into Doña Francisca's most efficient hands. The furnishing of our chapel has been her affair for some time now. I know that she has put many things in the chapel, pictures and a carpet and some candlesticks . . . last year she had a workman up from Bordeaux who made an altar-rail for us; but, although in former years I myself used to keep the chapel plain, I realize that some—most, indeed, of our members—are helped in their worship by the visible beauty of a statue or a lamp. So, though as a poor community we cannot spend a great deal on these things, I have allowed Doña Francisca to do as she wishes with the chapel, to please the younger sisters and"—she smiled her wise old smile—"the children."

Jennifer thought of the great concourse of saints and angels, soaring on wings of flame above the altar; she thought of the sanctuary rail, which no "workman from Bordeaux" had ever touched; she thought of the candlesticks, hammered from Florentine gold "to please the children" . . . there was more than one mystery, it seemed, about the Convent of Our Lady of the Storms. And if it involved golden lamps and El Greco saints . . . she recollected all at once the letter she had found behind the triptych, with what now appeared its highly provocative mention of "three million francs". A nerve twisted like a tiny painful needle, deep in her stomach.

"I see." She was angry to find that her voice was

shaking. "Well, it's very lovely. And Doña Francisca does it all?"

Doña Francisca's voice said, softly, behind her chair:

"Did you want me, Reverend Mother?"

*   *   *

"Ah, yes. . . ." The Prioress gave no hint of surprise: with the extra sense vouchsafed to the blind she must have been already aware of the presence of a third person. "I am glad you have come. Here's a matter that had better be cleared up straight away if possible. You have already met Mademoiselle Silver, of course."

"Yes."

"She has come—in some distress of mind—to see me, Francisca."

Doña Francisca did not look at Jennifer, but spoke still in that same colourless, composed voice. "Her grief is very natural."

"True. But it is not only a natural distress at her cousin's death that brings her to me." She turned to Jennifer, who sat frozen in her chair. "Doña Francisca is the person you should talk to, my child. Tell her what you have just told me—of your conviction that there's some mystery attached to your cousin's death."

Doña Francisca's eyes moved, with an almost palpable jerk, to fix themselves on Jennifer's face. Something flashed in them like the flicker of light off a knife-blade. Anger? Apprehension? Fear?

Jennifer, clutching Gillian's handbag with shaking fingers, tried vainly to avert a situation she had not had time to foresee. "It doesn't matter, *ma mère*. Perhaps—not now. We'd better leave it——"

"It is better now," said the Prioress decidedly. And turning towards the rigid figure of the bursar she related briefly but faithfully all the doubts and suspicions that Jennifer had recently laid before her. Jennifer dared not look at Doña Francisca, but she felt that unwavering regard fixed on her face. The woman stood like a statue, uncannily still and quiet, but for the red jewel that beat and sparkled on her breast.

"So I think it best," finished the Reverend Mother, "that mademoiselle should lodge with us here for a while and——"

Doña Francisca moved at that, as sharply as a jerked puppet. The ruby flashed. "Here? Stay here?"

Surprise touched the Prioress' face. "Yes. It seems to me that it's the least we can do for her; and if it will set her mind at rest to make inquiries, this is surely the best place for her to be."

"*Inquiries?* What inquiries can she possibly have to make?"

"This, for one," said Jennifer, and was surprised at the hard, level sound of her own voice. "What did 'Madame Lamartine' look like, Doña Francisca?"

The bursar turned to look down at her. There was a tiny, fractional pause. Then she smiled. "She was not very tall, and she was slightly made. She had fair hair, that curled a little, and eyes of a clear, true grey. A straight nose, and thick, straight brows." She spoke slowly, watching Jennifer from under hooded lids. "Is that a fair description, mademoiselle?"

"Very fair," said Jennifer hoarsely.

Doña Francisca turned back to the Prioress. Her voice sharpened, harsh as a saw biting wood. "You see, there are no inquiries to make, Reverend Mother. There is no mystery. Mademoiselle's suggestions are an outrage——"

"Francisca . . ." The old voice was soft, but the Spaniard stopped short in mid-tirade. She bent her head. "I am sorry, Reverend Mother."

"*La petite* is our guest," said the Prioress gently, "and we have wronged her. You may talk to me of this later—after Compline—but now I shall be glad if you will give orders for a room to be prepared for mademoiselle."

Doña Francisca said, in a still submissive, but quite definite tone: "We have no spare room, Reverend Mother."

"No? Who is in the one that Madame Lamartine had?"

"Sister Marie-Jeanne. She is suffering from a chill."

"Ah, yes. And the hospital room?"

"Two of the children——"

"I remember. Then it seems . . ." The blind face turned to Jennifer. "We can only offer you a poor kind of hospitality after all, mademoiselle. Perhaps you don't care to share a room? If that is so, you need not mind saying so."

"Share a room?" Doña Francisca cut in before Jennifer could reply. "There's no bed free."

"But surely—Sister Marie-Jeanne's, if she is in the spare room? Mademoiselle won't mind sharing with Celeste."

Jennifer heard the bursar above her, draw a little breath like a hissing snake. "Mademoiselle Silver will not wish——"

Jennifer lifted her head for the first time and looked the woman straight in the face. Blue eyes met black with the kiss of a sword's salute.

"On the contrary," she said. "I shall be delighted."

*   *   *

The sun was westering fast when at length Jennifer let herself out of the gate and began to hurry down the valley. Gradually the gold of the day had deepened, and the lengthening shadows of the western peaks lay blue across the valley, to shade the track where she walked. Once again she felt the loneliness of the place press on her, and she shivered and quickened her pace, as if by so doing she could escape the memory of the afternoon. So short a while ago she had thought this valley beautiful; she remembered the flowers and the spice-laden wind, the tumbling waters, and those three horses with their flowing gallop and the light slipping over their flanks. It was just here that they had plunged from the track to leap the stream; she could see the dash of white water, ghostly and unsparkling in the mountain's shadow. . . .

Her heart gave an uncontrollable twisted jump, and she stopped dead and stared upwards.

Above the valley, beyond the ghost-foam of the Petit Gave, sharply black against the rich sky, stood a horseman. The horse was motionless, save where the wind moved in his mane, and the rider sat, too, as if carved from the black rock. But about the set of the young shoulders there was no suggestion of ease, as there had been that afternoon; his head was thrust forward, sunk between the tense shoulders like the head of a hawk, watching, waiting.

The only sound that held the valley was the soft rush of water. Then the rider moved, and the horse, reined sharply back, reared as if at a sudden pain. There was the crack and clatter of hoofs on stone, and then horse and rider vanished beyond the ridge.

Jennifer reached the main road and turned towards Gavarnie. When, a few moments later, a big touring car stopped beside her and an English voice offered her a lift down to the village she accepted thankfully, and with the odd sense of a sharp return to normal. Soon she was being swept swiftly down the valley towards the hotel and the now immensely comforting prospect of seeing Stephen.

CHAPTER IX

INTERLUDE: *con desiderio*

SHE had not realized, till she walked into the hotel dining-room and failed to find Stephen waiting there, how much she had depended on seeing him straight away. She sat down, reaching mechanically for her napkin, and scanned the luscious menu with unseeing eyes. When the food came she ate without tasting, watching the door. But he did not come. He must, she thought with a sick disappointment that surprised her, be dining at his own hotel.

She felt drained and empty; suspended in that soul-destroying vacuum between the knowledge that drastic action is necessary, and the moment when the first move has to be made.

Between the acting of a dreadful thing.

And the first motion . . . and here she was, caught in the fantastic interim, in a dream made more hideous by the doubts that, in retrospect, assailed her. What if she *should* be mistaken? What if there was, after all, nothing wrong? And what, in fact, did she imagine could be wrong? The unlikely phantoms mocked her; Gillian alive . . . Gillian hidden away somewhere, somehow . . . kept under restraint . . . Gillian in danger. . . . She shook them away. Such things didn't happen. *Or did they?*

It was a stiff and tautly controlled Jennifer who, after dinner, sought out the *patron* of the hotel and apologized to him, in her easy flawless French, for her change of plan.

"I did give you to understand that this might happen," she finished, "but I didn't expect to go quite so soon. Of course, I'll pay you for tonight."

The *patron*, who had opened his mouth to protest, shut it

again, and, after another look at her face, became extremely helpful. His kindness and obvious sympathy did nothing to increase her self-control, and when at length she parted from him she almost ran out of the lighted foyer with one thought only in her mind, to find Stephen.

Twilight had deepened into dusk pricked with a few faint stars, but she saw him almost at once, walking past the end of the hotel, down towards the river. She ran after him, down the steep bank between the dark trees, stumbling unheedingly over the pine-roots that webbed the path.

He had stopped below her, on the stone-flagged bridge that crossed the fall, and was looking down at the boiling foam beneath. The rowans fanned out across it, their shadowy leaves whipped by the wind of the fall into a whitening dance, and the ravine was luminous with the froth of falling water. He stood, head bent, watching the torrent.

To Jennifer, running down the dark track under the pine trees, the sight of that familiar figure did much to strip from her the last vestiges of her careful control. While she had had the burden to bear alone, she had—somewhat to her own surprise—been equal to it; but now it was weighing her down, it must be shared. With the sharing, she knew, much of her tight grasp on herself must be loosened. And here was Stephen, representing all that just at that moment she needed most. Comfort, strength, reassurance . . . no more. Big-brother Stephen. She was suddenly glad that that was the way he seemed to want it. Elder-brother Stephen . . . that was the way it was. Jennifer, retreating into innocence like a snail into its shell, put out her hands and ran towards him, calling his name.

He turned his head and saw her. The noise of the fall had prevented him from hearing her approach, and all he saw was Jenny, a ghostly figure under the pines, running towards him with her hands held out.

His lips shaped the words: "Why, Jenny!"

"Stephen—oh, Stephen!"

He turned swiftly to meet her, holding out his arms. And then she was in them, folded close. His heart had begun to race, in sickening hammer-thuds. His arms tightened, his head went down, his mouth seeking hers. . . . But her head was bent, pressed hard into his shoulder, and his lips only found the silk of her hair.

He said hoarsely: "Jenny."

She did not lift her head.

"Jenny."

Still no movement. It was five blind and whirling seconds later that he realized that she was crying, oblivious of everything save her own distress. The trembling of her body was due, not to passion, but to tears, and her arms clung to him only for comfort. Big-brother Stephen. Hold your horses, fool: she doesn't even know it's you. . . .

Five lifetimes later he heard his voice repeat, unrecognizably: "Why, Jenny!" And then again, very gently: "What's the matter?"

She shook her head, burying it more deeply in his shoulder, so he remained silent, holding her closely, till her sobs began to subside. He had himself well in hand now: over her head his face was like a mask, but he was breathing fast, and the hand that crept up, in spite of itself, to stroke her hair, shook ever so slightly. It seemed that presently he noticed this, for his mouth twisted wryly, and he dropped his hand.

After a while she stirred in his arms and, pushing away from him a little, groped for her handkerchief.

"Have mine." He proffered it. "I don't know why men are always better equipped than women for these emergencies. Self-defence, I suppose."

Jennifer, dabbing at her eyes, managed a rather shaky smile. "Have I soaked your shoulder? I'm sorry. I must say you show up suspiciously well in the said emergency, Stephen. Do a lot of people run and cry on you?"

"Not more than three a day."

"Poor Stephen. I'm sorry."

"Silly child." The words mocked, but his voice was gentle, and his eyes considered her face gravely. Then he dropped an arm lightly across her shoulders and urged her towards the far side of the bridge. "Come away where we can hear ourselves think, and tell me all about it."

They began to climb the path that led to the mountain pastures, emerging almost at once from the cold shadows of the lower cleft. The warm air of evening met them, with its turf-scents and juniper-scents, and its caressing undertones of mountain breeze. Behind them the roar of the river sank to a murmur, and was finally lost under the darkness of its tossed boughs.

They found a low wall spanning the meadow, and there, sitting on the still-warm stone, with her eyes upon the grass at her feet, she told him. She told him of her reception at the convent, of her growing premonition of disaster, and then of Doña Francisca's bald announcement of Gillian's death.

"*Dead?*" said Stephen, in a shocked voice, and then gently: "Poor Jenny. I'm sorry. What a rotten thing to happen—and for you to run into it as you did. Damn it all, even if Gillian was about to retire from the world, they might at least have taken the trouble to tell you about *that*!"

Jennifer pressed her hands tightly together, and said, on a caught breath: "That's just it, Stephen. Listen. . . ."

And she went on to tell him the rest of the fantastic business; of the colour-blindness and the gentians; of the dying woman's extraordinary reticence; of the interviews that she herself had had and the things that she had seen. And through it all, like a black thread through a coloured tapestry, ran the voice and actions of the Spanish woman, now lying outright, now merely obstructive, but all the time palpably calculating and apprehensive of—what?

The moon was up now, full sail among the stars, like a swan serene on a lotus-pool. Mountain and meadow had withdrawn a little into the darkness. The wind moved silently, invisibly, across the turf. So quiet was the valley that they could hear the stirring of the tiny flowers at their feet.

Stephen spoke at last, and his words were sufficient of an anticlimax. He said: "It seems you've had a fairly trying afternoon, all things considered. Cigarette, Jenny?"

Across the flame of his lighter her eyes, wide and strained, studied him. "Stephen. You can't not believe me."

"I do believe you—up to a point."

"A point? What point?"

"The point where you start to make Grand Guignol out of facts—queer enough, admittedly—which will eventually prove to have quite simple explanations."

"You think so?" Her voice was tight, brittle, a danger-signal. He grimaced to himself as he heard it.

He said flatly: "My darling girl, look at what you're postulating: two young women, of similar appearance, somehow get interchanged. One dies, even on her death-bed pretending to be the other. The other one, a respectable and responsible Englishwoman, disappears without trace. You're left with two sticky problems: *one*—who was the dead woman? *two*—where is Gillian?" He shook his head. "It won't wash."

"Why not?"

He was deliberately brutal: "Because it's more reasonable to take, instead of two improbabilities, the one possibility that everyone else accepts, that Gillian is dead and buried."

She said, after a while, in a small shaken voice: "And I thought you'd help me, Stephen."

He made an involuntary little movement. "That's what

I'm trying to do, Jenny, can't you see? I don't want you to go building up some fantastic story—and perhaps getting yourself into an excessively awkward jam—by imagining accusations against people who're hardly likely to be the sort of criminals your story makes of them."

"It's only Doña Francisca, and she——"

"Fair enough. She lied to you, and you don't like her. That doesn't make her a criminal."

"I didn't say she was a criminal! But if you'd seen her today and talked to her, Stephen, you'd be convinced, as I am, that she's not all she should be!"

"Just who is the woman, anyway? What's she doing in the convent?"

She related what Sister Louisa had told her. "And later on I tried to pump the novice who showed me out of the convent. She was a nice girl and obviously in terrific awe of Doña Francisca. I gathered that she—Doña Francisca—pretty well runs everything that isn't directly a religious concern. I also gathered—not from anything the girl *said*, but from her general manner—that none of them like Doña Francisca very much, and they think she presumes on the Reverend Mother's blindness, but nobody likes to say anything. They're mostly simple souls and tend to take the woman at her own valuation."

"She seems to have a lot of authority for someone who's never professed."

"Yes. I almost think that's the very reason. I did get the impression that the Reverend Mother lets her have her head over a lot of things as a sort of compensation for not accepting her into the Order. You know what she made me think of? The good old days when queens and duchesses and high-up disappointed ladies retired into convents when politics got too much for them, and made perfect nuisances of themselves with lapdogs and visitors and condescending to the Abbess."

He laughed at that. "You didn't mention any lapdog."

"Well, you know what I mean. Even without the lapdog, and discounting the Velasquez get-up, she's—oh, she's *off-key*, Stephen! Not only over Gillian. There's the chapel. She's obviously been spending an incredible amount of money over that, and——"

"My dearest Jenny, there are such things as copies of El Greco. Could you tell?"

"No, of course not. But I can tell when things are made of gold and ivory, and even that kind of copy would cost real money! And where does she get it, tell me that?"

"You said she'd been rich."

"Her family lost their money. She brought nothing with her. Sister Louisa told me so," said Jennifer. "And if it's all above-board why does the Reverend Mother apparently know nothing about it?"

"Ye-es," said Stephen slowly. "I admit that's queer. But, once again, there must be some easy explanation . . . I mean, where can she possibly lay hands on that much money? There must be millions of francs involved."

"Millions of francs . . ." breathed Jennifer. She thrust her hand into her pocket and brought out a crumpled piece of paper. "Here, Stephen, read this."

"What is it?"

She told him how she had found it stuck in the frame of the triptych. He held the letter low in the shelter of the wall, and flicked his lighter into flame. The wayward breeze was lying still, and the flame burned steadily. Then he looked up, and extinguished the light. He was frowning a little.

She said quickly, "What d'you make of it, Stephen?"

"I? Nothing. But, all things considered, the mention of a sum like three million francs makes one wonder. . . ." He handed it back to her and she returned it to her pocket. Then he stubbed out his cigarette on the stone.

"Well?" inquired Jenny, the tautness back in her voice.

He said levelly: "If you still insist on your mystery, my dear, I can't stop you from hurting yourself. But neither can I see what the hell one can do about it."

"The police——"

His voice sharpened: "For God's sake, Jenny, no! You're a foreigner, and a Protestant, alone in a pretty wild part of the country. And Gillian was a French citizen by marriage. You can't go stirring up all sorts of stink without some pretty convincing proofs."

"N-no. I see that. Then there is only one thing I can do."

He looked at her doubtfully. "And that is?"

Jennifer stood up with an abrupt movement, and ground out her cigarette with her heel. "Go up and stay at the convent till I do unearth something."

He rose too, looming over her in the dusk.

"Jenny, will nothing I can say persuade you that it's all nonsense? That you'll simply get yourself embroiled——"

She said evenly: "No. You see, I've got to find out where Gillian is."

"My darling child——"

She flashed at him then, her precarious control snapping: "For heaven's sake, Stephen! You can call me every kind of a fool if you like, but *I just don't believe that Gillian's in that grave*! Can't you understand that simple fact? *I don't believe she's dead!*"

She faced him, her breath coming rapidly, her body taut and vibrating with anger and excitement. She stood there in the dusk, a glimmering ghost, but slender and alive against the background of dead rock and the threatening immensity of darkness. She seemed all of a sudden alone, touching, a trace forlorn in the bravery of her nonsensical defiance, and very young. Stephen, looking at her, felt a wave of desire so strong that it startled him, and he wondered that she could stand there, unnoticing, watching him with angry eyes.

He began shakenly: "My darling child——"

"And don't keep calling me your darling child!" snapped Jennifer.

He laughed then, capitulating so suddenly that her anger slid into surprise. It never occurred to her that he was grasping at any chance that would keep her in Gavarnie, the *princesse lointaine* outside her guarded bower. . . .

He said: "All right, my fragile little blossom. You win. Only count me in."

"You mean—you *will* help me, Stephen?"

"Oh, yes. If you're going to look for trouble, I'd rather you didn't do it alone. Only don't cast me as the hero of your story, Jenny. I'll do what I can, but melodrama isn't my line."

She drew a long breath, and smiled up at him, wondering even as she did so why there was no answering glimmer in his eyes, and why he should be watching her with a face as shuttered and remote as that of an Egyptian king.

"I knew you would!" Triumph and relief lighted her voice, and she moved towards him, her eyes brilliant in the moonlight. Almost without knowing what he was doing, he took her by the shoulders and drew her towards him. She came unresisting, taut with excitement . . . only to lift to him that enchanting face and ask eagerly, naïvely: "What do we do next?"

His grip tightened for a second. "Do you really want to know?"

"Of course!"

"For a man of my unstable temperament," said Stephen through his teeth, "I find myself remarkably single-minded." He dropped his hands then, and laughed down into her bewildered face. "Skip it, sweetheart. The next thing we do is to see you safely up to your convent." He put

a finger under her chin, lifting her face in the moonlight.
"A convent. That should suit you, Sleeping Beauty."

She moved her head away. "Why d'you call me that?
You're saying a lot of queer things tonight."

"It's the moon."

"And I'm *not* a fragile little blossom."

"You're telling me," said Stephen. "In fact, my heart at
this moment is bleeding with pity for Doña Francisca."

Jenny laughed, excitement still lifting her spirits. "And
well it may. . . . Well, I suppose if I've got to get up to the
Vallée des Orages——"

"I think I can borrow a car. Aristide Celton—he's the
local *gendarme*—is a drinking-companion of mine, and he
has a little Renault that I'm certain he'll let me use."

"That's marvellous. I was wondering what on earth to do
about my cases."

"If I can't get the car one of the muleteers will take your
heavy stuff up in the morning. One of them lives in your
valley at a farm above the convent; he's called Pierre Bussac.
I believe he ferries goods up when required. And there's a
lad called Luis who has horses——"

Her interest quickened. "Three horses? Chestnuts?"

"Yes. Why?"

"Oh, nothing. I think I saw him today."

They began to walk slowly down the hill. Jennifer, now
that the decision was stated, and a plan, however tentative,
was made, felt the tension in her slackening perceptibly.
She glanced sideways at Stephen. He caught the look, and
smiled. Whatever had been odd and withdrawn about him
had vanished. Things were normal again. He put out a
hand to help her, and she took it. They went downhill together, still holding hands.

"This boy," she said, "does he live in the valley too?"

"His home's at Argelès, on his uncle's farm, but he brings
the cattle up here in summer and lives with them, so to

speak, in a hut on the other side of the Vallée des Orages."

"You appear to know him very well!" said Jennifer, amused.

"Oh, he's come and had a look at my sketches several times. He's always up and down between Gavarnie and the Vallée des Orages."

"It's very brave of you to risk local criticism, Stephen! I'm sure it's devastating!"

He grinned. "They're pretty frank. Luis is always wanting me to draw his horses, which I couldn't do, and Madame Bussac—she had a look at my things once—said simply and flatly that paintings meant nothing to her and she preferred photographs. . . . Shall I see you tomorrow?"

"I don't know, Stephen. It's a long way——"

"I'll come. I'd like you to feel I'm there if you want me. I know, Jenny——"

"Yes?"

"If I collect some food and a bottle of wine, will you meet me tomorrow—say at the bend in the track below the convent—for a picnic lunch, and we'll exchange discoveries?"

"Of course. I'd like that. But—exchange, Stephen? What discoveries are you going to make?"

He said: "I thought I might have an idle chat tomorrow with the local doctor, and the priest. They both saw Gil—this woman, after all."

They were on the bridge. She stopped and turned to face him. "Stephen . . ." She added, slowly: "I know you think I'm crazy, and I expect I'll be proved a fool at every turn . . . but I must do this. You do see, don't you?"

"Yes, I see."

She touched his hand almost shyly. "And I'm terribly grateful. I—I'm awfully glad you're here. . . ."

He said, steadily: "That's fine. . . . Have you packed?"

"Yes."

He was looking at the luminous dial of his watch. "It's not late. We'll go and ask Aristide Celton for his car, and then, if you like, we might see the priest tonight."

"That sounds delightfully compromising," said Jennifer primly, and led the way up the path.

CHAPTER X

FOR ALL THE SAINTS (A. & M.)

THOUGH it was long past service-time, Father Anselm was in his little church. Having been directed there by his housekeeper, Jennifer and Stephen climbed the steps that led up the hillside behind the village towards the dark-spired bulk of the church. The triple-lanced light of the east window glowed above them, at once remote and welcoming, yellow against the stars, steadily asserting its three-fold link between the immensity of that star-hung darkness and the squat, earth-bound building that hugged the hillside. Within, they were met by the fragrance of dead incense mingled with the sharper smell of snuffed candles, a dusky fragrance, nostalgic as the scent of pot-pourri. It hung between the pillars, over the bristling taper-brackets, in front of the niches where lurked the little saints of stone and plaster.

There did, indeed, appear to be a veritable convocation of saints. To every pillar, three niches; to every niche, a saint . . . the side-aisles were lined with them, large and small, plain and coloured, merry and sad. And it was in front of a small, sad saint that they found Father Anselm prosaically busy with a duster.

He was a little man, with a thin face, sharp dark eyes, and a remarkable nose. He was not old, but what hair he still had was grey, and his shoulders were bent, as if with much peering at badly printed books. The grey hair, and the soutane which he wore, saved him from too closely resembling Dr. Beetle—a resemblance to which otherwise his nose might have condemned him. He greeted the visitors with a lively flourish of his duster, incidentally dispersing over a rather wider area the dust he had just laboriously gathered. They returned his greeting, and Jennifer began politely to admire the church. Father Anselm beamed with pleasure, and, almost before they realized what was happening, they were being carefully conducted from saint to saint.

"Polycarp . . ." said Father Anselm, pausing at length. "St. Britius; St. Machutus . . ." He stopped to whisk some wholly imaginary dust off the pedestal of St. Machutus.

Stephen took a quick breath. "We came to see you, *mon père*, about——"

"St. Remigius, Bishop of Rheims," said Father Anselm, and was off at a brisk trot, his duster at the alert.

They followed him to the next pillar. "St. Enurchus," he demonstrated. "St. Boniface; St. Alphège; St. Lucy . . ."

"—About a woman——"

"St. Perpetua, Virgin and Martyr . . ."

"—Who died about a fortnight ago——"

"St. Blasius, Bishop of Sebaste," and he was off again. "St. Simon, and, of course——"

"St. Jude?" supplied Jennifer automatically. This, surprisingly enough, had the effect of checking Father Anselm's hagiolatrous progress. As if aware of them properly for the first time, he turned and beamed at Jennifer.

"*And* St. Jude," he acknowledged. "Mademoiselle is familiar, then, with the calendar of the blessed saints?"

"Oh, no," she said hastily, "not really. Only some."

Father Anselm's face assumed an expression of pleased anticipation. "Have you heard," he asked, a thought anxiously, "of St. Bidulphus?"

"No."

"Of St. Onesimus?"

"No-o."

"Of St. Augustine of Hippo?"

"No indeed."

Father Anselm returned in triumph to his pillar.

"All here! Every one!" And he waved his duster with satisfaction.

Stephen, with a surreptitious glance at his watch, opened his mouth to speak, but was ignored. Jennifer and Father Anselm, evincing the liveliest satisfaction in one another's company, had already vanished round another pillar, presumably to identify St. Bidulphus and his rarer fellows. Stephen lifted an eyebrow and followed them.

". . . A most interesting church," Jennifer was saying with every appearance of delight. "And so unusual. All these statues . . . I've never seen another quite like it before, even in France. And at home we're as a rule quite content to deal with one saint at a time."

"Except for St. Simon——"

"And St. Jude," nodded Jennifer. They smiled happily at one another. Then Jennifer said, perhaps a shade too casually: "That's a remarkable statue of the Madonna that they've got at the convent, isn't it? I don't know when I've seen a lovelier."

The little priest looked puzzled. "Statue? Oh, you mean in the corridor? That's of St. Anne, my child."

"No, not that. The one in the Lady-chapel on the little altar. I thought it was wonderful. And so is that big picture in the chancel."

"As to that," said Father Anselm frankly, "that's a modern thing, isn't it? I can't say I've looked at it very hard. I'm a bit short-sighted, you know, besides being old-fashioned in my tastes." He chuckled.

And indeed the general standard of taste reflected in the crowded little church did not indicate any very noticing and critical eye on the part of the convent's priest. To Father Anselm it was quite probable that El Greco's stretched and skyward saints looked "modern" and no more. But surely, statue-minded as he was, he would have noticed the jewelled

Madonna? Jennifer looked up to see the same query in Stephen's eye even as Father Anselm answered it by adding: "And the statue you mention . . . I don't remember noticing that either. In the Lady-chapel? Surely they have a picture on the altar there, a pretty little thing, blue and gold? The children put flowers in front of it when I visit them."

So the treasures went into hiding, did they, on visiting days? Jennifer, not daring to look at Stephen, stifled the urge to ask if the gold candlesticks had similar vanishing habits, and said instead, with a gesture towards a particularly crowded pillar: "But you have plenty here, haven't you? All these . . . so strange . . . one feels so ignorant. . . ."

This attempt to turn the conversation had an immediate success. Father Anselm gave a curious little skip. "That's it! That's just the point! I have determined, in my church, that nobody—*nobody* (however obscure)—shall be forgotten. A few years ago"—he began absently to polish the already gleaming candlesticks of St. Augustine of Hippo—"a few years ago, I wrote a book on the saints of the Church. You can imagine, mademoiselle, that their stories led me into many strange and unexpected places. I speak metaphorically, of course."

"Of course."

"It took a good many years . . . but I think I may say that, in the finished work—compendium would be the better word—I have omitted no name, however obscure."

"Really?"

"And when I became Curé here, I made it my earnest endeavour to commemorate all those (however obscure), who had made their contribution to faith."

"I think it's a wonderful idea," said Jennifer warmly. "And you've got a wonderful church."

"Dedicated," said Father Anselm, with a sudden chuckle, "to All Saints. So you see, how could I help it?" He gave a final valedictory rub to St. Augustine's candlesticks, and looked up at Stephen, out of eyes that were all at once disconcertingly shrewd and wise.

"And now," said Father Anselm, with a flap of his duster, "you want to ask me a few questions about the woman who died on Tuesday the twenty-first of June, up at the convent in the Valley of the Storms? I am listening, my son. . . ."

*   *   *

But there was, after all, little new to add.

"They thought at first that she would get better," said Father Anselm, "but then, on the Tuesday night, she suddenly took a turn for the worse, and seemed to weaken very rapidly. I was sent for, and I was with her when she died. It was at about eleven at night." He looked up at Jennifer. "You say she was your cousin, mademoiselle?"

She nodded.

"I am sorry," said Father Anselm simply.

Stephen's eyes met Jennifer's, and, almost imperceptibly, he nodded.

"Father," she began.

"*Ma fille?*"

"I hope you won't think it very strange my asking you these questions. It's a very confidential matter, you see, and——"

"I shall tell no one."

"If I might just ask you certain things about this—about my cousin. . . ."

Father Anselm turned his disconcertingly bright gaze away from her, and spoke to St. Onesimus. "You may ask me anything you like, my child, and I will answer anything I can. What do you want to know?"

Stephen spoke. "We should like to know, *mon père*, what the woman looked like."

The little priest deserted St. Onesimus for a moment to

send Stephen a look of surprise. "My son, she was dying, and those who are dying——"

"I didn't mean in that sense," said Stephen hurriedly. "I meant the colour of her hair and eyes, and so on."

"But mademoiselle here——" Father Anselm broke off, and addressed himself once more to St. Onesimus. "She was fair," he said briefly, "and she had grey eyes or blue—I cannot tell you which. As to her height, I do not know. When I saw her she was very thin, and she had suffered much from the fever. A dying woman does not look as she has looked in life, my children, and I saw her only at the end. And by candlelight," he added.

"She spoke French to you?"

"But yes. All the time. Until you told me you were her cousin I had never supposed she was not wholly French. Her name, too, you see . . ." He began to chip a gout of candle-grease from St. Onesimus' pedestal with his finger-nail.

"She was sensible—I mean, she wasn't delirious when you saw her?"

"No. She was quite lucid. She knew she was dying."

"*She knew she was dying?*" said Jennifer softly.

"That is so."

"And she left no message with you, mentioned nobody by name?"

He shook his head.

"I know," she said awkwardly, "that you can't speak of anything said in confession, but you *could* tell me if she had left a message or mentioned a name, couldn't you, even if you couldn't tell me what it was?"

Father Anselm twinkled at her. "Yes, I could. But no, nothing of the sort was said. I am sorry, mademoiselle." His voice was grave again. "She did not, in fact, confess. The end came more quickly than we had expected. Too quickly. . . ."

There was a little pause. Then he looked up at her once more, his bright black eyes shrewd. He said suddenly: "Have you seen her papers? Everybody carries papers in France, you know."

"Yes, I saw them."

"Then," said Father Anselm, staring straight at St. Onesimus, "I'm afraid I can't tell you anything else that would identify her beyond doubt. . . ."

When they left him, he was unconcernedly engaged in cleaning a pillar positively swarming with Holy Innocents.

CHAPTER XI

NOCTURNE

STEPHEN said good night at the convent gate, and Jennifer, hoping a shade nervously that she would not meet Doña Francisca again that night, rang for admittance. She need not have been afraid. She was let in by a young nun she had not seen before, a pleasant-faced girl in the white head-dress of the novice, and crossed the yard with her to the sound of singing from the chapel. The novice led her quickly into the tunnel, then through the refectory, and up the stairs at the far end of the big room. These gave on to a long narrow corridor, lined with doors. At one of these the novice stopped, tapped, and on receiving no reply, opened the door and showed Jennifer in.

The room was as small and bare as might have been expected; there were two beds, two chairs, two chests-of-drawers, and a hassock placed beneath a small picture of the Virgin and Child. The window gave south on to the garden, and, far beyond, soaring miraculously above the darkness, the moonlit snows of Spain.

The novice pointed to the bed near the window.

"That will be yours, mademoiselle, and that chest-of-drawers has been emptied. I've written out for you a little list of meal and chapel times, but"—she smiled—"you mustn't feel bound to attend the latter. The Reverend Mother was most insistent that you must feel free to come and go as you please."

Jennifer thanked her, and the girl withdrew, leaving her alone.

She crossed to the window and stood looking out over the garden. Across the wall to her left, through a tangle of night-dim apple-boughs, she could see the graveyard, and the wall that hung its arras of roses and blue convolvulus over the grave. Well, here she was, ensconced in the heart of her mystery, and something, she told herself, must happen soon, For a beginning, anyway, there was Celeste.

She turned back from the window, wondering anew at the barren look of a room without personal possessions. There was nothing here to give a clue to the character of the owner. The dark cloak hanging behind the door, the string-soled slippers side by side under the chair—this was all. There were not even curtains on the window. No flowers, no pictures except the one devotional one, no books except a small scarlet missal lying on one of the chests-of-drawers. She picked this up, and then, her interest quickening, looked at it more closely. It was bound in scarlet leather, beautifully tooled with gilt, and the pages were illuminated exquisitely with medieval arabesques of gold and green and purple. She turned them reverently, marvelling at the work, until something familiar in her sensation of surprise brought her up short. This had happened before, and recently. In the chapel . . . the little dim plain building, with its flat white walls, its common windows—and the treasures of Italy and Spain glowing under its rich lamplight. . . .

And this repeated the effect, this beautiful little thing which lay so carelessly upon the ugly chest-of-drawers. She looked up at the picture of the Madonna and Child, and saw without surprise that the pictured lips were smiling down over the baby with the smile that Murillo had used to light greater canvases than this.

The missal had fallen open in her hands, and the pages had turned of themselves, to leave the book lying open at the first page, the fly-leaf.

On it was written: "Marie Celeste, from Maria Francisca, *un don en Dios*."

The Madonna smiled.

Then the door opened quietly, and Celeste slipped into the room.

Jennifer, with the book lying open in her hands, felt confused and guilty, as if caught in some questionable act. She smiled at the girl and said: "I hope you don't mind, Celeste. It was such a lovely little book."

The girl had flushed scarlet, as if with annoyance, but she muttered, "*De rien, mam'selle*," and, sitting down with her back turned, began to unfasten her slippers.

Jennifer, eyeing her back dubiously, decided that confidences were more easily extracted in the dark, and said no more. But by the time she had undressed, and had come back from the wash-room, Celeste was curled up in bed, with her face to the wall. If she was not asleep, it was at any rate obvious that sleep was the impression she wished to convey.

Jennifer gave a little sigh to herself, blew out the candle, and got into bed.

* * *

She woke to thick darkness, and lay for a moment, vaguely wondering where she was, then, more coherently, what it was that had woken her. The wind? This must have risen all at once, with the coming of the dark, because, though the evening had been still, she could hear now the soughing of the pines, and the intermittent flung rattle of rain against the window.

But it was some slighter sound than this, she knew, that had awakened her; some telling little sound that should not have been. . . .

The door. It had been the quiet closing of the door.

She sat up in bed and strained her eyes in the dark room, then, as things took shape, she saw that Celeste's bed was empty, and her slippers gone from under the chair. She groped for her handbag and, after one or two fumbling attempts, lit a match and surveyed the room by its small uncertain light. Yes, the slippers had gone, and the black cloak from behind the door. . . . Well, thought Jennifer, the corridors are chilly, and she may, after all, be on a perfectly normal errand. She must not, she told herself, run too eagerly on the trail of her mystery.

The match went out, but as it did so, something that she saw in its last flicker made her sit up straighter and grope again for the match-box. What she thought she had seen—yes, she had been right. Celeste's white cotton nightdress was flung down across the bed. Jennifer slid out of her own bed and went, cautiously because of the flickering match, across to the chest-of-drawers where, earlier that evening, she had seen Celeste tidily fold away her day-clothes. She opened the drawer. It was empty.

As she reached for the candlestick the second match died, and she stood there in the quiet darkness, her mind racing. If Celeste had only gone somewhere else in the convent—say, to Doña Francisca's room, or, which seemed possible, to the chapel, would she have dressed to do it? Her cloak would surely have provided warmth enough? But if she had gone outside . . . Jennifer padded across to the window and looked out. In the windy moonlight the dim outline of mountain and forest bulked huge and uncertain; rain was spattering the panes, and low clouds flung their moving and fitful shadows. Then all at once she saw another shadow, a slight black shadow, moving more purposefully across the garden below than the ghost of any cloud. It drifted below the apple-trees, through the gate, and vanished into the deeper darkness of the graveyard wall. Jennifer, leaning out, all at once excited, heard, in a sudden lull of the wind, the click of a latch. The door in the outer wall.

She did not consciously decide what to do; indeed, she could never afterwards say how she came, hastily but adequately dressed, to be letting herself out of that same door a very few minutes later. As she shut it softly behind her, and paused in the shelter of the wall with the wind plucking at her coat, she was telling herself that she was a fool. In this darkness, and with that start, Celeste would be already well out of sight and sound. Whatever she had hoped to discover—and on this point she was far from clear—it could not be discovered on a night like this.

Then, unbelievably, as a fragment of torn cloud, racing high, laid bare a patch of wet starlight, she saw it; it was barely seventy yards ahead of her, a hurrying black figure, bent against the wind, its cloak bellying like a sail.

Thankful now for the noisy darkness, Jennifer stole from the doorway and set off in pursuit.

The wind was not strong, but it came in flying gusts that took away the breath and made balance uncertain on the rocky path. Celeste headed, at a remarkable speed, straight up the side of the valley towards the edge of the pinewood belt, and soon she and her pursuer were plunged into its still and inky depths. Here the wind, faded to a far sighing overhead, did not impede progress any more; now it was the thick felting of pine-needles that silenced their going. But it was dark, a deep, velvet, heavy darkness that would have confounded Jennifer in a moment, had it not been that the path, running straight through the belt of pines, showed a glimmer of the paler night at its end, like the light at the end of a tunnel. As she hurried, almost running along the soft dry track, she caught a glimpse of her quarry outlined momentarily against a patch of lighter sky, before the figure turned to the left, and was blown on a gust of rain out of her sight.

When she reached the edge of the wood, she found, indeed, that the path turned sharply up the hill to the left, joining a widish track that ran up the mountain-side south of the pine-belt. Up this crude track Jennifer stumbled, not thinking coherently about where this was leading her, or what she was going to do, but simply determined to find out where Celeste was going, so secretly and so fast. Any lead into her mystery, however tenuous, was to be followed.

And this midnight sortie was, surely, mysterious enough? So she held the damp skirts of her coat above her knees, and toiled through the gusty rain, hoping fervently that Celeste was still moving ahead of her, and not awaiting her in the lee of the next rock.

Presently, however, she was reassured by the sight of the shadowy figure against the skyline above her, as it gained the summit of the track. A minute later Jennifer, too, breasted the last steep little rise, and stopped short.

The figure had vanished. But there, ahead, and a little to the right of the track, was a light. A little cluster of buildings huddled in the shelter of a low rock-face, and in the central building a wide chink of light glowed between rattling shutters. Somewhere a chain clashed, and a dog growled, and then fell silent.

So this was where Celeste had come. And Jennifer, with the memory of something Stephen had said, felt suddenly tense and excited, as if she were at last on the edge of discovery.

"There's a man lives in your valley," he had told her, "at a farm above the convent; he's called——" What had he been called? Bussac, that was it; Pierre Bussac. . . . She said the name to herself, staring at the lighted window, and then started as yet another memory hooked itself on to the name. The waiter at the hotel—he had mentioned Pierre Bussac too; Pierre Bussac, who had been down in the village on the night of the bad storm, three weeks ago. The night that Gillian's car had crashed into the Gave, and Gillian——

Jenny was trembling violently. It need not mean anything, of course, but if instinct were any guide, it did. And having come so far, fear or no fear, she was going to finish her mission. She had to find out, if possible, what was Celeste's business with Pierre Bussac. She began to edge forward across the short wet turf towards the lighted window, taking care not to cross the narrow path of light it threw, and moving cautiously because of the dog. The wind, with its accompaniment of creaking doors and rattling shutters, must have disguised her progress effectively, or else the dog was used to nocturnal visitations, for it did not hear her, or at any rate it gave no warning.

She softly crossed the weedy strip of rough cobbles below the window, and, pressing herself well back against the wall to one side of the frame, craned her head till she could see in through the crack in the shutter.

And got her second surprise of the evening.

It was not Celeste, the black figure which was advancing into the lamplit room of the cottage, shaking the raindrops from the voluminous folds of its cloak.

It was the Spaniard, Doña Francisca.

CHAPTER XII

ENIGMA

THIS, then, would be the explanation of how she had stumbled so easily across her quarry's trail. Celeste, as she had thought, must, by the time Jennifer had reached the garden gate, have been well started on her furtive journey. On the other hand, Jennifer realized with a slight quickening of the breath, she herself must have almost followed Doña Francisca out of the convent. Whether the bursar was ignorant of Celeste's pilgrimage, or whether something was arranged between them, Jennifer could not, of course, guess, but for the moment she was fully determined, if possible, to hear and see what was going on in the cottage kitchen.

She pressed closer, straining her ears through the flurries of the wind.

Doña Francisca had taken off her cloak, and flung it down across the table which stood in the centre of the little, low-raftered room. She stood facing the flickering light of the fire, talking rapidly to someone just outside Jennifer's range of vision.

Jennifer, to her chagrin, found that she could hear practically nothing of what was being said: the French was rapid, and the wind snatched at the sound and whirled it away in the whines and rattles of the night. But one thing was plain, that Doña Francisca was furiously angry. Her face, more drawn and sick-white than ever, was consumed from within by a passion of anger that frightened Jennifer, and made her picture that night-flight up the mountain as the avenging rush of a fury.

She had stopped speaking, apparently on a snapped question. From somewhere beyond Jennifer's sight, near the fire, came an inaudible reply, in a man's sullen growl.

Then, in a sudden lull of the capricious wind, the woman's voice came clearly, and what she said was significant enough to set Jennifer's blood tingling.

". . . her cousin," said Doña Francisca, "asking questions. I fobbed her off, but she was thoroughly suspicious, and now she thinks she's got this proof that she's right. She'll not let go." Her voice rose sharply. "What's more, she's staying at the convent, and if I can't think up some tale that'll satisfy her——"

The man muttered something, but Doña Francisca lashed back as quickly as a striking snake.

"But can't you see what you've done, you fool? You stupid, lustful fool!" The epithets came clearly, barbed with contempt. *"Obscène bête! Animal!* Can you not see what you may have lost? If she——"

The wind took the rest, but now Jennifer, by straining a little further, could see the woman's companion, who had taken a quick step forward, and stopped, growling something which, again, she could not hear. She saw a powerfully built man of perhaps forty-five, with the dark secretive face of the Pyrenean peasant. Black eyes scowled under thick straight brows; the nose was straight too, the mouth hard and angry-looking. It was a face that might, in its harsh animal way, have been handsome, but the man's whole being was disfigured by his anger and hatred. Eyes and mouth were sulky and cruel with it, and passion betrayed with its violence every movement he made.

Facing him, Doña Francisca looked all the more patrician, her thin high-bred face, with its gleaming fanatic's eyes, betraying no fear of his angry approach, only, as he moved closer still, a faint distaste. She began to speak again, her mouth biting off the words as if they were twisted and tinged with acid. But, although Jennifer nearly fell through the window in her attempts to hear, the wind defeated the voice almost completely.

". . . Only one thing to do, and you know it! Who knows how long this English girl will choose to stay, prowling about? She'll come this way—*ça se voit*—and she's bound to see her cousin!" The listener shut her eyes and leaned against the wall, while the night rocked round her with a roaring that was not of the wind; a roaring that subsided slowly with her own heart-beats into a lull where that bitter voice was still speaking: "What you've done was folly in any case, but now, it's suicide! *Comprenez, imbécile, le suicide!*"

The man said something in reply, but his voice was pitched so low that to Jennifer it was all but inaudible. Doña Francisca hardly paused for him, but flung her mordant contempt again into his face, and this time there were threats patently mingled with it. Jennifer strained her ears to catch the torrential French:

"*Vous feriez bien de vous rappeler.* . . . Don't forget, Pierre Bussac, what I've got in my possession! You should know by now that you can't play this sort of game on your own! There's only one thing to do, and you know it— *you'll get rid of her!*"

Pierre Bussac lunged forward at that, almost as if he would have struck her, but she never moved. He paused by the table, leaning his great fists on it, and snarled something across at her.

She said coldly, watching him: "But you know I'm right, don't you? I usually am. If you thought with your brains instead of your body you'd know that the only safe course is for us to get rid of this woman. Madame Lamartine"—her voice crisped a little, and the listener felt her nerves tighten —"Madame Lamartine is dead of a fever, and lies in the convent graveyard. She must stay there. . . . One question, one doubt, one spade in the side of the grave—and the hue and cry would be on in this valley—and the end of you, my friend!"

"And of you!" he countered fiercely.

She laughed. "Oh, I don't think so. I was an innocent part. All I stand to lose is my private income."

He raised his head at that. "All? All?" He gave a hard little laugh. "All you stand to lose, my fine lady, is the dream you live for—the dream of the power and the glory that money's going to bring you! Why else do you stay in this God-forsaken valley if it isn't that you're afraid to lose your 'private income'? Do you think I don't know the plans you hug to yourself in that chapel of yours, Señora Francisca, waiting—ay, and praying for the old Mother to die . . . waiting and hoping that when there's nobody left who knows you as well as she knows you, you'll get where you want to get? That's it, isn't it? Madam Prioress of Notre-Dame-des-Orages. Not a humble little orphanage any more, oh, no! but a grand place with its new buildings and its fine and famous chapel that folk crowd from all over the world to see!" His voice thinned into a sneer. "No, you'd never want to leave the pipeline from Spain that pumps the gold into your pockets and the power into your hands that it'd kill you to be without!"

She had listened without moving, but at this the heavy lids dropped over her eyes. He laughed again. "Ah, I know you, you see! Power, Doña Francisca . . . that's what your money spells to you. . . ." His voice dropped to a vicious whisper that came clearly in the lull. "And what do you care if it's sticky with blood?"

She moved at that, but stilled herself immediately. Her face seemed to hood itself, to become again the wooden mask that Jennifer had so mistrusted. The hooded lids lifted. "Tomorrow night. You'll get rid of her tomorrow night." The black eyes burned through the mask.

The man moved then. He was shouting something. He

had raised his great fists, and seemed to be shaking them in sudden rage, but she still held him away, it appeared, by the sheer strength of the personality that blazed from her eyes.

She said, still in the same clear, bitter tones: "I shall come up tomorrow night, after Compline, at the usual time, and see it's done. And you'll do it, my stupid friend!"

He said, hoarsely: "How?"

She lifted her shoulders. "That's your affair."

"There's nowhere—you know as well as I do that I've nowhere to send her!"

Her eyes held him. She did not speak. The wind still lay quiet. Jennifer could see Bussac, still leaning on the table-top, his head thrust forward, staring at the woman. His back was towards the window, but there was about his still pose some powerful suggestion of horror. And the horror was in his voice when he spoke again.

He said: "Are you suggesting—murder?"

She said sharply: "I'm suggesting nothing. I told you it was your affair. You got into it: well, now you get out of it. I know nothing."

"I'll not do it, damn you!"

Her lip curled. "You credit me with your own evil, friend. All I demand is that you get her out of sight, out of France. *Gésus Maria*, you, of all men, know the way to do that!"

"My bridge? Take her up there and show her the road to Spain? The way she is? That would be murder and you know it! You might as well cut her throat and have done."

"You exaggerate. If she's fool enough to lose her way, what concern is that of yours—or mine? If she were given her freedom, and the road to Spain, I should certainly not feel that her murder lay at my door! I repeat, all I'm asking is that you get her out of France. What happens after that . . ." She paused. The black eyes glinted at him. "You're mighty nice all of a sudden, aren't you? Who are you to prate of murder? What's another to you, more or less?"

He said nothing, but stood staring at her. There was a pause, then across the silence the wind began to whine again, clawing at the shutters, and whipping Jennifer's damp skirts flat against the cottage wall.

Doña Francisca's voice came again, clearly: "Then you understand. Tomorrow night. And if you refuse . . ." For the first time she moved nearer to him, and, though her body was still held stiffly upright, it was as if she had lowered her voice and leaned forward in hideous confidence: "If you refuse——"

The wind screamed through the broken eaves. Jennifer, in a fury of frustration, saw the bursar's lips moving dumbly. The man was shaking his head; he took a step forward and brought his fists down on the table as if in a passion of refusal. Doña Francisca, ignoring the gesture as if he had never moved, flung at him one last, contemptuous, vitriolic phrase. Then she turned her back on him and picked up her cloak.

Jennifer waited for no more, but fled into the shadows and down the stony track faster than even the wings of the furies would have carried her.

*   *   *

As she crept through the stone tunnel that led between chapel and refectory, she was halted by a faint sound, which seemed to come through the unlatched west door of the chapel. She hesitated a moment, then, reckoning that she had sufficient lead from Doña Francisca, she moved soundlessly to the door, pushed it open a further crack, and looked in.

At first she could see nothing, then, in the dim red glimmer of the sanctuary lamp, she saw, again, what she had encountered once before. Celeste was kneeling, crouching rather, before the altar of Our Lady of Sorrow. Jennifer could hear, faintly, spectrally, the tiny whisper of a sobbing prayer.

She drew back, but not before she had seen, on the shoulders of the girl's cloak, raindrops glittering in the red light like a scatter of rubies. Mindful of who was to follow her in a moment, she withdrew swiftly into the shadows, and closed the heavy door on that small desperate whispering.

CHAPTER XIII

CAPRICE ESPAGNOLE

IT would certainly be easy enough, now, to convince Stephen that she had been right. Jennifer, with one eye perpetually on her wrist-watch, saw the tiny hand ticking away the morning, herself in a rising fever of impatience and indecision.

No immediately useful purpose, she could see, would be served by laying her story straight before the Prioress: if Doña Francisca was to be exposed, it must be by those who could forthwith restrain her. There must be no risk of alarming her, and driving her before her time to "destroy the evidence" that was hidden away at Bussac's farm.

For this same reason she dared not hurry too early, and too eagerly, out of the convent to meet Stephen before the time arranged. She had, after all, accepted the convent's hospitality for the avowed purpose of making inquiries there, and to fail to carry out this programme might arouse the very suspicion that she wanted to avert. Nor could she have escaped at all easily had she wanted to, for, so eager was the Prioress to atone for the convent's "mistake", that she sent for Jennifer as soon as breakfast was over and asked her in Doña Francisca's presence what inquiries she proposed to make.

"Doña Francisca," said the soft old voice, "will do her best to help you." And the bursar, looking at Jennifer with those hooded, unreadable eyes, was understood to say that she would indeed.

But Jennifer had had a long time to think and she was prepared for this. She merely took Doña Francisca painstakingly and repetitively over what she knew to be safe ground—the car-crash, the storm, her "cousin's" arrival at the convent, the course of her illness, the summoning of Father Anselm, death. . . .

The bursar answered the questions with no sign of hesitation; her voice was even and pleasant, her face as usual expressionless, but her eyes watched. Jennifer, for her part, let it be seen from the beginning of the interview that this morning she was already repenting her unworthy impulses of yesterday. She began with slightly apologetic hesitation, and her artless questions, running the gamut of shame-faced persistence and, finally, reluctant conviction, brought the faintest shade of contempt into the line of the woman's mouth. Jennifer saw this with some pleasure, and saw, too, the slight relaxation of that steady, watchful stare. She proceeded, with a charming air of apology, to lull the watch-dog further. . . .

It was a performance that would have amused Stephen, and shaken Mrs. Silver to the roots of her being. The interview ended at last in as pretty an exchange of hypocrisies as could be imagined, Jennifer, in so many words, retracting her nonsense of yesterday, and Doña Francisca admitting that a mistake had undoubtedly occurred somewhere, and that if there was anything the convent could do she had only to let them know. . . .

Here the bell went for morning service, and, both in her rôle as the convent's guest and as repentant mourner for her cousin, Jennifer could do no other than accept the bursar's invitation to accompany her down to chapel, and there fret her way through what seemed an interminable service.

Nor was escape possible afterwards. When, after chapel, Doña Francisca suggested, in the kindest possible manner, that she might like to see her cousin's baggage and decide what was to be done with it, Jennifer could think of no convincing way of refusing. The idea did cross her mind that Doña Francisca was, as it were, deliberately keeping her close, and at this idea she felt a pang of uneasy fear. But to her relief she was handed over to Sister Marie-Annette—a fresh-faced woman of perhaps forty—while the bursar went about her own duties.

It was a full hour before Jennifer could decently tear herself away from the practical sympathy and obviously passionate interest of the gossip-starved Sister Marie-Annette. But she did escape at length, on the only possible excuse that would have made the good sister let her go alone—that of making another pilgrimage to her cousin's grave.

She hurried along the bright corridor, down the saint-watched stairs, and across the hall. The orphans, attended by two of the younger nuns, were congregated in the stone tunnel by the refectory, on their way to some lesson, so Jennifer turned aside, to pass through the western end of the chapel into the garden.

She did not see, till she had reached the middle of the nave, that both Celeste and Doña Francisca were in the chapel, busy with some sort of job of cleaning. She was instantly sorry she had come this way.

But they took no notice of her. It was doubtful, in fact, if Celeste even saw her. She was sitting on the shallow altar step, with a fold of tapestry pulled out from the wall towards her, mending it with tiny meticulous stitches. The bursar, who sat above Celeste in what must be the priest's chair, was polishing one of the candlesticks from the altar, her long fingers loving each curve, as they caressed, rather than rubbed it, into brightness. But she was not watching what she was doing; her eyes were fixed on the down-bent head of the girl, and Jennifer, with a vivid memory of that tormented, furious face of the previous night, saw, with a sense of shock, the expression that it now held. It was as if, from who knew what dark and bitter depths, a kind of fierce and yearning tenderness had been dragged up, and was straining like a passion at features which fought to deny it. Love, in a place that knew only barrenness and the fires of frustration.

Jennifer, shocked again at the wave of acute distaste which swept over her, moved quickly and quietly towards the south door. Doña Francisca's eyes lifted for a moment, watched her without expression, then fell to the task in her hands.

Jennifer, her heart beating uncomfortably hard, almost ran out into the sweet sunlight of the garden, and the healthy presence of the gardener.

*   *   *

It did not take her very long to satisfy Sister Louisa's un-exacting inquiries. The old nun was too relieved to see Jennifer restored, apparently, to sanity, to reopen herself the dangerous questions of yesterday. Jenny said enough to reassure her, then left her to her weeding, crouched happily under the peach-trees like a benevolent toad, and went back through the gate into the graveyard.

There she stayed just long enough to give colour to what she had told Sister Marie-Annette; then, with a glance at the shut south door of the chapel, she went swiftly over to the gate in the wall, and let herself at last out of the convent buildings.

*   *   *

Even then she was delayed, for as she skirted the outer wall of the garden she heard the sound of hoofs on the valley track, and rounded the corner to see the young man of yesterday's encounter approaching the convent. He was riding the same big chestnut stallion, and the other two horses followed as before.

She waited in the shade by the convent gate. It had occurred to her that it might be useful to know a little more about Pierre Bussac and his wife, and that this boy, who also lived, so Stephen had said, in the valley, might be able to tell her something.

He drew rein as he came up to her, eyeing her uncertainly, while under him the big horse sidled and fidgeted, raking at the bits and blowing gustily through flaring nostrils.

They made a sufficiently striking picture, the horse with the sunlight glancing and rippling off his shifting muscles, and the rider sitting him so effortlessly, his shabby jeans and stained blue shirt only serving to emphasize the beauty of his hard young body. He had the rather startling good looks of the young Spaniard, the long-lidded dark eyes, short upper lip, and proud, sensual, beautifully cut mouth. He waited, eyeing Jennifer, who was startled to see under the insolently drooping lids the unmistakable glint of dislike and suspicion.

It threw her off balance, and she could only say, lamely: "You must be Luis."

"Yes."

The two loose horses thrust forward then, eager to get into the shade of the wall. One shouldered the other, which turned with flattened ears and snapping teeth, and they crowded into the wall's shadow, heads low now and tails switching. Jennifer moved nervously away, and saw amused contempt curving Luis's arrogant young mouth.

The interview was decidedly not starting well. She began again, almost at random.

"I saw you last night."

This innocent gambit had a startling effect. Amusement vanished, and the dark eyes narrowed and hardened. She did not see him move hand or heel, but the stallion shifted his quarters, swishing his tail as if at some quick discomfort.

"Yes?"

"You were jumping the stream lower down the valley. You live over there, don't you?"

"Yes," said Luis for the third time, but his intent gaze had relaxed a little, and the stallion was quiet. Luis jerked a head westwards. "Over the ridge beyond the Petit Gave."

This positively garrulous reply encouraged Jennifer. She walked forward and put out a hesitant hand towards the stallion's neck.

"He's lovely. Is he your own?"

"They all are," he said proudly. "I hire out the other two, but"—his hand smoothed the glossy neck—"not this one. Not Foix."

She stroked the horse's shoulder softly. The skin was warm and alive under her fingers. "Does he bite?"

There was a gleam of a smile. "Only if I let him."

"Then please don't!" She glanced up at him, still feeling her way through that intangible barrier of unfriendliness. "Your name—Luis. You're Spanish, are you—not French?"

He said politely: "Half, mam'selle. My mother was Spanish, yes; but my father came from Orthez."

"Gascon? I see." She added, tentatively: "You must find it very lonely in this valley?"

"Perhaps." Again that imperceptible withdrawal.

"Does anyone else live in the valley, Luis?"

"Only the Bussacs. They have a farm higher up."

"Do you visit them?"

His lips curved. "Pierre Bussac doesn't encourage visitors."

"But you've been there? You've met his wife?"

"No."

"It must be a very lonely life for a woman. Has Madame Bussac no—companion?"

"I don't know. How should I? Why?"

His tone was hard again, almost rude. She said, ignoring it: "Do you know who I am?"

"Yes. You're the cousin of the woman who died here. Everybody knows that."

"Do they? . . . Then you'll understand why I'm interested in this valley. You live here throughout the summer, so I suppose you know most of the things that go on here? And quite a lot about the convent?"

Under his hand, perceptibly, the snaffle-rings jerked, and the horse flung up his head angrily, and began to sidle. Luis soothed him with hand and voice, but without taking his eyes off Jennifer's face. Not until the horse stood still again did he answer, and then his voice held no expression.

"Perhaps," was all he said.

She persisted. "You remember the night of my cousin's accident?"

"Of course."

"You never—saw her?"

"How should I?" he countered again almost fiercely, and she was suddenly reminded of the way she had seen him sitting his horse last night, with his head sunk between his shoulders like a waiting hawk.

"And no one else—you've talked to no one else who saw her?"

The rein gleamed and tightened along the glossy neck. Luis's heels moved. The stallion threw up his great crest and whirled round on his haunches towards the convent gate, almost shouldering Jennifer out of the way. She jumped aside.

"Be careful!"

He took no notice. His dark face was blazing. "You ask too many questions!" He flung it at her over his shoulder as the horse plunged past. He made no attempt to stop it, and in spite of her startled anger she caught her breath at the picture they made. A Centaur? That was hackneyed. This was a more than physical union. It was as if—so much a part of each other were boy and stallion—he used the great beast to express his own violent emotions. If the rider was flushed with anger, the stallion actually blazed with it. The hot light sparkled and flew off red-gold hide and glittering steel, the dry dust mushroomed up under the sledge-hammer hoofs; sweat sprang up dark along the bunching flanks as the beast shot forward in a series of vicious jarring bounds that were patently intended to hurtle his rider into the dust at his feet, there to be smashed at leisure. For perhaps thirty seconds Luis let him go, then wrist, heel and body moved together, and the great stallion came round and up to the bit, forced sideways, still viciously plunging, towards the convent gate. The wall's shadow quenched the silk-and-steel glitter of the sweating hide, and the horse was thrust—it seemed—sideways up against the gate, Luis holding him now with one thin brown hand. The other hand shot to the breast of his shirt, dragging out a package of letters which he threw, all in the same fluid movement, into a box on the gate.

The hand flew up to the bell; pulled it; then clamped down on the rein again beside its fellow, just as, inside the gate, the bell clashed, and the stallion, obedient to the boy's dropped wrists, shot forward from a fighting stand in one great leap that brought him and his rider flashing out again into the sun. There was a shrill whistle. The other two horses turned, churning the dry earth, trotting out a little ponderously into the stallion's smoking wake. Then they, too, seeming to receive some stimulus of excitement, threw up their heads and lurched forward at a faster pace, and presently all three swung into the familiar raking gallop that bore them swiftly from sight in a thudding flurry of hoofs.

"Now what in the wide world," said Jennifer, under her breath, "can be the matter with *you*?"

She was recalled to herself by the expiring jangle of the bell still quivering inside the gate, advertising to the convent hat its mail had been delivered. Someone would be coming to answer it, and she did not want to be detained again. She hurried to the corner of the wall, and stepped round it just as quick footsteps padded across the dusty courtyard towards the gate.

She waited. She heard the creak of the gate, and the rustle of the package being withdrawn from the box. The hinges complained again. The latch clanged down. The footsteps receded.

Jennifer turned away and hurried down the valley to meet Stephen.

CHAPTER XIV

HUNT AND STORM

THE day was stiflingly hot. What freshness of rain or dew had fallen on the grass last night was gone, sucked up by an ominously hot sun—ominous because, though the sun stood brilliantly overhead, the sky behind the mountain crests looked dull and thick, and the air moved heavily, as though charged with thunder. The little breeze that ran shining-footed across the bending grasses held the same hot presage of storm.

But Jennifer noticed none of this. She hurried down the hot track through the dust, almost running. It was already past noon, and still there had been no sign of Stephen. If he was late . . . if he failed to come . . .

But as she rounded the first bend in the track she saw him, less than a hundred yards away, coming, in spite of his slight limp, at a great pace through the still-quivering haze of dust that the horses had raised. If his face was grimmer than yesterday, she did not notice. She merely called out thankfully and ran the last few yards to meet him.

"Jenny! Thank heaven! I've been——"

But he did not finish. It was almost as if last night's little scene were being played again, but this time in the pitiless storm-charged sunlight which showed too clearly in her face the white distress that drove her towards him. And this time he knew his rôle.

He put out his hands and took hold of hers. She clung to his comforting grasp.

"Oh, Stephen, I was afraid you wouldn't come!"

"I said I would."

"Oh, Stephen——" She was shaking now. He lifted her

hands, still prisoned in his own, and held them against his chest, pulling her towards him.

"It's all right, Jenny. I did come. What is it?"

She began to tell him, trembling still, the urgency of communication making her stumble almost into incoherence, of which, in the first minute or so, the only word that stood out to convey anything was "*murder*". . . .

It was then that he detached her clinging hands gently, and led her off the dusty track into the shade of the cliff.

"Now sit down," he said calmly, "and tell me about it properly—no, wait a moment. I think some wine would be a very sound idea, don't you? And something to eat? We'll have our conference over lunch. . . . Here. Down with it. . . . Good girl. Now have a shot at a ham roll; I'll allow you to talk with your mouth full." He took one himself and settled his shoulders back against the rock. "Now tell me. Begin at the beginning."

His matter-of-factness, no less than the steadying draught of wine, had their effect, and Jennifer was able presently to give her tale some sort of shape. He listened in silence, the grimness settling on his face into a sufficiently forbidding expression as he heard of her mad flight up the dark valley on an errand—as was apparent now—so hideously dangerous.

"And Gillian's there, a prisoner!" cried Jennifer. "*Why* she's being kept there I don't know, and at present I don't care. But she's in danger—tonight. . . . Stephen, this isn't imagination any longer. It's sober truth. Stephen——"

His hand fell reassuringly over hers. "Yes, Jenny, I know. I'd found out for myself, already. I was worried sick to think what you might have got yourself into the middle of."

"You found out something? From the doctor?"

"No, from the police. I had a chat with my friend Aristide this morning, and without giving anything away I got enough information out of him to make me smell a pretty powerful rat."

"Pierre Bussac?"

"Yes, indeed. King Rat, our friend Bussac. And I found out who Isaac Lenormand was."

"Isaac—oh, the letter! Then he has got something to do with it?"

"Yes. Listen; I'll be brief. I got it all in the way of gossip, but the gist of it is that your Pierre Bussac is well-known locally as a smuggler—rumour has it that he has his own private and highly dangerous route into Spain. I imagine that's the 'bridge' you heard him refer to. Well, this has never worried anybody much—everybody smuggles in this part of the world; it's almost respectable. But during the war he started—still rumours this—a different traffic, that of smuggling wealthy people out of the country, away from the Nazis."

"You mean Jews and—oh! Isaac Lenormand!"

"Exactly. Three million francs Isaac paid . . . big money. Especially as he never got to Spain."

"Never got—what d'you mean?"

He said soberly: "His body was found washed down the Petit Gave. He'd been shot."

"I—see. And what did rumour say about that?"

"Plainly enough, that Pierre Bussac had murdered him in order to rob him of whatever other valuables he was taking with him into exile. But, of course, there was no proof, not a shadow, and at that time, during the war, no one was going to bother much. . . ."

"Stephen, it's horrible!"

He nodded grimly, and reached for his cigarettes. "But now they are, it seems, taking an interest in friend Bussac. There are still large sums of money to be earned by smuggling wanted individuals across the border—criminals, Jenny, escaping criminals; men and women wanted for serious crimes—like, for example, those bank-robbers from Bordeaux that they were talking about in the hotel yesterday. The Dupré gang."

Her face lifted to his, paling as aspen leaves pale in the wind. "Marcel Dupré's sister," she breathed. "The woman who got away. . . . Could it be?"

"Why not? She's completely vanished, according to Aristide. Supposing it was arranged that Bussac should ferry this Dupré girl over the border, and somehow she got wind of Gillian's coming up here, and wangled a lift. You remember that Gillian's letter said '*We* are leaving tomorrow'?"

"Yes. Yes, I do. I just thought it was a way of speaking about the car."

"It may have been. But also it may have referred to herself and her passenger."

"And then there was an accident."

"Yes. Something happened, we don't know what, and the Dupré girl somehow changed places with Gillian. Say she grabbed Gillian's money and papers, and set off for Bussac's farm, only to collapse at the convent gate. And, afterwards, found it safer to allow the nuns to assume she was Gillian Lamartine, than to admit to being Lally Dupré . . . only it didn't matter in the end. She died."

"And Gillian is at Bussac's farm," said Jennifer in a tight little voice, half of triumph, half of apprehension.

He glanced at her. "It seems so."

She drew in her breath. "And it's because she's seen the Dupré woman, and knows she came up here, that Bussac's keeping her prisoner!"

"Hardly. Why should he? Lally Dupré's dead now and —no, it doesn't quite hang together. Besides, it's Doña Francisca who wants Gillian put out of the way, not Bussac, according to what you said."

She pushed back the soft hair from her face with a sharp,

nervous movement, and got to her knees, making as if to rise. "We'll sort it out later. Just at the moment the only thing that matters is getting Gillian out of this, safe! The police——"

But he did not move. He was frowning thoughtfully at the smoke that spiralled up between his fingers. "No, Jenny. I don't somehow think the police are going to listen very hard."

"But—what I heard last night! Those plans to murder Gillian!"

His eyes lifted briefly. "There's only Aristide Celton at Gavarnie. By the time we've got through to Luz or Pierre-fitte, explained everything, made our depositions—probably in triplicate—that Doña Francisca, the bursar of the Convent of Notre-Dames-des-Orages, plans to murder a woman who's already officially dead . . ." He gave a hard little laugh. "Jenny, dear, don't you know your France better than that? If I accused you last night of inventing Grand Guignol, what the hell d'you think the police are going to say?"

The little silence seemed edged with the threat of storm. A lizard flicked on to a stone and then lay still, a delicately etched curve of dark jade, a Chinese ornament perfect in its artifice except for the tiny pulsing of the throat against the hot stone.

Jennifer said, in a small unemphatic voice: "Then we've got to stop it by ourselves."

He turned his head. At the movement the lizard flickered out of sight, and the stone lay hot and bare between them. He looked gravely at her.

"Oh—yes, we'll stop it. And it shouldn't be too hard, Jenny. In spite of the Grand Guignol set-up—mountain-valleys, murder, and mysterious goings-on in the convent— I don't think it's a case for heroics." He paused. "Or even the police. I still think it would be a mistake to get mixed up in what doesn't concern us—and Pierre Bussac's activities, however villainous, decidedly do not."

"But Gillian——"

"Oh, yes. She concerns us. In fact the whole affair boils down quite simply to that: to get Gillian safely away from Bussac's farm, and take her home with us." He hesitated. "And if that can be done quietly—without dragging in the police and accusing Bussac and that woman of felony—so much the better." He smiled at her expression. "Too unheroic by half, Jenny? Don't I measure up?"

She flushed. "It isn't that. It's just that—well, if they *are* felons——"

"We have a duty to do something about it? Perhaps. But think a minute"—his hand dropped lightly over hers—"if we rush into this with guns blazing, God knows what we may start, and Gillian's in the thick of it. If we can get her out of it by negotiation, as it were, don't you honestly think that would be better?"

"Of course. But *can* we?"

"I think so. I'm beginning to get a glimmering—the craziest glimmering—of an idea as to what she's doing up at the farm—though no ideas as to *why*. . . . And it makes me feel that our first move is obviously to go up there."

"What about Bussac?"

He grinned. "He won't be there. I saw him as I came up, away over the hill with a mule. That's why we're going straight away."

He got to his feet, and put down a hand to her, pulling her up. She said eagerly: "If Madame Bussac's there on her own, we can surely deal with her!"

He was looking down at her somewhat oddly. "If I'm right," he said slowly. "I hope we can."

"What d'you mean?"

He laughed, avoiding the question. "I told you I wasn't a story-book hero. I don't particularly want to face

King Rat, but I don't mind his wife. She's a friend of mine."

"Oh, yes, I'd forgotten. She's one of your painting critics."

"That's it. The one who prefers photographs." He turned to pick up his haversack. "And that brings me back to the crazy idea I was telling you about. I think—what the devil?"

From above a sharp sound had interrupted him. A puff of dust spurted from the cliff-top. Something moved. . . .

"*Look out!*"

He was on her in one leap. There was no time to get out of range. She felt herself whirled up into his arms, crushed there as he swung round with his back to the cliff and his body blocking the danger from her.

There was the whisper and hot smell of dust. The falling boulder whistled down, struck. . . .

It crashed into the rock where Jenny had been sitting, and smashed into a dozen vicious missiles. Ricocheting fragments flinched and whined round them. She felt Stephen's body jerk once, and as one arm fell away from her the other tightened in a momentary agony, so that she almost cried out. Her face was jammed against the rough tweed of his coat. A button was biting into her cheek. Her bones seemed to crack in his grip.

All at once it was over. A pebble flipped almost contemptuously on to a rock beside them; another came tapping harmlessly down on to her hand. Nothing else moved.

But, like a mocking echo from the top of the cliff, came another rattle which made her flinch again, then stiffen.

It was the retreating rattle of hoofs.

*   *   *

He still held her.

"Stephen!"

Fear edged her voice as she pushed herself back in his encircling arm, and lifted her head to look at his face.

"Stephen, you're hurt!"

A shudder went through him, so swift and sharp that it was as if he winced from another blow; then he seemed, with an equally rapid and violent effort, to gather himself together. The blank expression left his eyes, and he looked down at her. His face was very white.

"Jenny. Oh, my God, Jenny, I thought—are you all right?"

"Yes. Oh, yes. But what about you?"

"I'm O.K."

"Sure?"

"Quite sure."

She looked at him. "Don't lie to me, Stephen. You were hit. I felt it."

"Only a bump on the shoulder, I promise you. It's done no damage." He flexed his right arm cautiously, wincing a little. "Bruises, that's all."

"Honestly? You—you looked ghastly, Stephen."

"Did I?" He smiled a little. "Pure fright. If that damned rock had fallen a bit straighter——"

"Or if you hadn't jumped right under it to push me out of the way," said Jenny. She shook dust out of her skirt and looked up at him with grave eyes. "Not so unheroic, Stephen; don't belittle yourself, my dear. That should have hit me."

He grinned at her. The colour was coming back into his face, though a trace of pain still showed itself in the line of his mouth. "I live for others," he said lightly, then gave a quick upward look. "Let's get out from under, shall we?"

"You don't think there's more coming down?"

"I don't think so. But it's as well to be out of range."

Jenny said: "He's gone, anyway."

He looked at her sideways. "You heard it too?"

"Oh, yes."

He made no comment, but said, as they reached the safety of the track: "I think we can take the time to wash ourselves. It'll improve our morale, and I'm covered with dust."

"Is there anything left to drink?"

"Half a bottle of *vin topaze*; and it's intact."

The water was ice-cold and refreshing, the wind blandly heartening. Afterwards they climbed the grassy slope from the river back to the track in silence. The sun still glared down, hot and still, but, to the south, a slate-grey bank of cloud was slowly building itself up behind the mountain crests. What breeze there had been had dropped, and the air lay hot and heavy on the slopes. The green of the grass had deepened to a sultry olive, and even the papery heads of the mountain-everlastings failed to stir in any breath of air.

They reached the track, both pausing when they had gained it to glance, almost involuntarily, up at the cliff-top, which now showed nothing at its crest but the weight of the darkening sky.

Jennifer said: "Those horses——"

"Horse. There was only one."

She looked at him. "The boy, Luis."

He said nothing, but his eyes narrowed speculatively on the point from which the rock had fallen.

"Why, Stephen? He was awfully queer with me this afternoon, but why—that? You say you know him. Where does he come in?"

He shrugged, and then winced, so that she looked at him with renewed anxiety. "Your shoulder *is* hurt, Stephen."

He said, almost impatiently: "It's nothing. Come on, let's go."

He set off up the track, his limp perhaps a little more pronounced than usual. She followed, biting her lip, almost grateful now for the prospect of the action to come, leaving as it did no time to think too carefully about what had just happened. Attempted murder?. Even for Luis, with his instinct for the spectacular, it had been a pretty dramatic effort. To use the hills themselves as his weapon. . . . As she glanced back it touched her again, that feather-light finger of fear; the same shadow-tip of panic's wing that had chilled her yesterday when she hurried between the waiting hills towards the Dark Tower. . . .

Stephen had half-turned, and was waiting.

"All right, *mignonne*?"

His voice was warm and strong and normal. The pallor of his fear for her had gone, and he looked confident and a little grim. She smiled at him.

"Yes. Truly, Stephen. I'm fine."

The hazel eyes mocked her, gently. "Fragile little blossom. But seriously, Jenny, I——" He paused, then said abruptly: "I wish you'd stay behind."

"Oh, Stephen, no! You can't ask me to do that!"

"I'd be happier if you didn't come."

"Why on earth? It's not dangerous. Bussac——"

"I'm not thinking about Bussac. He'll not be there. It's just that I've a feeling the interview may be—distressing, and I'd rather you weren't in on it."

"Surely it'll be easier if I'm there? I mean, Gillian——"

"I—suppose so." He looked at her doubtfully. "It's only that . . . damn it, Jenny, I know you've done wonders so far, but you're not used to this kind of thing."

"Who is?" said Jennifer, not unreasonably. "Melodrama in the High Pyrenees? Come off it, Stephen; we're both amateurs."

He grinned. "Maybe. But I wasn't brought up in cotton-wool."

"And I was?" She spoke without rancour. "So what? You're surely not going to suggest that I go back into that beastly convent and just wait, are you?"

In spite of the light tone, something very like panic frayed the edges of her voice, so that Stephen glanced quickly down.

They were there, clear in her face, the faint but definite stress-signals. Serenity had gone; her eyes were dark with shadows, her mouth too firmly controlled. His heart gave a little jerk of pity and tenderness. The guarded bower of Cherry Close was a very long way away. . . .

He said, "All right. As you say, it may be easier with you there. But I'd as soon have seen you safe in out of the storm, in both senses of the word."

"More cotton-wool?"

He grinned. "It's your own fault. You shouldn't look so confoundedly fragile. Come if you must, but don't blame me if you get wet."

"I shan't," said Jennifer, and followed him past the convent walls towards the distant gloom of the pine-woods.

Round them, as they went, the sunlight seemed to thicken almost palpably, and the thunder-charged air sagged heavily on grass and scree. Away to the north the great storm-cloud mounted and darkened, and its indigo rim reached out to suck down the sun.

CHAPTER XV

THE BARTERED BRIDE

THE farm cottage was silent, shut, and apparently deserted, but as Stephen and Jennifer approached it across the weedy cobbles they saw a mule standing tethered outside one of the sheds. Its coat was dark with sweat, the hair on its belly tagged with points of damp.

Stephen stopped, and shot out a hand to grip Jennifer's arm.

He said, under his breath: "Damn and blast. That means he's come back. Jenny, for God's sake will you get away out of this? Quickly!"

But it was too late. A man had already emerged from one of the ramshackle buildings, and was making for them, bucket in hand. It was the big dark man of last night's adventure; Pierre Bussac, mountaineer and . . . murderer? Jennifer, rooted to the cobbles where she had played the listener last night, could only hope, through her dismay, that the Frenchman would not realize who she was.

The sunlight, cut across by a threatening shape of cloud, fell slanting straight into his eyes, so that, dazzled for a moment as he emerged from the dark byre, he took three or four steps forward before he saw them. He paused at sight of them, scowling uncertainly at Stephen, who had moved in front of Jennifer.

"What the devil do you want?" he asked roughly.

Stephen said: "You're Pierre Bussac?"

There was no direct reply to this, but merely a roughly dismissive, "You're wasting your time," in the thick Southern accent that had baffled Jennifer the night before. She realized with relief that the man had taken Stephen to be a tourist seeking his professional help as a guide. He added sourly: "I'm not taking any more up this summer. Didn't they tell you that in the village?"

And at that he turned, hunching one shoulder as if in dismissal. But his movement had brought him within sight of Jennifer, hugging her obscurity behind Stephen's back. He glanced, stared, his black suspicious gaze burning swiftly over her, taking in the pale-gold cap of hair, the tan-golden skin, the full-skirted frock of green cotton that she wore. . . .

The black eyes stared, widened. There was a clang as the bucket slipped from his unheeding fingers and struck the ground, tilting and overturning with an almost slow-motion unreality. He made no move to stop it. The dull clank of its fall brought two dogs running, but they stopped their rush as the thick stream of milk spread on the cobbles, and stayed behind their master, bristling a little and eyeing the strangers with snarling suspicion.

Bussac knew who she was; that much was obvious. And mixed with the anger in his eyes was unmistakably a shade of fear. His glance wavered, shifted, dropped, and then— irresistibly—he looked back at the closed cottage door.

But only momentarily. The faint clinking sound of the fallen bucket, as it rolled in an arc at his feet, seemed to recall him with a jerk. He stooped to pick it up, swore viciously at his dogs, and then turned back to Jennifer and Stephen with his self-command apparently unimpaired.

He said, flatly: "I've no time to spend talking. I've told you I'm doing no more guide's work."

He would have turned away again, but Stephen's voice doggedly stopped him: "Just a moment. . . . It isn't about making a trip that I want to see you, as I think you realize now, Monsieur Bussac: I want to talk to you."

Bussac smiled, not pleasantly. "I don't have to listen."

Stephen said quietly: "No. But I think you'd better listen, Monsieur Bussac. Or would you rather we went away now and discussed it with the police?" He took out a cigarette and lit it, eyeing the other man across the flame. "Or—say—Doña Francisca?" he added gently.

It was as if the name were a hawk—a storm-hanging vulture, thought Jennifer—the edge of whose shadow could strike the creatures below it into just this immobility. The man went still. His eyes held Stephen's. There was fear in them again, and along with it a new element that was difficult to determine—the kind of desperation that springs from an overwhelming and dreadful futility.

He said, licking dry lips: "All right. I'll listen. What did you come here for? Who are you?"

"I don't matter," said Stephen, "but I think you already know mademoiselle here. I saw you recognize her. Doña Francisca described her to you last night, didn't she? She told you, didn't she, that mademoiselle wasn't satisfied that her cousin was dead, and might come up here to inquire after her?"

"Last night? Doña Francisca? What are you talking about?"

"Don't bother to hedge. You were overheard."

The black eyes flicked to Jennifer, then back to Stephen. There was a glitter in them, but all he said was "So?"

Stephen eyed him levelly. "So I suggest we don't waste any more time. Mademoiselle's cousin is here, Monsieur Bussac, and we've come to get her!"

The atmosphere was suddenly electric. The sun had vanished now behind the towering bastions of cloud, and the air hung heavy and purple over the motionless pines. Away in the distance they could hear the first mutter of the storm.

Bussac straightened his great shoulders. "I'll not listen to this any longer. You're talking nonsense—lies!" He made a fierce gesture that sent the dogs swerving back from his heels. "You can get out, d'you hear? Go on, get out, you

and your woman too! What if I do know who she is, and
the story she's telling? What if Doña Francisca did come
here last night to warn me she'd be sneaking about my
place? I'm telling you both, there's nobody here but me
and my wife, and we don't like strangers in these parts."
He swung on Jennifer with so menacing a look that she
stepped instinctively back. "As for you—your cousin's
dead and buried—d'you hear me? Dead and buried, and
you've got no call to go scrabbling about the grave. So get
out of here before I set the dogs on you!"

Stephen spoke sharply: "One moment, Bussac! You can
bluster all you like, but you know—and we know—that it's
all bluff." He added in a reasonable tone of voice: "Listen
to me for a moment—no! I assure you it's worth your while
to do so! We know that mademoiselle's cousin is here, just
as we know that you're up to your neck, you and that
woman at the convent, in a dangerous game. What it is I
don't know, *and believe me, Monsieur Bussac, I don't care!*"

"I don't know what you're talking about!" The man
came a threatening step nearer, his dogs at his heels.

"What's it to us," said Stephen, without moving, "what's
it to us what happened to Lally Dupré?"

Pierre Bussac stopped as if he'd been shot. The breath
whistled through his nostrils.

He said: "*What do you know about Dupré?*"

Stephen eyed him blandly. "I know nothing—if you'll do
what I'm proposing you should."

Pierre Bussac waited, still as a rock, his handsome head
sunk a little between his shoulders, his dark eyes unreadable.
They flickered once—towards the cottage door—then fixed
again on Stephen.

"Well?"

Stephen said, pleasantly: "We might strike a bargain,
Pierre Bussac. Let me repeat that your affairs are no concern of ours except as they touch mademoiselle's cousin.

All we care about is her safe delivery into our hands. Now, I gather that her presence here is an embarrassment, perhaps even a danger, to you and your"—he looked down at the cigarette in his hand—"your partner. I'm proposing that you let us relieve you of this danger, now."

The man's eyes flickered and he appeared to hesitate.

Stephen said: "*Now*, Monsieur Bussac. And we'll remove her from the district as quickly and privately as we can, and nothing said."

Something struggled in Bussac's eyes, some dark glint of passion or fear or urgency, underlined with something that might—had it not seemed absurd—have been shame. His gaze fell from Stephen's queerly. The hand which he put up to drag the shirt away from his throat was trembling.

Stephen pressed home his apparent advantage. "You understand me?" he said, smoothly and urgently. "The police—Dupré—Doña Francisca—they don't come into this. All we want is the girl, safe and sound." His voice sharpened. "I'm offering you a bargain, man—a good one. We'll relieve you of the evidence, ourselves, Monsieur Bussac, *now*. When that woman comes up tonight your—your lodger will have vanished, and by this time tomorrow she'll be half-way to England. And 'Madame Lamartine' stays buried—and no one will ever find Lally Dupré! . . . What about it? What d'you say?"

But what Bussac might have said they were never to know, for even as he lifted his head, his great shoulders stiff, his hands clenched into fists, there came an interruption—dramatic enough in itself, but rendered positively theatrical by the threat of the approaching storm.

Behind Bussac the door of the cottage opened. A solitary beam of yellow light, spilled somehow through the piled clouds, stabbed steeply across the cobbles to spotlight the woman who stood there.

She was slim and fair, and she had grey eyes. From where

she stood, faced by the beam of light, she could not see Stephen and Jennifer, and she spoke straight to Bussac's back.

"It's going to rain," she said. "You'd better come in, hadn't you?"

Across Bussac's startled oath as he turned, across the nearer growl of the thunder, cut Jennifer's cry.

"Gillian!"

CHAPTER XVI

DISCORD: *con forza*

"IT's Gillian!" cried Jennifer again, and started across the cobbles.

And then everything seemed to happen at once.

At that first cry of wild and incredulous joy, the fair girl in the doorway started and stood rigid, the words freezing on her lips. Her eyes, wide, and very clear grey, met Jennifer's in a single startled look, then, as Bussac's oath ripped out, she shrank back into the shadow of the cottage doorway.

"*Gillian!*"

Jennifer ran towards her, hands outstretched. And the cottage door slammed in her face.

As she recoiled, Bussac moved. With another oath, whose violent meaning there was no mistaking, he seized Jennifer by the arm, and dragged her back from the door. The hand bit into her arm, and she cried out. Stephen leaped forward, his cigarette whizzing like a tiny meteorite down into the runnel of milk that seeped, bluish, between the cobbles. Bussac, thrusting Jennifer violently aside, swung to face him.

It is doubtful whether Stephen meant to do more than surprise the man into releasing Jennifer, but any choice of action was now brutally torn from him. For Bussac, head low and fists swinging, attacked like a crazed thing.

Jennifer, bruised and sprawling on the cobbles, had a momentary and flashing vision—as if the eye of a camera had clicked open and shut—of the male musk-ox, horns down, charging his enemy; charging danger, while his females stood protected at his back . . . but of course (she scrambled, confused and shaken, to her feet) it was not Stephen who was the enemy and Bussac the protector; it was the reverse. Bussac had Gillian a prisoner in his beastly little cottage, and Stephen and she must get her away. Now.

Bussac, with a tearing grunt, had broken Stephen's hold, and the two men flung apart. They stood, glaring and breathing heavily, the space of air between them already quivering with the next attack. Bussac rushed—another bull-like rush—and Stephen side-stepped, but not neatly enough. The other's fist caught him above the heart, and then the two were locked again, in a horrible battle of straining muscles and grunting animal breaths.

Jennifer turned and ran for the cottage door.

But she had reckoned without the dogs. As she reached out an arm towards the door-latch, the foremost of the two flung himself straight at her hand. She snatched it back with a cry of terror, and the dog's body crashed into the door. She whirled to face them, her heart thudding, her mouth dry with fear, and backed against the wall to meet the next attack. But it did not come. The dog which had fallen had recovered itself from its sprawl on the cobbles, and now crouched two paces away, snarling its hate over a hurt paw. The other wove restlessly back and forwards, just out of kicking distance. Jennifer stayed where she was, crucified by her fear against one of the open shutters that hung between the cottage window and the door. The bodies of the two men, locked together, lurched and swayed within a few feet of her. Helpless, she stood and watched, her breath caught in her throat with a dry sobbing, and she gripped her underlip between her teeth to stop herself screaming. . . .

In common with most civilized young women, Jennifer had never before seen men fighting hand to hand. Nor had she pictured such a fight as being in any way like this. This was no clean, hard-hitting tussle between villain and gallant hero of the kind to which romance and the cinema have accustomed us; it was a thoroughly dirty and shocking business, a grunting, swaying, battering fight with no holds barred, and Jennifer sickened as she watched.

And Stephen seemed to be getting very much the worst of it. Both men were soaked with sweat; Bussac's shirt was black with it, and clung to his back, outlining the bulge and strain of the great muscles beneath. Stephen's face was streaked and greasy-looking, and there was an angry mark on his cheek-bone. His mouth was open and ugly, and blood was running into it from the bruise on his cheek. The breath rasped, short and hard, in his throat, and, as Jennifer watched, appalled, there came from him a small sound, at once furious and desperate, as Bussac's grip shifted, and his knee came up in a blow that is against the rules in any language. Stephen twisted to avoid it, and the driving knee glanced along his thigh; at the same moment he thrust with a vicious and unskilful short-arm jab at the other man's throat. It missed, and cracked harmlessly enough on Bussac's collar-bone. But the Frenchman, seeing it coming, had winced from it, and this movement, coupled with Stephen's own ungainly twist of the body, set the two staggering, locked as they were. Then Stephen trod in the blue treacherous slime of the spilled milk, and went down heavily, with Bussac on top of him.

Jennifer turned her head away at the impact, shuddering back against the window-frame. It rattled against the wall, and, like a bigger and more terrible echo, came the rattle of the approaching thunder. A small herald of hot wind ran whispering along the tops of the pines, and the steep shaft of sunlight dimmed and shifted and then brightened again, so that the heaving, struggling bodies on the ground, half in and half out of the single pool of light, suddenly took on the unreality of a moving picture. The sobbed breathing, the scrape and shuffle of bodies on the ground, the guttural noises of pain and effort, seemed to be coming from far away, like effects supplied from behind the old flickering screen. Stephen's face, its angles high-lighted with sweat, jerked into the light, like a head horribly disembodied by a guillotine. There were hands at his throat now, and he was tearing at them—dark hands with hairy backs. Thin threads of bright blood crawled among the hairs, where his nails had ripped. They looked like the fantastic scarlet veins in some anatomical drawing, painted outside the flesh . . . the dark fingers moved, ever so slightly, and the scarlet threads gleamed suddenly like silk, and ran together in a thick red bangle across the wrists. . . .

Jennifer screamed. She turned her head away from where Stephen was being strangled in the pool of light, and screamed again. Behind her, in the dim little room beyond the blank glass, there was a slight movement. She strained her head round to look, and one of the dogs snarled softly . . . but she could see. She could see the other girl's face, white in the darkness behind the blank glass. The white face moved again, swam forward, was pressed against the window, the wide grey eyes staring out into the storm-purple afternoon. They lit on Jennifer, within a yard of the pane; on the brutes holding her at bay; on the ominously locked bodies beyond. . . .

"*Call off the dogs! For God's sake call off the dogs!*" Jennifer shouted it with all her strength towards that blind window.

The face wavered, and vanished. As if at the touch of a button, the shaft of light switched off, and with a rumble the storm pressed nearer.

Then the cottage door burst open and the girl ran out. The dogs backed and swerved in front of her, and her shout

sent them, tails down, flying through the cottage door.
She spared no glance for Jennifer. She flew across the
cobbles as if she were winged, and fell upon Bussac, where
he still straddled Stephen's fallen body.

Jennifer, with a sob that was a prayer, followed her.

The girl had grabbed one of Bussac's arms, and was tug-
ging with all her strength to break his grip. Jennifer, with a
force she had not known she possessed, laid hold of the other
wrist with both hands, and put the whole weight of her body
into the strain. She was shouting she did not know what—
some incoherence born of terror—and the girl she had called
Gillian was shouting too, to Bussac, in rapid indistinguish-
able French that nevertheless, after what seemed an aeon of
screaming time, got through to him through the red mists
of murder.

The dark hands slackened, slipped—and Stephen, twisting
like a fish beneath him, had broken the grip and rolled
clear.

He wasn't dead. Stephen wasn't dead. Jennifer, who had
gone in this last moment beyond fear, thrust Bussac away
with all her force, and flung herself to help Stephen. He had
rolled, dazedly, on to one elbow, and his breathing was raw
and horrible, as if it came from torn lungs, but when he saw
Jennifer between him and the other man he made a desperate effort to rise, putting up a hand to push her out of the
way.

Bussac had risen slowly, gulping for breath and shaking
his head for all the world like an angry bull. He towered
over Stephen who, sick and battered as he was, strove to
push himself upright to meet the fresh attack. The red
glare was still in the Frenchman's eyes, and if he had
attacked again the fight could have had only one result,
but, just as he lurched forward, the girl who had been
clinging to his arm gave a low cry, a curious little moaning
sound that was no more than just audible, but which

nevertheless stopped the man in mid-lunge as a shot
stops a charging bison.

He swung round. She had dropped his arm as he moved
forward, and stood now, paper-white, and swaying on her
feet. One hand went gropingly to her head. She looked
shockingly ill. Even as Bussac whirled with a quick breathless "*Qu'as-tu?*" she swayed again, put out a hand blindly,
and crumpled where she stood.

Bussac moved like lightning. He caught her before she
struck the cobbles, swinging her up into his arms as if she
had weighed no more than a doll. Her head hung helplessly,
her face ashen in the uncanny light. Then he spoke over his
shoulder.

"Get out."

Stephen was, albeit unsteadily, on his feet. Jenny, ash-
white herself, glanced desperately from him to the unconscious girl.

"Monsieur Bussac——"

"You heard me. Get out." He strode for the cottage
door. The dogs lurked there in the shadow, red-eyed and
uneasy. Jennifer started forward, to be checked by
Stephen's hand on her arm. At her movement one of the
brutes snarled viciously, bristling and crouching, then slunk
back into the shadows as Bussac reached the door. He
went in without a backward glance, and kicked the door
shut behind him.

Jenny, starting forward instinctively once more as he dis-
appeared from view, found herself yet again blocked by the
uncompromising square of the cottage door.

Stephen's hand closed round her wrist, holding her.
She said, unbelievingly, like a child:

"But it was Gillian. It really was Gillian. I know it
was. . . ."

Then futility, like the heavy air, seemed to press down
and engulf her. She turned blindly, stupidly, and allowed

his unsteady hand to urge her away; back across the cobbles, back down the track, back into the choking blackness of the pine-woods. . . .

In the far distance, behind the towering immensities of cloud, came the sword-gleam of the first lightning.

CHAPTER XVII

ENTR' ACTE: con amore

THE pine-woods reached out to engulf them. The trees parted, accepted them into a sheltering darkness. The wood had been quiet before, but now, with the blanket of the storm sagging thickly on to the tree-tops, the silence was charged, heavy, ominous. The carpet of pine-needles sucked at the feet, like a bog, drowning the footsteps; the progress of an army along this track, one felt, would make no more disturbance than a troop of ghosts, a current of air, a sigh. The very noise of breathing was a violation of this silence. . . .

His breathing, hoarse and raw, ripped horribly at the stillness. He limped beside her, his hand still on her arm, urging her on over the soft, clogging pine-needles, away from danger, away from Gillian, away from that murderous devil. . . .

Jennifer, hurrying dazedly, obedient to the pressure of Stephen's hand, checked against it, and half-turned as if in rebellion. Then she stumbled, and the ranked stems of the pines seemed to tilt and recede . . . to surge forward again outlined in light . . . to waver, and then right themselves, painfully. . . .

She was sitting with her back against a tree, where the pines thinned at the northern edge of the wood. Stephen sat beside her. She turned her head, with a long, trembling breath, and looked at him.

His head was bent, and he was fumbling ineptly in a pocket. He looked both grim and indescribably weary, and there was still a trace of the ugliness that had frightened her in the set of his mouth, marred as it was by the marks of dried blood. His hair was matted and damp on his fore-head, and when he put up a hand to brush it back, she saw blood—Bussac's blood—under his nails.

"Have a cigarette, Jenny." She was shocked anew at his voice. It was little more than a thick whisper. "No wine . . . this time . . . I'm afraid."

"Oh, Stephen. . . ." There seemed nothing that could be said. She took the cigarette, and saw with an awful pity how his hands shook. Not only exhausted, she thought; beaten. He—we, are beaten.

She looked away, downhill through the thinning pines to where the convent crouched under the dark sky, its white-washed walls purple in the lurid storm-light. As she watched, a distant flicker lit it to quivering life, and, seconds later, the thunder trundled itself closer over the mountain-tops.

Thunder, off. That, too, she thought to herself, but dully and without bitterness—that, too, had to round off the im-possible little drama which was even now playing itself out. Her own part in it had been futile enough, and Stephen's— yes, futile was the word there, too. What had he said to her, only yesterday? *Don't cast me as the hero of your story, Jenny.* But she had. She had run to him, had put the burden of her apprehension and fear into his hands, con-fident that he would not—could not—fail her. The story must have the right ending. The hero, the strong man, the elder brother . . . he would not let her down. But he had. He had.

She turned her head and met his eyes.

And in that moment something happened to her. She saw, beneath the chagrin and weariness of his eyes, that he knew what she had been thinking, and with the knowledge came shame, and some instinct, pricked into being by her pain for him, that in a breath withered the ineptitudes of innocence with which she had deceived herself. *Today put on perfection.* . . . With her new adult's eyes she saw it all; that it was she who had done the betraying, the "letting-down", she who had allowed the queerness of the situation to build up in her a set of values as strange as they were worthless. Stephen's half-casual, half-jesting rejection of "heroics" went, in fact, very deep; he was the kind of highly civilized man who would loathe violence in all its ugly manifestations as he would loathe the plague. That was, in fact, how he would see it, as a plague, a creeping cancer of the modern world—and he would fight against accepting it. Clever, sensitive, gentle . . . and, however much the paper and celluloid supermen strutted in their invincible physical splendour, it was the men like Stephen, the thinking men—no more than *moyen sensuel*—who were the true constant.

He had said he was no story-book hero. It was true. And it was the measure of the magic of the place that she had been betrayed into accepting that as a confession of weakness. It was, she saw now, the reverse. A story-book hero had by definition no place in life; he battered his way through twenty victorious chapters, faded out on a lustful kiss, and was gone for good. But at the end of this story there was still a new chapter to open. England, Oxford, Cherry Close . . . herself and Stephen. . . . It came to Jennifer quite clearly and quietly just what the next chapters must contain.

But first she must give him back himself. *Today put on perfection.*

She said: "Stephen, dear. Don't mind so much. Please." He did not answer, and she put out a hand and touched his, softly.

"Stephen."

He looked away. "I lost your game for you, Jenny."

She cried out at that. "Don't say that! It's not fair! I won't have you say that!"

"It's true."

She turned on him almost fiercely.

"It's not true! You lost nothing! If I'd done as you told me and stayed behind it wouldn't have happened that way. And he's twice your weight, and you'd hurt your shoulder, and besides——"

"Besides?"

"You're lame," she said in a small voice.

The word dropped between them into a little silence. Then he heard a tiny sound, and at last looked at her. She was crying. The tears starred her lashes and spilled on to her cheeks. His heart twisted in his breast, but he did not move.

"Jenny. Oh, God, Jenny, don't I'm sorry. Gillian——"

She said: "It's not Gillian. It's just that I—I can't bear you to be—hurt any more. Not for anything. Not— *you*."

He said shakenly: "Oh, my darling. . . ." And then she was in his arms and he was kissing her at last, but gently, her tear-stained lashes, her mouth. . . . "My lovely Jenny. My love."

The pine-trees stirred high above them, the dark boughs sighing with the far-away hollow soughing of the sea-waves in a shell. Lightning stabbed nearer. A shower of hail raced up the slope and over the crested woods, its million tiny ghost-feet pattering and galloping overhead like a wave sweeping the shingle. As it ebbed into silence the lightning stabbed again: a flash, a crack, and then at one stride the storm was in the valley; the growl and roar of thunder rolled and re-echoed from the mountains on either hand, and the sword of the lightning stabbed down, and stabbed again, as if searching through the depths of the cringing woods for whatever sheltered there.

Jennifer gasped and shrank in Stephen's arms. He held her still, and close, her head pressed into his shoulder.

"It's all right, Jenny. It'll pass."

"Should we—I mean, the trees——"

"It's all right," he said again. "It's going."

As he spoke, the lightning drove down again, with a crash as if Roland's great sword Durandel itself were splitting the mountains wide again.

"The crack of doom," said Stephen, then, as he felt her shiver: "That was away beyond the wood, Jenny. It's going fast."

She lifted her head from his shoulder. "Towards the farm." She shivered again.

"Fightened? There's no need."

"Not of that. The other thing. The Gillian thing. We—we shouldn't have forgotten it like that: I didn't mean that I didn't care what happened to Gillian. I only——"

"Darling, nobody imagines you did."

She lifted scared eyes where tears still clung. "The thunder. You called it the crack of doom. It *was* like that; all day it's been like—something waiting, waiting in the wings to pounce. Disaster. An evil omen, Stephen. And the evil's happening, now."

"Not yet."

She said, on a little sob: "But it will. We can't stop it."

"No?"

There was a new note in his voice which made her blood tingle. She pushed away from him, her hands against his chest, her eyes searching his face. The change there was startling enough. Fatigue, depression, pain—all these had vanished, as if on the tail of the now retreating storm. The marks of his defeat were still there, bruises, cuts, ugly smears where blood and sweat had dried crustily, but he was smiling, and his eyes were steady and confident and—yes, excited.

She said sharply: "You're not to go back there! You're not to!"

He laughed, then pulled her to him and kissed her. "I don't propose to—though the way I feel now, I could turn friend Bussac inside out with one hand!" He put a hand under her chin, and tilted up her face, still smiling. "Your magic, Jenny . . . talk about moving mountains! I could shift the whole range, by God, before breakfast, and wash my hands, saying—how does it go?—'*Fie upon this quiet life, I want work!*' "

He got quickly to his feet and reached a hand down to her.

"You and the thunder between you, sweetheart, have cleared the air! There's a way out of your precious melo-drama yet, if we'd only brains enough to see it!"

He slid his hands up to her shoulders, and shook her gently. "Don't look so stricken, my darling. This isn't going to be a tragedy after all! Listen."

Away among the peaks to the south the thunder crashed once more.

"Thunder—on the right," said Stephen. "There's your omen, Jenny, and not on the sinister side. *Thunder on the right*—the best of omens! A happy ending!"

She found herself smiling back, with a quite illogical lift of the heart.

"All right," she said, "let's go and move those mountains. Only—we'd better be quick."

* * *

Not wishing to be seen approaching the convent by the track leading directly from the farm, they turned downhill, keeping within the borders of the wood.

The way down between the pines was steepish, but the thick dry pine-needles made it safe and easy. Everywhere underfoot the mat of dead stuff gapped and broke to show curved croziers of pale green stems butting their way up into the light. Here and there wax-white orchids nodded above the finished star of leaves, slender taperlights clustered over with the fragile swarm of tiny wings. Occasional shower-drops from the melting hail spattered down, shaking the tiny swarms to life, and the rich tarry smell of the pines thickened in the warm air.

Stephen reached a hand to help Jennifer over a fallen pine.

"The first mountain we move," he said, "and it may well be difficult—is the police."

"The police? But you said they wouldn't listen. You said there was no evidence——"

"My God, isn't my face evidence? Things are a little different now, my dear. We've seen and identified Gillian ourselves, and in any case, now, I can insist that the man is at least interviewed about this." He touched his damaged cheek.

"But—oh, Stephen, there isn't time! I do agree about the police, and I don't see what else we can do, but surely it's not going to help! All we've done is warn Bussac, and frighten him into acting straight away!"

"I know." His voice was grim. "I haven't forgiven myself for that yet, though I suppose the fat was in the fire as soon as he recognized you. And there *was* a chance that he'd accept our bargain and let us take Gillian off his hands. At least, I thought so, until I saw her."

"What d'you mean?"

He shot her a look. "You haven't guessed?"

"Guessed what?"

He seemed to be choosing his words carefully. "It must have occurred to you that Gillian wasn't—isn't—exactly a prisoner."

"Of course it did. I haven't had time to think it out properly, but I suppose with him and the dogs about, she couldn't have got very far anyway—oh!"

"Exactly. The dogs did as she told them. And so,"

added Stephen meditatively, "to some extent, did Pierre Bussac. . . ."

Jenny said uncertainly: "Perhaps she and Bussac's wife——"

He said, "She *is* Bussac's wife."

She gasped and turned, and would have tripped if his hand had not shot out to steady her.

"Careful there. I'm sorry, and I don't understand it any more than you do, but it's true. There's nobody else at that farm with him. She is 'Madame Bussac'."

"She can't be! It can't be true! You've guessed wrong, Stephen!"

"No. You forget, Jenny, I've met her before."

"You *what*? When?"

"I told you. I was painting once, early in the morning. I must have been quite near the farm without knowing it, on the far side of the hill. I'd walked over from Gavarnie—it's quite incredibly lonely over there, and very bad walking; I doubt if anybody goes there in a hundred years or so. . . . Anyway she—your Gillian—must have gone out early too. She came on me suddenly, and I don't know which of us was the more startled. She shied away at first, looking quite scared, but I spoke, and we talked for perhaps five minutes. No more. She still seemed uneasy, and eventually hurried off. But it was certainly the girl you called Gillian, and just as certainly she told me she was Madame Bussac, and lived over here."

Jennifer said, fastening half-dazedly on the one word that seemed to make sense: "You said she was 'scared'?"

"Perhaps that's too strong a word. Uneasy, apprehensive —she must have known Bussac wouldn't want her to be seen. I doubt if she ever told him about the encounter."

She put a hand to her head. "And she wouldn't come away with us. . . . She didn't know me, either. Of course, it's a few years since we met, but I'd have sworn it was Gillian."

"Oh, yes, it was Gillian."

She turned bewildered, almost panic-stricken eyes to him. "But I can't believe it! It gets crazier and crazier!" Her voice rose with a quiver of hysteria. "The whole damned valley's crawling with girls who look like Gillian!"

He put an arm round her shoulders, and turned her towards the edge of the trees. "Come on, darling. Out of the wood." The arm tightened momentarily, and he smiled down at her. "Another omen. . . . And don't panic, sweetheart. It's mad, but not that mad; there's still only one Lally, who's dead, and only one Gillian, who's alive—*and* likely to remain so."

They had reached the edge of the wood, out of sight of the convent, emerging from the very scented twilight of the pines into the thundery darkness of the open valley. The storm-centre had moved to some distance now, but the sky was still low and dark, and in the intermittent electric flicker the mountain-shapes showed a curious light olive-green, lighter than the indigo clouds beyond them. The lower meadows and slopes shone paler still, stretching ghostly and frost-like where the shower had left its evanescent hoary glimmer. Dark sky, pale mountains, phantom-grey meadows . . . it was like looking at the negative of the normal daylight picture, a magically inverted landscape through whose pale foreground drove the sharp ink-black furrow of the Petit Gave.

They were out in the open now, and the meadow-grass, stiff with its bedded hail-stones, crunched and rustled under their feet.

"Something else I told you," he said. "Remember? I told you Madame Bussac didn't like my pictures. She preferred photographs."

"Well?"

"What's the main difference," said Stephen, slowly, "between a painting and a photograph?"

"I don't get it. Why? I suppose one's, oh, a mechanical reproduction of the thing as it is, and the other——" Then she caught her breath. "No. No, it's not that. Is it that one's black and white, and the other's in—colour?"

"Yes, indeed. Perhaps colour doesn't mean very much to Madame Bussac," said Stephen. He glanced down sideways at her. "Not any kind of proof in itself, but under the circumstances a very sufficient pointer. I think we can call it conclusive. I mean the whole damned valley can't be crawling with *colour-blind* girls who look like Gillian, can it?"

"No." But her smile was strained. "All right, it's Gillian, married to that man. And where does that get us? She's alive, but—for how long? Oh, God, Stephen, it's like a nightmare, and just about as sensible!"

"Think, darling! The fact—weird though it is—that she's married to Bussac, does guarantee that, as far as Bussac's concerned, she stays alive! *As far as Bussac's concerned*. Think back to that conversation you overheard last night. Didn't you tell me that Doña Francisca was forcing him to take some course that would result in Gillian's death, and that he was passionately refusing?"

"Y-yes. Yes, I did."

"And the way he acted just now, wasn't it a repetition in a way of the same scene? He knew he ought to let her go, for his own safety's sake, but he didn't want to. Did she act as if he frightened her? On the contrary; I'd have said he was fond of her, and that squares with his reactions both to me and Doña Francisca."

Jennifer said in a tight, flat little voice: "When did he marry her?"

"I—what?" He was patently at a loss.

"*When* did he marry her?"

He was silent.

She said: "Unless they were married in Bordeaux before she even came here, there hasn't been much time, has there? And they weren't. When she wrote to me the night before she left Bordeaux, she was still planning to enter the convent." She kicked at a tuft of grass, and the melting drops flew from it in flashing arcs of spray. "Father Anselm didn't marry them either, or he'd have told me."

He said, gently: "I know. I'm sorry, Jenny."

"Last night," said Jenny, not looking at him, "that woman was cursing him for wrecking their plans for—for lust. That squares, too, as you put it, doesn't it? *Obscène bête*, she called him, and *animal*——"

He gripped her arm. "Steady there. Whatever Gillian's up to, it's her affair. All that matters to us is her safety, and this affair with Bussac, whatever it is, is a guarantee of just that. He'll not hurt her. I'd stake my life on that, and it's one reason"—he smiled ruefully—"one reason why I came away from the farm when I did. No, the real danger to Gillian lies in another direction."

"Doña Francisca?"

"Our gentle Francisca. To put it bluntly, as long as Gillian's above ground, and therefore traceable by us or the police, there's the danger of an inquiry starting about the identity of the body in the graveyard."

"But even if they proved that that was Lally Dupré, there's no evidence that Doña Francisca knew anything about it! She said herself that she'd lose nothing but her private income."

"Exactly. And Bussac gave some indication, didn't he, of just what that would mean to her? There's big money involved, Jenny—it's fifteen years since Isaac Lenormand's three million francs were paid over, and in fifteen years there'll have been a fair amount of traffic, one way or another, over Pierre Bussac's private bridge. Damn it, what did that El Greco cost? Even if she got it cheaply in the general muddle of the war, when Rembrandts went for nothing and Botticellis lay about in barns—no, the loot those two have been handling is something more than pin-money. Big money, ambition, love of power and fear of scandal . . . that spells danger to me, Jenny. She won't relinquish her dreams very easily, if your account of her is true. And to keep those dreams she has to keep Bussac, and get rid of Gillian—*somehow*."

Jennifer gave a little shiver. "Love of power . . . yes, that's her all right . . . that lean and hungry look . . . like someone burning-up inside. I wouldn't like to get between her and anything she dearly wanted."

"Gillian has," said Stephen soberly.

They had rounded a shoulder of the mountain meadow, and now the convent lay close below them. He stopped, frowning thoughtfully down at it.

"Look at it from Bussac's angle," he said slowly. "Some-how—never mind the hows and wherefores—he has got Gillian there, living with him willingly as his wife. Your inquiries make Doña Francisca tumble to the fact that it *is* Gillian, and not Lally Dupré. She urges him to put her out of the way before you recognize her and start a fuss which can only end in exposure for both Bussac and herself. Bussac refuses—or at any rate would like to refuse. . . . Then we turn up. We recognize her. We offer to take her away and nothing said. Bussac refuses again."

He lifted his head, and his gaze rested, still unseeingly, on the long flank of the hill behind the convent. "Now, how is he placed? Whatever Doña Francisca does, it's obvious that *we* will go straight to the police. And though we can't get him over Gillian, as she's apparently staying with him of her own free will, we are bound to start an inquiry that will lead to Lally Dupré, and through her to Bussac's criminal connections. Add Doña Francisca's threats to this, and what decision d'you suppose Bussac will come to?"

"In his place," said Jenny, "I'd disappear myself."

"And so would I." He looked at her gravely. "As I see it, friend Bussac will light out at the earliest possible moment along his private route to Spain. With Gillian."

She turned and began to walk, leaden-footed now, down the slope towards the convent gate.

"And Gillian wants to go."

"It would seem so."

"She—she might have told me."

He said nothing.

"Do you suppose she's somehow mixed up with his criminal affairs too? And that's why she didn't tell me, and wouldn't recognize me?"

"Hardly, Jenny. She'd have written to stop you coming, if that had been the case."

There was a pause. "It doesn't get any clearer, does it?" she said.

"Not much. No."

Somewhere away to the south-east, the thunder murmured. She looked up. "Thunder on the right. . . ." Her voice was not quite her own. "The happy ending, Stephen. It seems that all the drama's been for nothing, after all. The heroine doesn't want to be rescued. There's nothing more to do."

"Oh, yes there is. Plenty." His voice had quickened. "We can't just leave it at that, Jenny. There's too much that's unexplained about Gillian's part in this. Damn it, darling, there's one thing, from first to last, that's been sticking out like a sore thumb: *why did she write to invite you here and then not write to stop you?* She's had three weeks, and surely a letter keeping you away would be simpler than cutting you dead after you'd come?"

She put a hand to her head. "Of course! If she *were*

involved with Bussac in his criminal activities, she'd have moved heaven and earth to stop me coming!"

"And Bussac," said Stephen grimly, "would have personally posted the letter. No, whatever the state of friend Bussac's emotions towards Gillian, I don't think we can assume anything about Gillian's for him. If Doña Francisca has a hold over Bussac, he may in his turn have one over Gillian. It would explain quite a bit if he had."

They had reached the cover of the convent wall. She stopped and faced him, speaking low.

"What can we do? Try and stop them?"

"I think we must."

"They'll have gone already."

"That's only too likely. But the sooner we get to the police the better. They can be picked up in Spain. And there's one other—circumstance—I'd like to clear up, while we're about it."

She glanced instinctively at the convent gate.

"Her?"

"Her. Don't forget she's promised to go up there after Compline. If she finds them gone, she may follow to make sure he doesn't quit. She probably knows the way. And I'm not sure that I like the idea of her being free to follow Gillian."

She shivered. "We'll have to stop her. We'll have to. Will the police believe us?"

He said grimly: "I'll see they do. Listen." He took her hands in his and held them hard. "It's just possible that Bussac mayn't be able to get away as quickly as all that. It's a long trip and I imagine a hard one, and he may still have preparations to make. Also, remember, Gillian fainted . . . that might put a fairly effective brake on for an hour or two."

"You think there's a chance?"

"There's always a chance. Even if the police aren't in time to stop Bussac, they might be able to follow and catch him up, if we can only get them to move straight away. Now"—his grip tightened—"can you get straight in there and get to the telephone without being seen?"

She said tightly: "There's no telephone."

"What? Oh, my God, I suppose there's not." His voice was savage and weary. "I should have thought of that. So much for the mountains I was going to move, Jenny, my darling. All we needed was a blasted miracle, and they don't happen any more. Well, we'll have to content ourselves with catching the she-wolf. At least there's plenty time for me to get down to Gavarnie and drag the police up to the farm by the time Compline's over."

He loosed her hands then, and lifted his own to cup her face. He said, very gently: "Don't worry, my darling. I'd stake my life Bussac won't hurt her." He bent his head as if to kiss her, but in the very act she felt him stiffen, and he lifted his head from her, turning sharply, as if listening. Then he dropped his hands and straightened up. He spoke softly, but his eyes were beginning to blaze.

"And there's my miracle, by God," he said. "Who said they didn't happen any more?"

Then she heard it too. The swift heart-beating pulse of hoofs coming down-hill from the north-east.

"Luis? Miracle?"

"Transport," said Stephen, and laughed.

There they were, the three of them, the big stallion leading, coming down the long slope with manes flying, their chestnut coats glowing richly in the queer light. Luis's face gleamed pale as he turned to look towards the convent. Stephen raised an arm, beckoned urgently, and began to run, limping, towards him. Luis, lifting a hand in reply, brought the stallion's head round. Stephen stopped at that, and waited.

"Spectacular young devil, isn't he?" he said in some amusement.

"Stephen"—Jennifer came breathlessly behind him—"what are you going to do?"

"Borrow a horse, my darling."

"But Luis tried to kill us."

"What? Oh, that. No, Jenny, that was Bussac. Didn't you see his mule? It was sweating. He'd just got in. He must have seen you running out of the convent to meet me, and taken an impulsive chance on shutting you up or frightening you away. He got a bad start when we turned up at his cottage within the hour. . . . Don't you worry about Luis. He's a friend of mine."

"Not of mine. He was horribly rude, and he looked as if he hated me."

He grinned briefly. "You must have been probing a bit near the bone. Had you been asking questions about the convent?"

"I suppose I had. What's that to do with Luis?"

"The whole world. Celeste."

Before she could do more than blink at this intelligence the horses were on them, the big stallion coming to a sweating, plunging halt not four yards away. Before it had stopped, Stephen was at its head.

"Luis, *mon ami*——"

"*M'sieur?*"

"Listen, Luis, I can't explain, there's no time. But I've got to get to Gavarnie, and quickly. Will you let me have Foix?"

The young man sat like a rock, looking down at Stephen, his dark eyes inscrutable under their long lashes. The stallion jerked his head viciously, but Stephen's hand dragged him down and held him hard.

"*Eh bien, Luis?*"

"It is nothing to do with me—or—mine?"

The hazel eyes met his steadily. "Nothing."

Luis nodded. "Then I lend him with pleasure." His

teeth flashed in a smile. "If you can ride him, m'sieur. He's a devil at the best of times, and Beelzebub himself when there's thunder about. . . . But he can hurry." He swung out of the saddle and slid to the ground. "You know what you're taking on, of course? He'll probably try to kill you."

"I'll risk it." Stephen was busy with stirrup-leathers, and spoke absently, but Jennifer cried out.

"No, Stephen! He means it! He's not joking!"

"I know." Luis had the three bridles now in his grip, and Stephen came quickly over to Jennifer, pulling her to him. "But this happens to be one thing that I *can* do. This'll be one fight I'll win today. . . ." He held her close, speaking urgently. "I'm going now, sweetheart. Get straight into the convent and stay there till I come. The rest's for me and the police; you'd better keep out of it."

"Very well, Stephen."

His eyes glimmered for a moment with a smile. "That's my girl. If I can get help up here in time, so much the better; if not, we'll certainly get up to the farm in time to arrange a reception committee for you-know-who after Compline. Till then—keep out of her way, my darling."

"I will."

"And whatever happens, today the drama *hasn't* been for nothing, Jenny. . . . Didn't you see the golden gates opening for us, up there in the woods? Didn't you hear the trumpets?"

"All the trumpets."

He stooped to kiss her once, a brief hard kiss, then he turned quickly away. A hand from Luis, a swift heave, and he was astride. The big stallion, white-eyed, threw his head up, laid back his ears, and began to sidle, swishing his tail. Luis, still holding the bridle, spoke softly to him, then flung an anxious glance upwards.

"Are you sure, m'sieur? He doesn't like strangers, and he's always queer in thunder, even with me."

"I'll manage. By the time I've got to Gavarnie he'll be quiet enough, thunder or no thunder! Let him go, Luis—and thanks!"

Luis stepped back.

The big horse, ears flat, nostrils cracking, moved backwards and sideways, and raked his great head down to get a grip of the bit. But he was held hard, and brought up to the bit with an expert kick that wrung from the watching Luis a small sound of satisfaction and relief.

Stephen was fighting now to turn the circling horse back on to the track. He dragged the wicked head round on to the off side, and drove in his left heel. Foix, held as he was, still plunged viciously to the left, trying to pitch the rider over his exposed shoulder.

"Blast you," said Stephen cheerfully, and pulled him round again.

This time he went straight, in one long arrow-swift leap, only to stop dead as he shot out stiff forelegs to brake in the dust.

Jenny made some little sound, but Luis' eyes were shining, and they heard Stephen laugh as he drove in his heels again.

"Gee up, Dobbin," he said, between his teeth. Then he slashed the stallion hard across the neck with the reins, and, in a tempest of angry hoofs, they were gone at a gallop down the valley.

Luis, with another of his dark unreadable looks at Jennifer, vaulted up on to one of his horses, and, with no more than a muttered word to her, turned the pair of them down towards the stream. The trotting hoofs echoed, queerly in the stillness, the rapid dwindling gallop to the north.

The valley seemed all of a sudden empty, desolate. . . . She turned quickly and pushed open the convent gate.

CHAPTER XVIII

PATIENCE: *marcato il tempo*

THE rain had started. Big drops, thrown singly against the window, struck the glass with soft, vicious impacts. Beyond the pane the valley swam in green, liquid light, eerie under a slate-blue sky now scored across by the pale diagonals of the rain.

The convent seemed deserted, the nuns being either occupied with their teaching tasks at the other side of the building or else about some silent business of their own. Jennifer had passed no one on her way up to the corridor above the refectory. She had bathed and changed her soiled and crumpled dress, and sat now on the window-seat at the corridor's end, hugging a coat round her in the chilly shadow, and straining her eyes for as far as she could see down the dim valley.

It was empty, but for the silver arrows of the rain.

She sat still, her hands quiet in her lap, holding her thoughts, too, quiet, schooling herself to wait . . . wait. . . .

Outside, the valley was empty but for the wet wind.

But no; she was wrong. Something was there. Something—someone—was running up the hill from the Petit Gave, towards the convent gate.

A gust of wind shook the vine that clothed the window, shaking its drops even more thickly on to the streaming glass. She peered down, and a chord of memory vibrated at the sight of the slight figure, cloaked against the rain, that flitted across the grass below her. Celeste, driven in by the storm from some more-or-less guilty foray, some assignation down by the Petit Gave. . . . It was true, then: Celeste and Luis—it was true. Jennifer's lips curved involuntarily as she saw that the girl was carrying flowers—more gentians, perhaps, for the poor mound in the graveyard? If the gentians had been nothing but an excuse for going out to meet her lover, then the girl's hesitation and guilty demeanour were explained. It was to be noticed that she had not minded being questioned when the bursar was not by.

Other memories flashed—the look of almost fierce possession with which Doña Francisca had seemed to brood over the girl; the flicker of impatient jealousy in her eyes at Celeste's evident care for the grave; the lovely little scarlet missal, the "gift in God" . . . Jennifer stood up as Celeste reached the gate below. She had no wish to be caught watching the valley. She walked quickly down the corridor to her room, her own miserable preoccupation shot through with a sharp feeling of pity for the girl, so young, so ignorant, so bound in by ties of training and faith, now cruelly torn—for so she must be—between the sunlit promise of the young Gascon's passion and the narrow white life which was the only one she knew. No wonder there were tears and agonies in the little chapel. And no wonder, thought Jenny, at a vivid memory of Luis sitting the big golden stallion, no wonder she risks what she does to see him again, and yet again. . . .

Celeste must have left her tryst once more in time for chapel; there was a certain obvious symbolism about the way the bell began now to ring for a recall to devotion. Three notes again, blown away by the wind. And again three. She looked at her watch, incredulously. The Angelus? Six o'clock? Two hours since Stephen had gone down the valley, and still the track showed no light, no car, no hurrying posse of rescue. . . .

She bit her lip savagely as she felt the scurry of panic in her brain. He wouldn't hurt Gillian; about that, surely, they had been right; and if he took her away he would be traced. *He wouldn't hurt her.* The only danger was Doña Francisca, and she was safely held till half past ten, when Compline finished.

Or was she?

The bell was beating steadily now, calling Vespers. Jennifer cast a quick glance in the mirror, ran a comb through her hair, and set off to find out.

*   *   *

Her steps tapped hollowly down the dim corridor; the wooden stairs creaked and echoed emptily; the tiles of the empty refectory rapped at her heels. The tunnel was full of whining wind, and the remote cold voice of the bell.

The chapel, warm and mellow with a blaze of half a hundred candles, was like a different world, a place of floating lights and shadows musky with incense and the smell of burning wax. The chords of the voluntary marched and thickened in steady progression. Over the ranked lights on the high altar saints aspired and angels soared. She knelt down in a shadow corner near the wall, just as the music gathered and swelled to its close, and the bell stopped.

Doña Francisca sat in her usual stall, a little apart, stiff and still like the carving of the screen behind her. Her face, withdrawn, austere, gleamed stilly in the light of the candles like the face of a statue, empty alike of evil and of good. Jennifer, watching her as it were with new eyes, saw the rigid control that was stamped on mouth, hands, eyelids—the woman's whole being disciplined to the same patience of waiting . . . waiting. . . . But on her breast the ruby beat like a pulse.

It was still raining. The darkness drew in more thickly round the lighted building; outside the windows it was night already, and the black panes glimmered only with the reflection of candle and sanctuary lamp. The rain beat against the walls, fistfuls hurtled against the panes with the rattle of grape-shot, but over the doors the arras hung still, and the ranked flames of the candles were steady. The music swelled and soared in a sober Latin ecstasy. Jennifer, kneeling in her corner, gripping the back of the chair in front of her, was trying not to think, to blot from her mind's eye the picture of the squat little farm with its shut door and blind windows and Gillian's face in the swimming darkness. They would be there now. Stephen and the police would be in time. There was nothing she could do. Nothing but wait.

Somehow, the service came to an end, and they were all filing across in silence to the refectory. She found herself sitting next to the Prioress at the high table, and managing, even, to eat, but, though she should have been hungry, the convent's excellent stewed mutton tasted like ashes, and the apples that followed it might have been Dead Sea fruit. She was devoutly thankful for the custom that appointed a nun to read aloud during meals from some devotional work, for this meant that she need not talk to the Reverend Mother, to be questioned within Doña Francisca's hearing about how she had spent her day. She stole a glance at the nearest window—a futile gesture, for the windows were nothing but blind oblongs of roaring blackness against which the lamplight blandly purred. And still the voice of the reading nun went placidly on, and the hooded eyes watched her from the foot of the table, and her heart beat sickeningly in her throat as she gazed down at her plate and waited. . . .

All at once it was over. Chairs scraped, grace was sung, the Prioress led the black-and-white file of nuns out of the room, Doña Francisca followed without a backward look, and Jennifer was once again free of the novices' corridor and her heartbreaking sentry-go between the windows. And if the corridor had been blank before, now in the deeper darkness its emptiness rang mockingly hollow. Her heart still jerking unevenly, she paused at the head of the stairs, glancing down the line of shut doors, then flew again to the window that gave on the valley.

Nothing. Nothing but the dark.

She turned and ran to her room, pressing her face against the window there, then, in an agony of frustration, flung the casement open. She held it against the kicking wind, leaning out into the rain, her eyes straining towards the pinewood on the southern slope. She was met by the roar of the trees and the rich smell of a thousand herbs pounded and pashed by the rain. Nothing else.

And it was getting late. She drew back slowly, fighting vainly now to recover her lost calmness. If they had been in time to stop Bussac, they would surely by now have been coming back down the valley, with Gillian safe, and the convent as their objective? Or would they wait up there, all of them, till that cold bell rang again for Compline in three hours' time? All at once weariness seemed to envelop her. She bit her lips as she pulled the casement shut. Three more mortal, crawling hours. . . .

Then as the casement closed, a light sprang to life in the darkness beyond it. Her heart jumped painfully, but in the same moment she saw that the light was not out in the night, but behind her, in the room. She turned, to see Celeste standing there, framed in the doorway, holding one hand in front of a streaming candle-flame.

Jennifer latched the window, and the flame steadied. Across it the girl looked at her with dark inscrutable eyes.

"I want to talk to you," she said, and her tone was abrupt almost hostile.

Jennifer came away from the window. "Very well." She spoke wearily, and without much interest. All her being was concentrated on that dead darkness beyond the window. "What is it?" She sat down on her bed and waited. As well, she supposed, spend the time this way as any other.

Celeste shut the door and stood with her back to it, the candle still in her hand. In the golden liquidly flowing light she looked very beautiful, a creature of long shadows and wavering glory. She also looked very dramatic. Jennifer, who was tired and strained to the point of exhaustion, noticed this with misgiving.

"You'd better put the candle down," she said.

The girl obeyed, setting it on her chest-of-drawers, so that the Madonna's face flickered with an uncertain smile, and the gold tooling of the missal gleamed richly.

She said in an unnaturally loud, defiant voice: "I've been out tonight to see my lover."

"Yes. I saw you."

The dark eyes widened. "Then—you know?"

"Oh, yes. I saw you go last night, too, though I didn't then realize where you were going. I think," added Jennifer, with a glimmer of a smile touching her strained face, "that you'd better see him a little less frequently if you don't want to be caught out." Celeste, looking considerably taken aback, abandoned her heroic pose against the door, and sat down on her bed, looking doubtfully at Jennifer.

"You don't mean to tell?"

"I? No. It's none of my business, after all. What would happen, incidentally, if I did—tell the Reverend Mother, I mean?"

Celeste shrugged, a sulky little gesture. "Nothing very much, I suppose. Reverend Mother's told me many a time that I've no vocation. She says I ought to go out and get a job and live an ordinary life and some day marry and—and have children."

Jennifer was startled, and showed it. "But, good heavens, Celeste, surely you don't delude yourself that the Reverend Mother would countenance these comings-and-goings of yours? Surely——"

The girl flashed round at her: "There's nothing wrong in them!"

Jennifer raised her brows, and said nothing. The dark eyes met hers defiantly, then Celeste flushed and looked away, her fingers plucking at the counterpane. "Well, there isn't. Only because they're secret!"

Jennifer was silent, her gaze bent out of the window down the dark and empty valley. It was decidedly none of her business, as she had said, to interfere between Celeste and her conscience. But then as she turned back to the room she met the girl's eyes, and the bewildered youth in them touched some chord of pity in her that stirred her, perhaps unwisely, to offer some help.

She said gently: "But you'll have to make your mind up soon, you know, Celeste. You can't go on like this! It's not fair to you, or to Luis, or to the Reverend Mother. If you've no 'vocation' to become a nun yourself, and the Prioress knows it, why don't you go and tell her——?"

Celeste's fingers dug into the counterpane. She sat up with a jerk.

"You're not to tell her!"

"I've said I shan't." Jenny spoke wearily. "That's for you to do. And you must, you know. You must decide. And if you've no 'vocation' then for goodness' sake accept the Reverend Mother's advice and go out and live an ordinary life. It has its—rewards."

Celeste said nothing, but her fingers started plucking and pleating again at the cotton counterpane. Then she said, with difficulty: "But I *have* a vocation, really. Doña Francisca says so. She won't hear of my going out of here, ever."

Jennifer said, more sharply than she had intended: "You're the only one who can decide about that. Are you in love with Luis?"

"Yes," whispered Celeste, and her eyes filled with tears.

Jennifer looked at her. Of course she was: how could she help it? And how, if it came to that, could Luis? She remembered the smouldering frustration of the boy's whole attitude, and his voice as he asked "*Is it anything to do with me—and mine?*" Well, he would have a hard fight to claim his own, if Celeste refused to take any other advice but that of a powerfully possessive woman whose nature had soured into rank evil. If she hadn't mis-read the expression she had surprised on Doña Francisca's face in the chapel, the Spaniard would exert every ounce of her powerful personality and influence on the girl beside her. Meanwhile, there were other dangers. . . .

She said bluntly: "Has Luis said anything about marriage?"

Celeste's head went up, and on her lips hung a proud, shy little smile that was exquisite and very touching.

"Oh, yes."

"Could he keep you?"

"Oh, yes! His uncle has a farm down at Argelès, a big farm, Luis says, with a dairy herd and—oh, everything! There are no sons, and it will all belong to Luis! He says that we could——" The glow faded abruptly, and she added, in a mechanical and slightly priggish tone: "But, of course, it's not possible. Not when one has a vocation for a higher life."

"Are you so very sure you have?"

"Of course. Doña Francisca says so."

Jennifer bit her lip and then said quietly: "You make me very sorry for Luis."

Celeste looked surprised. "For Luis?"

"Certainly." She went on gently: "Celeste, it's very natural that you should be—fond of Doña Francisca, as I'm sure she's fond of you. . . . But consider a moment. You know that Doña Francisca has wanted for many years now to enter the Order here, while—various things—have prevented her from doing so?"

The girl nodded, looking bewildered.

Jennifer said carefully: "This is hard to explain, Celeste, but I honestly believe it may be true. Couldn't it be that Doña Francisca somehow sees you as *herself*? That she's not considering *you* and *your* life, so much as making you a sort of projection of herself, a kind of second chance?" She paused. "The Reverend Mother tells you that you've no vocation. As she once told Doña Francisca. Now, Doña Francisca insists that you have, that you should stay here against (be honest, now!) your inclination, that you should, in fact, let her . . . how can I put it? . . . realize *herself* in you. . . ."

But here she saw the bleak incomprehension in the girl's eyes, and stopped. She smiled, and added gently: "You know, Celeste, the Reverend Mother is surely the best judge in the matter of vocation. Can't you just let yourself believe in your own heart, my dear? Especially when the Reverend Mother tells you that you may?"

For a moment the girl seemed to hesitate, then she said stubbornly: "Doña Francisca doesn't agree with the Reverend Mother. I know, because she told me they've talked about it, often. Reverend Mother's old, so very old, but Doña Francisca's clever as well as good, and she knows me better than anyone!"

"Does she know about Luis?"

The girl went white as paper, and seemed to shrink. "No."

"Then she doesn't know you all that well, does she?" said Jennifer dryly. She was astonished at the wave of revulsion and—yes, hatred, that had swept over her at the soft, almost reverent, reiteration of the bursar's name. She turned her head quickly away towards the window, clenching her hands tightly in her lap as if by doing so she could get a grip on her emotions, and curb the impulse to hurl a denunciation of the woman into the face of this unhappy child. But she had her own fears to contend with; she was not prepared—nor qualified—to interfere further in a matter which seemed to her a simple affair of warped possessiveness, but which must appear to Celeste as a choice between mortality and God.

So much, indeed, Celeste was trying to explain, in a hesitating little whisper of which Jennifer caught only a few odd phrases of broken French. "So wise," she was saying, half to herself, with averted face, "Doña Francisca . . . *that* sort of life—husband, children. . . ." And then again, more softly still, Jennifer heard the one word: "Sin. . . ."

She stood up. She yanked open a drawer with a bang, took out her cigarettes, and slammed the drawer shut again. She walked deliberately across the room, thrust the cigarette into the candle-flame, drew on it, then straightened up and exhaled a long and grateful breath. The smoke drifted across the little room, its sharp pungency shocking in that sterile convent atmosphere. But it brought the world—the pleasant ordinary soiled and sinful world—back between her and the raw emotions of a scene which had become un-endurable. She said: "It wasn't this that you came to see me about. What was it?"

Celeste had stopped talking, and was watching her with shocked eyes. Jennifer felt a twinge of wry amusement.

She drew on her cigarette again and repeated the question: "What was it?"

Celeste looked momentarily taken aback. She hesi-tated, then, at some remembered indignation, flushed. She sat up straight on her bed and went uncompromisingly back to the beginning of the conversation.

"I saw Luis this evening!"

"So you said."

"And he told me"—the flush deepened, and the lovely

eyes met Jennifer's angrily—"he told me that you had been asking more questions about Madame Lamartine's death, you and your lover!"

Jennifer's cigarette was arrested half-way to her lips. "I and my *what*?"

Celeste looked at her almost with hatred. "Your lover. Luis said that's who he was. Isn't he your lover?"

Jennifer sat down slowly on the bed. "I—well, yes, I suppose he is. I hadn't . . ." She looked across at the other girl with a kind of surprise. "Yes, he is," she said, and it was she this time who smiled.

Celeste, hardly heeding her answer, had swept on: "Why are you still asking these questions? Why does Luis say that there's something wrong about Madame Lamartine's death?"

"Does he say that?"

"Yes! He says that you and the Englishman seem to suspect some sort of mystery—it's true, isn't it? That's why you asked *me* all those questions! What are you accusing me of?"

"You? Nothing."

"That is not true!" Celeste's breast rose and fell, her face was flushed and her eyes blazing. She looked very lovely. Jennifer saw, with a sinking heart, that she had escaped one emotional storm only to run into another.

"Do you think I poisoned her?" asked Celeste burningly.

Jennifer fought to keep the sharp impatience out of her voice. "Oh, Celeste, don't be silly! Of course I don't! It's nothing whatever to do with you! I assure you——"

"Then what *do* you think was wrong? What do you suspect? What could be wrong?"

"Nothing! Nothing that you could have anything to do with! Please believe me, Celeste! No one could possibly imagine for a moment that you did anything but your best for—for Madame Lamartine."

"But yesterday you asked me questions, you accused me of keeping the news from you when I assured you I did not know——"

"It's not that. I'm sorry I questioned you like that. I was puzzled, and I had to find out. But I believe you: honestly I do."

"Then what *is* the mystery?" demanded Celeste.

"Look," said Jennifer wearily, "there isn't any mystery, as far as you're concerned. The questions that we—the Englishman and I—have been asking are purely our own affair. They do touch Madame Lamartine's death, *but they do not touch you*. I swear it. Now, will that do?"

But Celeste was still smouldering. "I nursed her," she said stubbornly, "and I was with her almost till she died. It does touch me. I have a right to know what you suspect."

Jennifer grabbed at the last rags of her patience, and pulled them round her with dignity. She said quietly: "I can't tell you, Celeste. If you won't accept my other assurances you'll just have to accept this fact. I can't tell you anything—tonight."

"Tonight?" The girl's voice went up on the word, and she sat forward, her body tense and shaking, her eyes brilliant. Jenny recognized with horror the symptoms of rising hysteria. She said quickly: "Listen, my dear——"

But the girl paid no attention. She leaned forward on the bed, head out-thrust and eyes accusing, and cried again: "Tonight? Yes, tell me that, *madame l'anglaise*? What is happening tonight? Why do you look like that, with your face white and your hands unsteady and your eyes—yes, your eyes *waiting*?"

Jennifer said sharply. "What on earth d'you mean?"

"All day you've been like that," cried Celeste shrilly. "I've seen you! Prowling and watching, and wondering about us—I've seen you! Oh, yes, *I* watched *you*, too! And now tonight . . . What are you waiting for? What are you watching for out of the windows? What are you looking for in the valley—*tonight*?"

"Celeste, for heaven's sake——"

Celeste shouted it at her: "*Is it the police?*"

There were steps in the corridor outside, the soft-slippered footsteps of a nun. Jennifer came to her feet, shaking.

"Hold your tongue, you damned little fool!" New terror grating on nerves already raw had brought her, too, nearer to hysteria than she realized, or she would never have spoken like that. But the brutal words had an effect. Celeste gasped and shrank down on the bed, and when she spoke again, though her voice was still shaken and hostile, it was lower.

She said, almost triumphantly: "I was right, you see! Luis said the Englishman had seen the *gendarme* this morning, and that he'd gone off for the police tonight. So you needn't try to fob me off by telling me there's nothing wrong!"

"I didn't say that! I said it didn't concern *you*!"

Celeste slipped off the bed, and faced her. Her eyes gleamed in the candle-light.

"But it concerns the convent, mademoiselle, and it is not right that you, a foreigner and an intruder, should bring trouble on us like this. I shall not let you, I!"

"*Celeste, where are you going?*"

The girl turned, her hand on the latch.

"You say it doesn't concern me, mademoiselle . . . that may be so—but there are those whom it will concern!"

Jennifer started forward. "No, Celeste! You are not to bother the Reverend Mother——"

"Reverend Mother?" Celeste flung another of her burning looks over her shoulder as she turned away. "I'm not going to the Reverend Mother! It's Doña Francisca who's concerned, and we'll see how you answer *her*, *madame l'anglaise!*"

She wrenched open the door.

Jennifer's leap was purely instinctive. In one shattering moment the situation had changed: where it had been merely exacerbating it was now thoroughly dangerous. So she took drastic measures without a second thought. She leaped across the little room and gripped Celeste by the arm. She pulled her away from the door and kicked it shut.

The girl whirled to face her, quick as a cat.

"Let me go!"

Jenny, panting, tried to speak calmly. "Listen to me, please!"

"Let me go!" The girl began to struggle wildly, wrenching her arm out of Jennifer's grip and hurling herself once more against the door. As she clutched the latch Jennifer's hand clamped down over hers and held it hard.

"Let me go!" Celeste gasped and sobbed, writhing against the door in Jennifer's grasp. "I'll tell . . . Doña Francisca. . . ." Beyond the door footsteps sounded once more. A latch clicked somewhere. "*Let me go!*" And Celeste drew in her breath for a scream.

Jennifer said desperately: "*To warn that murderess?*"

The girl's body stiffened in her hands; went still. The sobbing breathing seemed to stop. Jennifer let go of her and moved away. She felt sick and dazed. She sat down on her bed and looked at the floor. The stub of her cigarette lay where she had dropped it, lazily smouldering. She put her foot on it and squashed it out.

Celeste said: "What do you mean?"

Jennifer looked up reluctantly to meet her eyes. She was still standing against the door, but this time there was no conscious drama in her attitude. Nor did she look beautiful. Her face was pinched and sharp, her body huddled bonelessly back against the door, as if only the door held it from falling.

Her voice was small and toneless, like a child's. She said: "You'll have to tell me now, you know."

"Yes," said Jennifer. "Yes, I'll have to tell you now. You'd better sit down."

"I'm all right."

Jennifer looked away from her, out of the dark window, down the valley where the storm wind blew across the bending grasses. No light, no movement. But she felt too tired, now, to worry.

Celeste said from the door: "Go on."

Jennifer, with a little sigh, began to talk. . . .

It had been, perhaps, a mistake to talk to Celeste in the first place, but one that could hardly be avoided. Inevitable, too, had been the blurting out of the final terrible accusation. And, that once uttered, the third disastrous step had to be taken. If Jenny was at all conscious of the risks attendant on smashing an idol in front of its worshipper, she had borne too much that day to apprehend fully the danger of the step she had been forced into taking. Exhausted herself by the storms of the day, she avoided looking at her companion, and, keeping her voice impersonal and her eyes on the darkness beyond the window, she told her story.

She spoke flatly and uncompromisingly, talking of the gentians, of her own surprise, of mistrust and uneasiness deepening through suspicion to certainty. She told of the letter she had found behind the triptych, of her determination to investigate the riddle of her cousin's death, and, finally, she told of the midnight flight up the mountainside, and what had happened there.

"And what my cousin's doing there, I don't know," she said, "but that doesn't matter: I'll know soon enough. What does matter is that your Doña Francisca's in it—in it up to the neck, and it's something so dangerous that she'll stop at nothing to keep us from asking questions. And I stood there and heard her, plain and clear, blackmailing Pierre Bussac into murdering my cousin Gillian. . . ."

Then she looked up, and anything more she might have said was frozen on her lips.

The girl was crouching against the door, still as an animal, and her skin was like wax in the candle-light. The flesh of cheek and temple seemed to have shrunk, sharpening her features into an ugly mask. The great dark eyes were blank, like the eyes of a ghost.

Jennifer's heart twisted; she leaned forward and spoke urgently: "Don't look like that, Celeste! My dear!"

The lips moved to a thin whisper. "Is it true?"

"I—yes, it's true. But——"

"Do—you—swear—to—me—that—it's—true?"

"Celeste——"

"Do you swear it?"

Jennifer said woodenly: "I'm not sure about the blackmail, but the other——"

"The murder. You heard it?"

"Yes, I heard it." She stirred and put out a hand. "I—I'm sorry, Celeste. I can't tell you how sorry. I wish you'd never had to know."

"I'm glad I know." The whisper was barely audible, and Jennifer glanced sharply at her. She said uncertainly: "I think the Reverend Mother—you'd better let me take you——"

"No." Celeste straightened herself, quickly, and reached for the cloak which lay across her bed.

"What are you doing?" asked Jennifer sharply.

But, without replying, the girl opened the door and was gone like a wraith down the dark corridor.

CHAPTER XIX

TRAGIC OVERTURE: *stringendo*

THE candle-flame, streaming sideways in the draught, was ripped off by the slam of the door. The smell of smoking wax wound through the darkness.

Jennifer said, "*Oh, God!*" on a dreary little sob of apprehension and flung herself towards the door, blind hands groping. The blank surface met her, defeating her urgent fingers. Her hands slid over it, patting, touching, slithering, for an agony of moments before they found the latch.

She wrenched the door open, and ran out into the corridor, making blindly for the head of the refectory stairs.

"Celeste!" she called, in an urgent undertone. "Celeste!"

But the girl had already vanished. And where she had gone Jennifer did not care to guess, but it could only be towards disaster. She plunged down the stairs at an increased speed, towards the oblong of dim light which was the refectory door.

The refectory was empty too, but a ghostly smell of warmth and food still hung about it. A single lamp, high on the wall, dealt a small uncertain light. The door into the tunnel was open, swinging in the wind, and the tunnel itself was filled with the cold and moaning sounds of the storm. The heavy arras across the chapel door was swaying, as if someone had just brushed through . . . of course. The chapel. That was where Celeste would be. For the torn ship, the harbour. . . .

Jennifer, with her hand already on the arras, stopped, hesitating between pity and relief. But even as she wondered what to do, the decision was made. Doña Francisca's voice said, sharply: "Where are you going?"

Every nerve in Jennifer's body jumped and tingled. Her hand jerked away from the arras as if the stuff were electrified. Then she realized that the voice came from beyond the arras, inside the chapel.

It had happened, then. Celeste, whether by accident or design, had run straight into the arms of the bursar.

Jennifer pulled the edge of the arras aside slightly. One leaf of the door it masked was shut. She slipped through into the heavy darkness between the curtain and the door. She peered into the chapel, her heart thudding.

The chapel was not lit for service, but a couple of lamps glowed on the walls, and in various nests and niches in the aisles the pyramided tapers glimmered. The sanctuary lamp glowed a clear and steady red, and in the side-chapel a smaller one hung like a still ruby.

Under this stood Celeste, rigid and upright. Doña Francisca, interrupted at some task about the little altar, faced her. Through the dusky incense-laden air wove and flickered an organ fugue of Bach, as Sister Marie-Claude, in her little enclosed loft, played on unawares.

Jennifer stayed, frozen, in the shelter of the arras, her mind a whirl of horror and indecision, when, through a thin phrase of music, she heard Celeste speak. She spoke in a cold hard little voice that Jennifer had not heard from her before.

She said: "That's what I came to tell you. I'm going away from here, *señora*, now, tonight, and I'm never coming back again. Never again, do you hear me?"

The bursar stared at her as if she had run mad.

"Celeste! What are you talking about? Are you ill? My child—my dear child——"

She took a step towards the girl, but Celeste, without moving, said clearly: "Get back from me. Don't you dare touch me."

"Celeste!" The hard voice sounded stupefied, then it

quickened with anger. "How dare you speak to me in that manner? Are you mad? Do you know who you're talking to?"

"Oh, yes." The answer was gentle as death, and every bit as cold. "You are Doña Francisca, the person that all these years I thought I loved. That's all finished. No, don't touch me. I'm trying to explain why I had to come and say good-bye . . . because of all those years, because I can't quite forget"—her voice quivered, and she said on a note of horror—"even tonight, that you were good to me in your own way."

"*Tonight?*"

Jennifer, her hand flying to her dry throat, saw the Spaniard stiffen, saw the black eyes narrow in the candle-light.

"*What are you talking about, Celeste? Why 'even tonight'?*"

For the first time the girl moved; only her hands, which clutched whitely at the folds of her cloak, but the gesture was a curiously powerful one. She said, her voice hardening: "That gets you, doesn't it? It's true, then. It's funny, but I knew it was, straight away, as soon as she told me."

Doña Francisca spoke very softly. "Who told you, Celeste?"

"The English girl. You wouldn't expect me to stay here, would you, after what I heard?"

Then the woman moved like a striking adder. Her long hand shot out and grabbed the girl by the shoulder. She said, on a hiss: "*What does she know?*"

Celeste did not move. "Murder," she said softly. . . .

Through the silence the music poured, remote, angelic.

Then Celeste, with a swift violent movement, wrenched her shoulder from the Spaniard's grip, and the cloak pulled aside as the thin cotton of her blue dress ripped and tore. She lashed at the older woman's clutching hand with a vicious fist, and her voice, subdued still automatically to quietness in that building, came in a whisper that was more shocking than a scream: "I'm going now! I'm going from you and your fine talk and your pious ways! I'm going out now to my lover—*aah!* you didn't know that, did you? I've a lover I've been meeting, for weeks and weeks, out on the mountain there—*you'd* call it sin, no doubt, Doña Francisca! Sin! Maybe it is! I don't care! If it is sin, it's better than your kind of holiness!" She had backed away as she spoke, towards the south door, and the rich candle-light flickered and shimmered over her. She paused in the doorway, and the contempt that had stiffened her face like frost broke and melted, crumpling into tears. She opened her lips to speak again, but no sound came. She turned away blindly and wrenched open the door.

The black cloak swirled round her like a cloud. One moment she was there, held in the glancing light against the shadows of the great door. Then she was gone, and the draught from the outer night made the candles bow and stream along the air.

*   *   *

The chapel door, framing a square of black and wind-ridden night, swung heavily, once, twice.

Doña Francisca stood there for a long moment, rigid in that queer bird-like stance, the clutching hand that the girl had struck aside still reaching out, claw-like, towards the blank doorway. The other was against her breast, a taut fist clenched on the rubied cross. It was as if some malignant sorcery had stricken her to a statue of wood, old, dark wood, with the deep lines of the sunken face scored heavily by some primitive craftsman.

Even when she moved the illusion was not dispelled. Slowly, like the arms of a doll, whose limbs fall with their own weight, her arms dropped to her sides, and hung there, the hands twitching loosely. Something else dropped like a falling spark . . . the cross, its chain snapped in that convulsive grip, flashed to the carpet, to be quenched in the shadow of the silk robe. She had not noticed. That carved face was expressionless still, the eyes hooded over like a vulture's.

Then, slowly, the dark gargoyle of a face turned towards the door where Jennifer hid.

"The English girl . . ." said Doña Francisca softly, and came straight towards her.

*   *   *

Jennifer was not conscious of having moved at all, but before the Spaniard had taken more than two paces in her direction she had dived out of her hiding-place like a bolting rabbit, and was running down the echoing tunnel towards the garden. The darkness closed round her, but a glimpse from some half-shuttered window showed her the way. It had stopped raining, but the sounds of her flight were drowned by the wind that still roared in the trees. Above her head the apple-boughs tossed whistling leaves; the little orange-trees swayed like blown dandelion-clocks as she ran between them and, wrenching open the iron gate, dived through into the darker shelter of the close.

Her plunge into the dark had been a purely instinctive one, but she realized, through her panic, as she stumbled across the wet mounds of the graveyard, that she had been right. She must make straight for the farm, and Stephen. She must warn them—but Jennifer did not attempt to persuade herself that she was flying to warn Stephen and the police. She was running, for the third time, into the sheltering comfort of Stephen's arms. Reason had caught up with instinct; however he might deny himself the rôle he was, quite simply, the hero of any scene that Jennifer played in. And Jennifer had no doubt at all as to the kind of scene she was involved in now. If ever murder had looked out of anyone's face, it had looked out of the Spanish woman's as she turned to find her quarry.

Her quarry. . . . But if the storm hid Jennifer's flight from the hunter it also effectively drowned the noise of pursuit.

Doña Francisca could not have seen her go; nor was it at all probable that she had heard anything. She might still be on her way up to the corridor above the refectory to look for "the English girl"—but she might also, even now, be sweeping after her prey like a blacker shadow through the black graveyard . . . Jennifer's outstretched hands met soaked and tossing leaves, where the roses swung in a curtain over the wall near the outer gate. Her hair whipped wet and blinding across her eyes. Thorns tore at her groping hands and wrists, and dragged at the skirts of her coat, catching at her like claws. Something struck her heavily on the arm, and she bit back a cry of terror, only to realize that it was the gate, swinging open in a squall of wind.

She plunged through it out on to the bare mountain side. To Bussac's farm. Stephen would be there, Stephen and the police from Luz and Gavarnie. Stephen . . .

She could see better now that she was clear of the convent walls and trees. She ran up the grassy track towards the pine-woods, sobbing for breath, driven headlong by terror which gained on her even as she fled. She raced on into the path of the storm with never a backward look. As she came above the level where the convent buildings afforded protection, the storm seized her, driving her before it as if she had no more weight than a wisp of cloud. Her shoes slid on the slippery turf; twice she stumbled and fell to her knees, so that her hands were grazed and her coat torn and filthy; but neither falls nor the unheeded pain of bruises checked for a moment her headlong speed, and the impelling storm, thrusting against her as against a sail, drove her like a small scudding ship up the steep way towards the woods. It threw her, half-blinded, almost straight against the column of the first sentinel pine, then she was swallowed by the silence of the wood, which lopped off the roar of the storm behind her as a cliff shuts off the sounds of the sea.

The blackness was intense, so that to move at all was to thrust one's body, wincing, against palpable darkness. But she dared not stop. She dared not even look behind, for fear of seeing a blacker shadow moving under the trees, of feeling another breath than the breath of the cold wind on the nape of her neck. She ran on.

And then she was out of the trees, racing up the steep track which led to the farm.

The track, rocky enough and treacherous at all times, was tonight like a scree of hell's mountain; a dozen new-filled rivulets had spilled into it, so that, instead of a track, it was the bed of a new stream, a shallow treacherous torrent that poured over the smooth-worn rocks, or slid in slabbed mud between them. On and on . . . up and up . . . no longer running, but slipping in the mud, dragging herself up the steepest bit, heaving her weighted limbs over boulder and stump. . . .

On . . . up . . . now she was above the main source of the stream and running over rock wet only with the rain . . . on, on . . . to pelt, gasping, round the last shoulder of rock. . . .

And there before her, huddled low under the leaping wind was at last the farm, its lighted windows blinking behind flapping shutters.

"Stephen!" cried Jennifer, and flew across the cobbles with the tears of relief stinging her eyes.

She thrust open the cottage door and plunged inside. Warmth met her, and the smell of stew and new bread.

She gasped again: "Stephen!" and stood, blinking in the little room's lamplight, while the door slammed shut behind her.

Across the table she met the startled and questioning gaze of the girl with the grey eyes.

There was nobody else in the room.

CHAPTER XX

CONTE FANTASTIQUE

THE girl was sitting on a high stool that was drawn up to the table in the centre of the little room. She still looked very pale; her face was drawn and tired, and the movements of her hands were clumsy and badly controlled. She had been engaged in cutting a crusty loaf into thick slices, and beside her on the table was a pile of sliced meat. The remains of a hasty meal still littered the table, and the rest of the room showed every sign of hurried preparations for departure. There was very little furniture; the table, a few chairs, a couch piled with blankets under the window, and, oddly, an ancient English grandfather clock in a corner. An open door opposite the window gave on to what appeared to be an empty bedroom.

So much Jennifer noticed in the shocked, half-dazed second before the girl spoke. She put down the knife she was holding, and said: "Mademoiselle?" She seemed considerably startled—as well she might.

Jennifer said breathlessly: "You've not gone. It's all right! You've not gone!"

"No." The girl spoke in French, on a note of puzzlement. "I was ill, and then he found the mule was lame so we couldn't leave. But what——?"

Jennifer went forward a little shakily towards the table. "Then it's all right! Oh, Gillian!"

"Mademoiselle?" The grey eyes held nothing but bewilderment, and then apprehension in the swift glance they flung at the door. "Why have you come back? You saw how angry he was this afternoon. If he comes in and finds you here——"

Jenny's hands groped for the back of the nearest chair, gripped whitely. "D'you mean . . . they've not been here yet? He—they've not taken him——?"

"They?" The other's voice sharpened. "Who are they?"

"The Englishman." Jennifer answered automatically, her tired brain whirling anew with frightened conjectures. "The police."

"Police?" The grey eyes narrowed, then flared wide with alarm. "*Police?* Why?"

But Jennifer was not watching her. She, too, had turned her head towards the door. She said shakily: "Something must have gone wrong. We've got to get out of here—*now*. . . . That woman may be on her way, and Bussac—where's Bussac?"

"At the farm in the next valley. Corentin's. I couldn't have managed it on foot, and he went to borrow a mule. He'll be back any minute."

Jennifer straightened up as if at the crack of a whip. Her face was a white blaze of excitement. "Then we must go now! Quickly! Don't wait for anything—there's no time! It's pitch black outside, and the storm'll hide us. . . ." Then, as the other made no move, "My God, Gillian, what's the matter? What *is* this? Are you trying to tell me you *still* don't recognize me? I'm Jenny, Gil, your cousin Jenny! Don't you know me now?" She put out an urgent hand across the table. "There's no time for explanations, Gil, but you're in danger here, and this is our chance! Believe me, whatever you've got involved in, it won't matter! Just come with me now and we'll sort it out later. *But you've got to come!*"

But the other girl drew back from her desperate outstretched hand, and in her face bewildered apprehension had deepened into naked fear.

"I—I don't understand. Why should I go with you? What are you talking about? *Who are you?*"

A gust of wind sent the shutter crashing back against the wall outside. But Jennifer never heard it. Gone was the storm, gone the dangers that might even now be converging on the cottage. Blue eyes met grey across the cluttered table. In the stillness between them the lamp sang.

"I've told you. Your cousin Jenny."

"My—cousin?" The girl was as white as the table-cloth. She shook her head. "I—don't understand."

"Are you . . . trying to tell me . . . you're *not* Gillian?"

"I don't—I don't know what you're talking about. I am Marie Bussac. I don't ever remember any cousins." Her hands shook as she moved a plate on the table.

Round Jennifer the little room seemed to swell and darken, while the lamp shrank to a hissing point of light. She began to tremble. She said, stupidly: "Marie—Bussac? Marie?"

"Yes, mademoiselle. But of course. His wife." She picked up the knife in an unsteady hand, as if to continue her task, but held it slackly, staring at Jennifer with a pale, almost dazed look on her face. "Please, mademoiselle. You must explain. The police—why should they come here? What have they found out about us? For God's sake, mademoiselle, you must tell me what this is all about! And who are you—really? Why have you come here?"

Jennifer groped shakily for the nearest chair, and sat down. She pushed the wet hair back from her face and gazed dumbly at the other girl. The latter, almost mechanically, reached for a bottle of red wine, tipped some into a glass, and pushed it across the table. Jenny took it and drank greedily. The harsh tang of the stuff steadied her, and seemed to set the chilled blood flowing again to brain and fingers.

She said, "I thought I was your cousin, Jennifer Silver, but now I don't know. I—I——" She looked at the other again and said unsteadily: "You wouldn't do this to me, would you, Gil? Surely you can trust me? If you're mixed up in this game of Bussac's, living with him here—and—oh! what does it matter? I swear I'll help you."

The pale face opposite her seemed to freeze, and fear touched in its lines and shadows.

The girl said rapidly: "I don't know you. I don't know what you're talking about."

Jenny said in a whisper: "Then you're her double. And she's dead. But you're still alive, Mademoiselle Lally Dupré!"

*   *   *

The pale face opposite her never changed.

"*What* did you call me? Another name? Are you crazy, with your names and your cousins and——?"

But Jennifer with a cry had jumped to her feet. "Of course! What a fool I am! We said there couldn't be more than one who looked like you!"

She stepped aside into the full light of the lamp, and pulled open the draggled skirts of her coat. "Marie Bussac, Madame Bussac, what you will—*what colour is my dress?*"

The girl looked at her as if she were mad. "I—I don't understand. You must be crazy!"

"No. Just answer me that one question, and if you get it right I'll go." She thrust the damp folds forward in the lamplight. "What colour is it?"

The grey eyes glanced, faltered. The straight brows drew together. "I—is it grey? A pale yellowish grey?"

The tears stung behind Jennifer's eyes, and brimmed over on her cheeks. She said, shakily: "No. No, it's not," and let the blue folds fall. She put cold hands to her cheeks and scrubbed away the tears with a childish gesture. She looked across the smoking lamp at Gillian.

She said: "I knew it was you. I don't get this, Gil. Why don't you trust me?"

Gillian stared at her, her body hunched on the stool as if exhausted, her hands clutching whitely at the table's edge. The lines of fear and weariness deepened in her face. She looked ill. She said uncertainly: "I don't—I can't——" Then a hand went to her head with a sudden, almost frantic gesture. "*Oh, mon dieu, que j'ai peur! Je n'y comprends rien!*"

Jennifer stood quite still. She said, on a long breath: "I . . . see."

She put both hands flat on the table-top and leaned forward. She said: "Madame Bussac, you don't remember, anything, do you?"

Gillian's head was in her hands. It shook slightly.

"How long have you been here?"

Another shake.

"When did you get married?"

"I—a year ago. Why?"

"Did he tell you that?"

The muffled voice said: "Yes."

Jenny bit her lip, but her voice was still gentle: "But you don't actually remember getting married, Madame Bussac?"

Gillian lifted her head. "No, mam'selle. That was before . . ."

"Before the accident," said Jenny softly. "Yes."

Across the hissing lamp the grey eyes met hers again, bemused, uncertain, the blank child-like gaze of the person whose past has been wiped out. . . .

There was a little pause.

Then Jennifer straightened up, with a little shivering breath that was almost a breath of relief. At least, now, she knew where she was. And the issue lay before her in all its plain impossibility.

She had to get Gillian away. Whatever Bussac's intentions towards her it was, of course, out of the question to leave Gillian with him. All other considerations apart,

Gillian was ill. . . . She must, somehow, be made to listen, and to trust. She looked down into the grey eyes, now so pitifully lost and bewildered.

"Then you must let me remember for you, Marie. It's true I'm your cousin, but never mind that now. You must trust me. There's no need to be frightened of Bussac. If you'll come away with me now——"

"I'm not frightened of him. But the police——"

"Why should *you* be afraid of them? You've done nothing. They can't hold you responsible for anything he's done."

Gillian's hands twisted whitely together in her lap. "They can. They can. They want me too. That affair in Bordeaux——"

"So he told you you were mixed up in that, did he? I suppose that was one way of ensuring that you'd keep out of everyone's way. I begin to see. . . ." She ran round the table and laid an urgent hand on Gillian's arm.

But Gillian had turned her head at some sound outside. The storm slammed against the shutters, and, as Jennifer's heart leaped into her throat there came, like an echo, another slam that was not of the storm.

The door opened on a gust of wind, crashed shut.

"*Eh bien, mademoiselle?*" said Pierre Bussac grimly, and slid the bolt home behind him.

CHAPTER XXI

DEATH AND THE MAIDEN

ALL at once it seemed as if the sounds of the storm had receded, leaving the kitchen still and quiet. A log hissed; the clock ticked quietly, the lamp sang; but the small sounds held the silence tensely, while Jennifer, dropping Gillian's arm, backed away from the anger that blazed in Bussac's eyes.

He said: "What have you come back for?"

Gillian put out a hand. "Pierre——"

He paid no heed to her. He looked at Jennifer across the table. "What are you doing here? What have you been telling my wife?"

She said, more bravely than she felt: "You know quite well what I've been telling her. She's my cousin, Gillian Lamartine! And what's more, you know it, Monsieur Bussac!"

"That's nonsense," he said roughly. "She'll tell you her-self——"

"She can't tell me anything, as you must be perfectly well aware. She doesn't remember anything. But she's my cousin and I can prove it!"

He took a quick step forward at that, and she saw a gleam in his eyes that frightened her. He said softly: "Can you indeed? And you came up here . . . alone, mam'selle?"

She licked her lips. "I—no, I——"

"He said: "Where's your friend? Where's the English-man I thrashed this afternoon?"

Gillian had been standing, supporting herself by the table, following the exchange with the same expression of dazed bewilderment. Now, when Jennifer did not answer, she said, soft-voiced: "She says he's coming."

Jenny moved sharply, but Bussac only laughed. "Let him come."

"With the police. Now. Soon."

He looked at Jennifer, his eyes narrow and dangerous. "So he did go for the police?"

"Of course!" Her voice was shrill with defiance. "He went as soon as we left here! What did you expect? You must be a fool, Monsieur Bussac, if you thought we'd do nothing."

"No. Not such a fool as that. I thought he might go. But you see there *are* no police to find on a Wednesday, mademoiselle. It's Aristide's day off, and he goes—in his car—to play in the pelota match at Luz. Your friend will find it's a long way to Luz, when there's no transport!"

"There's a telephone," said Jenny harshly.

"There is also," he said pleasantly, "a thunderstorm. Corentin tells me that the lines have been out of action since three o'clock."

He smiled down into her eyes, the smile deepening at what he saw in her face. She opened her mouth to speak, then shut it again, lifting a hand in a boneless little gesture which was poignant in the helplessness it conveyed. Something of this must have touched Gillian, for she seemed to rouse herself now from her weary apathy. She turned to Bussac and touched his sleeve.

"Pierre—what is it, Pierre? What's all this about? She said she knew me. She said I was her cousin." The eyes she raised to him had a lost, hesitating look that under any other circumstances would have been heart-breaking. Now, it made Jennifer want to scream. "What does it all mean?" asked Gillian.

His hand closed over the one she had laid on his arm. The gesture was one of protection, even of tenderness, and his voice and look were gentle. Jennifer, though prepared for something of this kind, was startled by the suddenness and completeness of the change in him. Why, she thought, I believe the man loves her. *That*'s why he wouldn't listen to Stephen's proposals. And now I'm trying to get her from him. . . . Oh, Lord, oh, Lord, it only needed that. What do we do now?

Bussac said gently: "It means nothing, *ma mie*. It's she who's confused. She's mixed you up with somebody else. I've told you who you are. You belong here."

"But this cousin——"

"Is dead. *Dead*, d'you hear me?" His hand tightened over hers, but he was speaking straight at Jennifer. "She was the woman who died at the convent; I told you about her. Remember?"

Jennifer could stand this no longer. "Marie! Listen to me!"

"Be silent, you!" His voice blazed, as he turned, from gentleness to such fury that she shrank, and obeyed him.

He lifted Gillian's hand gently from his own and held it for a moment, bending over her with an urgency in his deep voice that was uncommonly convincing.

"*Ma chère*, you heard all this talk about police. It's true. You remember what I told you before, that the police were looking for us over what happened in Bordeaux?" She nodded dumbly. "Well, they've found us out. This girl and the Englishman have brought the *flics* down on us. That's why we're leaving. I didn't tell you before because I didn't want to scare you. But that's why we're getting out, and fast." He patted her hand, smiled at her, and dropped it. "Now we must go. I think there's probably still time enough, but the sooner we go, the better."

"What about—her?"

He was smiling at Jennifer again. He looked huge in the lamplight, a big, confident, handsome brute whose shadow dwarfed the room. He said softly: "She wanted to meddle in my affairs. She mayn't find it quite so easy to get out of them again. . . ."

Gillian made a sharp little movement. "You're not to hurt her, Pierre!"

He said, not taking his eyes off Jennifer: "Oh, no, I shan't hurt her. . . ." But his eyes were dangerous.

Jennifer said desperately: "We've told you we'll forget about your affairs. We don't want to interfere with you. All we want is for my cousin to be safe——'

He said roughly: "Your cousin's dead, you little fool, and the sooner you realize that the better it'll be for you. As for my wife, she's safe enough with me."

"Where are you taking her?"

"That's my affair." He swung round on the other girl. "Now, enough of this foolery: it's time we went. Are you ready, Marie?"

She nodded.

"I got Corentin's mule. It's in the shed. Can you manage to saddle it? Good. Hurry if you can. There's a lantern out there."

She turned to obey him, with a troubled look over her shoulder at Jennifer standing white-faced by the fire. "You'll come soon?"

"Yes, yes. Go now, quickly."

The door slammed. The lamp fluttered in its globe, and was steady again. Jennifer said shakily across the table: "Monsieur Bussac, please listen to me—*please*, just for one moment. . . ."

"*Eh bien?*" He had taken a coat down from a hook in the corner, and was hastily cramming the packages of food into the pockets, keeping all the while, between Jennifer and the door.

She forced herself to speak calmly. "Let's be honest with one another, Monsieur Bussac—now that there's nobody to listen. You were expecting Lally Dupré that night. Did you know her by sight?"

He hesitated, then said flatly: "No."

"Then you—and Doña Francisca—both thought that this girl you call Marie was Lally Dupré. But when I started asking questions Doña Francisca realized fast enough who it was you were keeping here. When I asked her to describe the woman who died she described Gillian—Marie. She'd guessed. And she came straight up here last night to tell you that whereas before it had been folly not to send your —guest—straight into Spain, now that 'Marie' was certainly Madame Lamartine, keeping her was suicidal. I followed her here—you know that. I heard her. You must have known then, Monsieur Bussac, what had happened on the night of the storm."

The black eyes held hers for a moment. "And if I did?"

"Nothing," said Jennifer, "except that you know and I know that I'm telling the truth."

"Oh, yes," said Pierre Bussac indifferently, "you're telling the truth."

"Then for goodness' sake believe me when I say that I'll make no trouble for you! You know she's hardly fit for this journey, whatever it is. Tell her some tale—you can do it— and let her come with me!"

His voice was rough. "Damn you, can't you grasp what I tell you? I want her with me!"

"You've no right!"

"She's my wife."

"*Is* she?"

He shot her a look under lowering eyes. "What d'you mean?"

"She only came up here three weeks ago. I suppose she was hurt in the car crash, and lost her memory as a result. She tells me she has been married to you for a year. Why did you tell her that lie, Monsieur Bussac?"

There was a pause. Then he spoke quietly. "All right. You wanted it; you can have it. You've guessed the rest fairly enough. I was being paid by Marcel Dupré's lot to

smuggle Lally out into Spain. She was to have met me in
the gorge below Gavarnie, at a place called Chaos. I'd
been told she was getting a lift from a woman called
Lamartine. I took the mule down that night, but she wasn't
there. After a while I went on along the river, and I came
on the car, smashed up. She—Marie—was there. I must
have missed the real Lally Dupré in the dark. Marie was
lying near the car. I thought she was dead at first, then I
found she was just unconscious. I looked for her papers,
purse—anything that would identify her. I couldn't find
any, so I assumed this was Lally Dupré—the description
I'd had fitted fairly enough—and that the Lamartine woman
had picked up her own stuff and gone for help. I knew that
Lally had got to be got away quickly before anyone came,
and besides . . ."

He had thrust his way into his coat while he was talking.
In it he looked bigger than ever. He took a step forward and
put his fists on the table, leaning towards her with a dark
look that blazed.

He said: "She was lying on the grass in the torchlight
with her hair spread out and her clothes half torn off her.
She was lovely, and I wanted her." His teeth showed.
"Just—like—that. Do you understand that, you pale little
English miss? *I wanted her.*" The black gaze held hers.
"So I picked her up and brought her here. And then in the
morning I heard about the other woman at the convent.
I'd been worried about her, because in the normal way I'd
have had my passenger over the hills and far away before
morning, and no evidence to prove she'd ever been near
me, and here I was stuck with a girl who couldn't be made
to travel. But my luck held." He grinned briefly. "It
always does. The woman at the convent held her tongue.
Lally must have wondered why the police didn't ask about
the 'passenger' she'd left for dead in the wreck, but she'd
be too thankful for the ready-made alias to risk breaking it

by asking questions. If she'd known that the *señora* was in with me . . . but, of course, no one knew that." He paused. "At any rate she played safe and kept quiet. I simply assumed she'd been too ill to recollect having a passenger—and then she died. More luck."

"And luck too," said Jennifer unpleasantly, "that my cousin had lost her memory?"

"As you say. She wouldn't have stayed with me else, would she? As it was, when I found she remembered nothing, I was only too pleased she wasn't in a hurry to leave for Spain. I told her she was my wife—there may have been other tales in the village, but she never left the farm, and no one interferes with me."

"And you told her, I gather, that she'd been mixed up in the affair at the Bordeaux bank?"

"Of course. I had to give her some reason for keeping her close. I thought it was true, anyway. I didn't tell her it was murder; I told her just enough to keep her in hiding and not enough to make her anxious to leave. . . . And when I found out who she really was, I saw no call to change my story. It came to the same thing in the end, didn't it? She'd stayed here with me, though God knows she must have found the life up here hard and a bit strange, and me, perhaps, not exactly what she'd been used to. . . ."

He smiled at her as he straightened up his big body. "I thought it would shake you, *mademoiselle l'anglaise* . . . you little Snow Queen of an English girl; you're all the same. She has it too, that look . . . I find it—exciting." The smile widened. "No, don't look at me like that. I've other things on my mind just now." And he turned aside to pull open the table drawer.

"You're—*vile*!" said Jennifer shakily.

He had taken an electric torch out of the drawer, and thrust it into his pocket. He lifted an indifferent shoulder. "You think so? She seems to like me well enough."

She said hoarsely: "Where are you taking her?"

"Where you'll not find her."

"They'll follow you."

"They won't, not the way I'm going." He gave a hard little laugh. "How d'you think I've evaded the frontier guards so long, my dear, if I hadn't my own road into Spain?"

"You fool!" cried Jennifer. "Even if you do get away, you can't hide for ever."

"No? Spain's a big place. My money's over there, and I have friends."

"She'll recover," said Jennifer brutally. "She'll remember. Do you imagine she'll stay with you then?"

"Why not? I'm good to her."

She said desperately: "You're crazy! You'll never get clear!"

He snarled at her then, with something of a resumption of his old manner. "Shut your mouth, you little fool! D'you think I've run the risks I have, keeping her, to let her go now? You may as well save your breath, *petite anglaise*. She goes with me."

"And I?" said Jenny quietly.

He eyed her. "You'll stay here. But I'm not leaving you loose to spy on the way we go. I said I'd not hurt you, and I won't. But I've got to put you out of action for a while, my dear. It might be quite some time before they think of looking for you in the outhouses, and by that time we should be well away."

He lifted a coil of rope from the back of a chair, and moved towards her.

*   *   *

Before he had taken more than a step the cottage door opened again. Jennifer whirled towards it, hope widening her eyes and parting her lips. But it was only Gillian, breathless from the buffeting of the storm, which had whipped colour into her pale cheeks, and set a sparkle in her eyes.

She said: "The mule's ready, Pierre."

"Good. Get your coat. We're going."

Gillian ran into the inner room. Bussac came round the table towards Jennifer, rope in hand. She shrank back, and, as he grabbed for her, she dodged his hand, and ran round the table, facing him again breathlessly. He cursed, and lunged after her. His hand scraped her sleeve, but she ducked and ran, facing him again. It was like some dreadful nursery game, playing tag with terror round the lamplit table, dodging and panting on the edges of the little pool of light, while behind them their shadows danced and swelled, hugely, up wall and ceiling. There was no sound but the scrape of feet, and their quick, hard breathing, and the quiet voice of the clock in the corner ticking the seconds away . . . but to Jennifer that monstrous pouncing darkness was pierced with her own silent, frantic cry—*Stephen! Stephen! Stephen!* . . . He would come; he had to come; *he had to come.* . . .

The terrible little game went on.

The shadow loomed, struck, as Bussac flung himself across the table, a long arm shooting out to grab. She jumped backwards from the clutching hand. He overbalanced, falling heavily forward. The lamp rocked. In the split second when his weight was on the table, she sprang through the reeling shadows towards the door. Her hand was on the latch when he caught her. His arms closed round her from behind in a powerful grip, and he dragged her back from the door. She struggled, wild now with terror, and lashed out with her feet. kicking him on the legs. He cursed again and shifted his grip. One arm was tight round her body; his other hand bit into her arm. Vaguely, through whirling panic, she heard Gillian's voice say:

"*Pierre!*" and his breathless, almost savage reply: "Go on. I'll catch you up in a minute. You know the way as far as the fall."

"But the girl?"

"I can't leave her to follow us, you know that. I've got to shut her up. Now for God's sake, Marie——"

"All right."

The door opened. The wind whirled in. Jennifer screamed once: "*Gillian! Don't go!*"

His hand clamped brutally over her mouth. The door banged. Seconds afterwards, surging back on the wind, came the beat of retreating hoofs.

She felt his muscles relax a little. She jerked her head sharply, and the hand loosened. She bit viciously, blindly, like a terrified animal, and felt the skin break under her teeth. He pulled his hand away with an oath, and his grip tightened fiercely. She was held helpless against him, his one arm round her, pinioning her, while with the other hand—the bitten one—he forced her head up till her eyes met his.

She saw through her sick terror that he was laughing.

"Snow Queen, eh?" he said, thickly. "So you bite, you little devil? Who'd have thought it? It's a pity I've no time to teach you your manners."

Before she realized what he meant to do, he bent his head and kissed her full on the mouth.

She made a tiny sound of protest, then the shadows whirled up to engulf her, and she went limp in his arms.

*   *   *

The gap in her consciousness cannot have lasted many seconds, but Bussac had moved fast. She found herself lying on her back on what appeared to be a bed, blinking up dazedly, half-sick, at the low ceiling where the lamplight swelled and dwindled in the draughts. The sound of the clock came unnaturally loud, distorted by her semi-conscious state into a hurrying rattle, like the faraway clicking of rapid little hoofs. . . .

Gillian.

Memory flooded back. She moved sharply, only to find that something was gripping her hands, holding her down. Her whole body was weighted as if with lead . . . helpless, stifled. . . . She realized, incredulously, that she was lying, bound and gagged, on the bed in the inner room of the cottage.

Her first feeling was one of pure rage that anyone should have handled her so. The rope was not cruelly tied, but the knots seemed to gnaw at her wrists and ankles, and the gag was sheer horror. Something had been stuffed into her mouth, and then a scarf tightly bound round the lower part of her face. It pressed on her tongue, drying her mouth painfully, and setting her teeth screamingly on edge. She made a frantic little sound of protest, and turned her head agonizingly to where the lamplight streamed in an oblique shaft through the half-open door.

Then shrank into herself, watching with wide open eyes and thudding heart.

Pierre Bussac was by the jamb of the door, his big body filling the wedge of light. He was not looking at Jennifer. He was standing very still; his whole attention riveted on something in his hand.

A letter? She thought she recognized the torn folds. He must have found it in her pocket. . . . Yes, she knew it now . . .

It was Isaac Lenormand's letter.

She thought wildly what this new discovery might mean. He now had part—half—of what must be Doña Francisca's blackmailing lever in his hand. He would know that Jennifer, too, had read it. And he might think that she knew where the other half was still concealed. But if he

was going away tonight, surely neither Jennifer's knowledge nor Doña Francisca's defeat could matter? And he
had said he would not hurt her. . . . The flesh seemed to
flinch on her bones as she went small in her bonds, her dazed
mind insisting, childishly, on that one brittle hope. . . .
He had said he would not hurt her. . . . He was not all bad;
his treatment of Gillian, self-interested though it was, surely
showed that? True, he had compelled Gillian to accept
him ruthlessly enough, but he was a creature of his passions,
ferociously indifferent to any claims but his own, and
driven by desires and hates equally compulsive and uncom-
plicated. Hates? She remembered the look in his face as
he confronted Doña Francisca the night before, and, oddly
enough, felt reassured. Pure hatred, banked and smouldering through long years of frustration towards some sudden
and terrible explosion . . . compared with what she had
seen in him then, his conduct to her tonight had been almost gentle. He wouldn't hurt her. All he wanted was to
put her out of action for a while. That was what he'd said.
He wouldn't hurt her. *He wouldn't.* . . .

He thrust the letter into his pocket and turned towards
the bed. His shadow seemed to swell and darken all the
room. He took a step towards her; the shadow reared up
the wall, over the ceiling, and hung there, waiting.

He had stopped and turned his head to listen.

Outside, the wind whined down a petulant diminuendo
scale. Feet clicked across the cobbles.

Stephen! . . . It was a soundless, mindless scream. It
seemed to her to fill the night and drown the wind. . . .*At
last! Stephen!*

The outer door opened quickly. From her place in the
shadowed corner Jennifer could not see it, but Bussac had
stiffened like a pointer, and now he whipped out into the
lamplight, pulling the door to behind him.

CHAPTER XXII

DANSE MACABRE

THE door failed to shut, and swung back a little way, creaking, its wedge of light once more widening across the roughly boarded floor. She could see the corner of the table with the loaf still on it as Gillian had left it, the bottle of wine glowing like a ruby, the slim glitter of the knife under the lamp. Beyond the table-leg glimmered the dying logs of the fire.

Bussac had moved out of sight, towards the door. She saw the logs sputter sparks in the draught, then the outer door closed quietly.

She heard him say on a quick-drawn breath: "You! Already? How did you get away so early?" Through the breathed words came soft footsteps and the whisper of silk.

Jenny stirred in her bonds. She had forgotten—unbelievably she had forgotten the other terror that stalked the stormy night. Doña Francisca's voice came, pitched low: "You've let her go?"

The words were softly spoken, but it was apparent that she was furiously angry, and Bussac's reply was automatically defensive. He hedged. "What are you talking about?"

"Don't be a fool! I heard your beast! *Where has she gone?*"

"Where you'll not find her, my lady!"

There was a pause. "You're going to do as I told you?"

"I'm going to do as I please. And now get out of here. I'm going too."

"I'll wait. I'll see you when you come back."

He said deliberately: "Then you'll wait a long time. I shan't be back."

"What d'you mean? No, wait. Wait! Fool! What d'you intend to do? You can't have thought——"

He interrupted roughly: "We'll not start that again. There's been enough talk of fools and folly, and this particular folly's over for me. You can do as you like, but I'm going. Now get out of my way."

"Pierre Bussac! You don't mean this?"

"No? Will you get away from that door, or do I have to make you?"

Her voice blazed with fury and contempt: "Don't dare lay a hand on me, you clod!"

He laughed, and there was a self-confidence, almost a triumph, in his voice that must have shaken her. He said: "Do you want to wait here with me for the police?"

"The police? Here?"

"Yes. Here."

She said on a long-drawn breath of hatred: "The English girl. . . ."

"As you say." His feet scraped the floor, and Jennifer, rigid in her shadowed corner, waited for exposure. But he had only moved to the table. She saw his hand lift towards the lamp to turn it out. He said over his shoulder: "Now will you go?"

But she moved quickly to cross the room. Her long robes swished across the glow of the fire. She was in Jennifer's field of vision now, as she leaned over the table towards Bussac. Her face, lit from below by the lamp, was like a mask thrown dramatically on a screen, a thing of sharp shadows and hard highlights, with great pits of darkness for eyes.

She said, almost breathlessly: "No. Wait. Has that girl really found anything out?"

"Just about everything, I imagine," he said coolly.

"About me?"

"Oh, yes. She was up here last night and heard our conversation."

Her hands went down flat on the table with an urgent little slapping sound. Beside them the knife-blade jumped and glittered.

"She's been up here tonight as well?"

"Yes."

"And what have you done with her? Let her go to tell her story?"

There was a fractional pause. The blade gleamed stilly by the thin hand. Jennifer's whole body shook to the thudding of her heart. The darkness was alive and vibrant with her terror; it seemed as if they could not fail to feel it. Then Bussac said slowly: "There was no point in keeping her. She'd already told it."

The woman made a sharp little sound, and her teeth gleamed as she bit her lower lip. "Then—I can't stay here either. I don't want to face an inquiry. I can't. You must know I can't."

He said unpleasantly: "Then that's just too bad for you. You should have thought of that before you blackmailed me into giving you half my takings. You should have stopped to consider that you were making yourself equally guilty— and that there'd come a time when diamond could cut diamond, Doña Francisca!"

He, too, had moved right up to the table. He was leaning across it towards her, and his face came into Jennifer's range of vision, dark, formidable, with a look in the black eyes that Jennifer had seen before—the same flash of naked ferocity on which he had attacked Stephen, but this time without either fear or uncertainty to cloud it. This—it was patent—was no longer the angry brute that Doña Francisca had been used to hold at bay; this was a dangerous animal all at once very sure of itself. As their glances met and locked she must have seen this, for her gaze widened as if in surprise, and she drew back a little, shifting her ground.

"You're talking nonsense. Equal guilt! It was never the

same, never! It's just that I don't *choose* to face an inquiry, and perhaps have to return what I've purchased with your money!"

He gave his hard little laugh. "Yes?"

She said fiercely: "They can't touch me! All I did was take the money from you, a common criminal—a murderer, and use it for good! For good! I took nothing for myself! It was for the house of God!"

"That's as may be, but you knew where I was getting it. You knew I was helping criminals, and murderers, to escape. You were condoning murder, Doña Francisca. . . ." He smiled unpleasantly. "They call it being accessory after the fact, don't they?"

Her nostrils quivered to a sharp breath, and the thin lips thinned still further. Jennifer, through her terror, could not help a sharp thrill of elation at seeing her thus out-faced and brow-beaten. She leaned forward again with one of her swift striking movements, her face sharp in the lamplight. "All the same, Pierre Bussac, we're in this together. Diamond can cut diamond both ways, my friend! I'll not sit here waiting for the police while you walk out and leave me! . . . You've got to take me with you!" Her voice dropped to a thin urgent whisper. "I know the way you go," said Doña Francisca. "Take me with you—to Spain. . . ." And something that might have been sorrow plucked at the strings of her voice.

But Bussac, if he heard it, paid no heed. He laughed in her face. "Not on your life!" he said. His hand went again to the wick of the lamp. "Now get out. You're wasting my time, and I've still—something—to do before I go."

The Spaniard straightened with a jerk, and the old fierce look of contempt was back in her face. "Then go, fool! After all, what have I got to fear? I can swear I took your money innocently—as a salve to your conscience! There'll be a scandal, but such things pass, and I—I am who I am!

You will be gone, and who'll believe that whey-faced English girl!" The hooded lids lifted, and her eyes gleamed hard as onyx. "And I'll see you're hunted, Pierre Bussac! Even in Spain, my friend, I can reach you! In Spain, I am still somebody, I and my family! You will see, Pierre Bussac, that I still have teeth!"

There was a smile in his voice. "If you mean the letter from Lenormand, you might find the teeth have been drawn."

There was a pause. "What d'you mean?"

"That." There was a rustle of paper, a quick gasp. Then she said rapidly: "That's only one piece. I've got——"

"No doubt. But is half a letter any use—without its signature?"

"Where did you get it? *Give it me!*" Her hand flashed, quick as a snake, but just as quickly he whipped the paper back out of her reach, and laughed again. "Oh, no, you don't! This is my passport to freedom, *señora, and* my warrant for your good behaviour! You can try your Spanish tricks if you will, but I warn you that as sure as you try to trace me, I'll bring you down as well. And if you think you can prove yourself an innocent party to my—trade, shall we call it?—you'd better think again. Accessory to murder, my fine madame! There's a witness to where this letter was hidden——"

"That proves nothing! It wasn't in my possession!"

"No ? Life in a convent's a bit communal for that, isn't it? But I wouldn't mind betting it'd pay to dig a bit deeper where this was found!"

Her breath hissed in a sharp little gasp. He gave his rough laugh. "That bites deep, doesn't it? Your little cache, your private hoard, your fine power-house of money stolen from me . . . including, of course, half of what Dupré's lot paid—*in notes stolen from the Bordeaux bank, damn them, and the number of every one published in the police record!*"

"No!" It was little more than a breath. Her eyes were black pits in a grey face.

He said: "It's true. I found out tonight. Corentin heard it from Aristide Celton." His teeth showed. "So you'd better hurry back to your treasure-chamber, hadn't you, before the *flics* find it—or maybe our little witness has taken them there already?"

"*No!*" This time the word was a scream, with some quality in it that turned the listener's blood to ice. The woman's breath was coming now in short gasps. She was almost crouching, and sweat gleamed thickly on her face in the lamplight. There was something more than fear and anger in that drawn and furious mask . . . to Jenny, watching in sick fascination, came hauntingly a phrase that hitherto she had dismissed as fancy. *Possessed with devils . . .* this woman was so possessed, driven by the demons of that devouring will-to-power from which springs all human tragedy. And now the dream of power was dissolving into mockery, slipping like dust through her hands.

Her hands. . . .

Her hands moved, as if blindly, on the table-top. Her right hand touched the knife that lay beside it. Still blindly, it groped, closed. . . . The knife shivered in her grip like a guttering flame.

Bussac had turned his head away. He was putting out the lamp. The lighted wick dwindled, faded, dimmed to an amber thread. Then it sank into darkness, and the firelight took possession of the room. The woman was a black shadow across the red glow. The knife was invisible.

She came round the table behind him. The rich silk rustled. She caught his arm.

"You can't go like this." Her voice was hoarse and strange, almost pleading. "You can take me. You can——"

"You? You can go to hell, my lady." And he laughed.

"Now go your own way to damnation, and leave me to go mine!"

And he pulled his arm away with a rough movement that sent her staggering.

She reeled back against the table's edge with a cry. There was a moment of silence, then, on a shuddering breath, she began to speak, still in that hoarse strange voice, a stream of soft, thick, unemphatic Spanish that brought Bussac swinging round to face her.

And as he turned, she leaped for him.

She was on him. The two shadows flowed together, towered grotesquely. Something glinted, flashed home with a small thickening thud. A curse, a gasp, and the locked shadows fell apart as Pierre Bussac crumpled where he stood, and went down in the firelight to lie at his murderer's feet.

She stood there for a long moment, like something stricken, black and immobile against the firelight. Then she moved slowly, stiffly backwards, to stand gazing down at him. The red light glared on her face and made flame of the knife in her hand.

And Jennifer saw.

She saw the saliva crawling, like the track of a slug, down the side of the woman's chin. She saw the thin mouth split open like a crack in rotting wood. She saw the eyes.

The woman lifted her head and looked slowly round the cottage kitchen. Her gaze hesitated on the door of the room where Jennifer lay.

And as she looked, some stray gust of the storm-wind, rattling the shutters, breathed a draught across the kitchen, and the door swung open a little further. The faint glow of the fire probed the shadows. The door creaked yet more widely. The woman was gazing straight at her now: the cruel firelight leaped and flickered to catch the gleam of her terrified eyes.

She shut them, hardly breathing, hardly living.

The door creaked again.

Something in its desolate sound must have spoken of emptiness, of a deserted house with a dead man on the floor and a woman fleeing alone into the bare mountains. . . .

With a sound like a tiny moan of pain, Doña Francisca turned and leaped for the outer door.

CHAPTER XXIII

NIGHT ON THE BARE MOUNTAIN

A DESERTED house; a dead man on the floor, and a woman fleeing alone into the bare mountains. . . . If it had been nightmare before, this was the very stuff of horror. Melodrama? That term with its attendant irony, belonged to another lifetime, where such things didn't happen. This had happened. This was real. She was in it; now; here.

She lay, her body one shivering ache, her mind beaten into numbness, her eyes fixed in a sort of fascination on the huddle of the murdered man. This was real. This was happening. To her, Jennifer. Here and now.

She had forgotten about Stephen and the long break-neck road from Luz; she hardly, even, thought about Gillian and the knife following her through the darkness; she lay in a kind of vacuum of fear, in what would have seemed a suspension of time itself but for the clock that steadily flicked second after second out into the dark well of the little room.

With that same empty creaking, like the scream of a mouse in a deserted wainscot, the door inched wider. A log broke, sending up spurts of yellow flame, little probes of light that fingered the crumpled body on which her helpless vision centred. The door squeaked again, with another ghostly movement that breathed cold pimples up her spine. The fingers of firelight plucked at the dead man till you could have sworn he was moving. . . .

He was moving.

Jenny's head jerked sideways on the pillow, her eyes strained till the eyeballs seemed to crack in their sockets. Her body went rigid. She held her breath, her whole being concentrated in a new ache of terror on the body that lay huddled half on its face on the kitchen floor.

He was moving. As she watched, held in the nightmare-helpless grip of her bonds, there was a tremor of the hunched shoulders and a perceptible movement of the man's head. And now a hand moved; it quivered against the flagged floor, then spread, stiffly, in pain, and dragged its flattened way in under his body, as if to clasp the wound the knife had made. There was the sound of a sharp, gasping little breath, which whistled suddenly through clenched teeth, while the man's body went still again, hunching itself round its hurt as a hedgehog curls to protect its tender parts.

Then he seemed, from some source, suddenly to gather strength. The other hand went down, and he lifted the upper part of his body, slowly, until it was clear of the floor. For a very long time, it seemed, he stayed there, stretched rigid, shoulder muscles bulging, frozen into a grim arabesque of pain and effort, then he got one knee beneath him, and lifted himself with a grunt of pain. For a moment it appeared as if the effort had been too great; he lurched forward, and might have fallen again but for the leg of the table, which struck and held his shoulder. Instinctively, it seemed, a hand shot up to grip the table-top and with an effort that even to watch brought the sweat pricking between Jenny's shoulder-blades, the man had pulled himself upright, and was leaning over the table, doubled on to his fists, breathing with ragged hurtful gasps.

And there he stayed without movement other than the convulsive clapping of a hand to his injured side, and the distressed heaving of his fight for breath, while the clock in the corner ticked gently on, and the small noises of the fire held the quiet kitchen, infinitely more compelling than the fitful roar of the storm without. And still the man stayed there, leaning on his hand, and Jenny lay stiff in her bonds and watched him, and the wind plucked at the shutters and then raced on up the gullies and into the clefts of the bare mountains, like a dark vengeance pursuing Gillian. . . .

Pierre Bussac lifted his head. Slowly his body straightened, one hand still clamped to his side. The other groped blindly among the debris on the table, stirring up a clatter of crockery whose homely domestic note sounded oddly in the charged silence. The searching hand found; clenched. He shook his head sharply, once, as if to dispel the last of the rack of pain. Then, still slowly, with a sort of terrifying deliberation, he lifted a knife from the table and turned towards the bedroom door.

This part of the nightmare had happened before. Once before she had shrunk in her bonds as she watched him approach the bed where she lay. But there comes a point where terror anaesthetizes itself, a point beyond which it has no more effect. And Jennifer, mercifully, was beyond terror now. She simply lay still, her back arched stiffly away from the bed, as if in resistance to the blow that was coming. Her eyes flinched from him. That was all.

He had paused to lean against the door-post, his big body blocking out the firelight. His breathing was rapid and harsh. He seemed to stay there interminably, a shadow of menace, before he gathered himself with a visible effort, and came forward, faltering only a little, across the room.

Once he turned his head back, as if listening, and she saw the sideways gleam of his eyeballs. Then his shadow fell over her. She felt his hand groping, gripping her wrists. He pulled her over on to her side, jerking at the rope that bound her. The cold line of the knife slid between her hands and the rope. It sawed viciously at the bonds.

"Marie," he muttered thickly. "She'll have gone after Marie. . . ."

The ropes slackened, parted, fell away. As he thrust the

kitchen knife under her ankle-bonds Jennifer reached numbed hands and managed to rip away the ghastly gag. She spat out the rags with which her mouth had been stuffed and passed a dry and bruised tongue round a mouth that felt unmentionable, fighting back a wave of nausea. She began to chafe the blood back into her wrists.

Bussac muttered in that thick slurred voice: "She'll get . . . Marie." He hacked at the rope, but the knife was blunt, and his hands were unsteady. Jennifer tried to say, "Give it to me," but failed to make any sound but a little croak. She leaned forward and took the knife from his un-resisting fingers, and sawed afresh at the now-fraying rope that bound her ankles. Bussac straightened himself.

"Marie . . ." he said again, and lurched like a drunken man back across the little room and into the kitchen.

And then Jennifer was free. It could not have been so very long that she had lain there—those aeons of terror-filled time—because the rope had not yet deadened her limbs. Her feet tingled, and her body ached, but she got up from the bed with little more than a slight giddiness, and walked with a reasonably steady gait into the kitchen after Bussac.

He turned from the table, with a chipped cup in his hand, and she caught the heady reek of brandy.

"Got to go," he said thickly. "You've got to help. I'm hurt. That damned Spaniard hurt me. You'll have to help. Here." He sloshed more brandy into the cup and held it out to her. She took it without hesitation, and gulped a mouthful. It's sour pungency bit and burned her sore mouth, then ran like fire down into her body. She gasped and shuddered, and drank again, and this time the spirit pierced her like a new life, hot and red, that licked through her veins till it tingled in her finger-tips and set her body glowing.

She managed a hoarse, breathless whisper: "Yes. She

ran out with the knife. She looked crazy enough to do anything. Which is the way? Tell me the way to go."

"You'll never find it. It's my own . . . secret way. I'll have to show you. . . ." But his hand was still clamped against his side, and in the glimmer of firelight his face looked sunken like that of a dead man.

Jenny said, on a little sob: "Oh, dear Lord. . . . Where did she hit you? Let me see."

"Let be, woman," he said roughly. "There's no time."

She said sharply: "Don't be a fool. You'll not get fifty yards like that."

She thrust him down into a chair, and he went, unresisting. She pulled open his coat and ripped away the shirt, which was slimy and matted over a place that showed black and oozing in the firelight. It was a small wound, with the dark blood slowly gathering and swelling, to trickle sluggishly from its lip as the water gathers and then drips from a leaking tap.

If she had gone beyond fear, she was also past feeling shock. Quickly and calmly, as if she had treated knife-wounds every day of her life, she tore an unstained piece from the shirt, tipped brandy over it, and gently dabbed the edges of the wound clean.

Pierre Bussac did not move, but his hand clenched sharply, once, and stayed close.

"The Englishman," he said in that blurred, painful voice, that yet held a hint of irony. "We could . . . even . . . do with him. Perhaps he . . . did get . . . transport."

"He had a horse. Luis's."

He gave the ghost of a laugh. "That won't get him very far."

"The stallion," said Jenny shortly.

He made a little movement, as if of surprise. "*That* one? He must be . . . a man . . . after all."

"Man enough," said Jenny through her teeth, "to get

lamed in his country's service, where others spend their
wars at home making money out of robbing refugees and
murdering them."

She flung the brandy-soaked rag on the fire, where it
flamed to vivid blue light.

It showed a gleam of amusement in his eyes, overlying
both anxiety and pain. She shot him a glance of reluctant
respect. A brave brute, this. King Rat? No, Stephen had
been wrong. *A man, take him for all in all. . . .*

"You'd better shut up," she said crisply. "You'll need
all the strength you've got."

The gleam persisted. "All right, Snow Queen . . . all
right. Perhaps you'll neither of you get such a . . . bad
bargain, after all. . . ."

She was not listening. She sat back on her heels, glancing
swiftly round the primitive kitchen for something with
which to make a thick pad. A clean handkerchief in her
pocket; good, that would go against the wound. But what
else? Her eye fell on the cloth spread over one end of the
table; it had looked fresh, she remembered. She grabbed
a corner of it, and, without a second's hesitation, yanked
ruthlessly at it, so that cups, bread, spoons, fragments of
meat, all slid together in a clattering confusion. She ripped
the cloth from under them, sending the whole gallimaufry
down in a crash of crockery, Bussac, with a surprisingly
quick movement, whipping the brandy-bottle out of the
tumbling chaos even as it fell.

With swift fingers she folded the cloth, wrapped the
handkerchief round it, then pressed the pad as tightly as she
dared against the wound. She felt the man's strong body
flinch, but all he said was "*Hurry*", as he tilted the bottle
greedily to his mouth.

"A scarf," said Jennifer. "Is there a scarf to tie it with?"
He jerked his head. "On the door."

She flew across the room, groping in the dark corner

among the clothing hanging there. She found the scarf. A few seconds later she was dragging the knots tight, and he was pulling his coat close and heaving himself to his feet. His face was livid in the firelight, but it was grim with purpose, and he moved, if not with more ease, at any rate with a kind of dogged strength that could out-face pain.

As she got to her feet his arm came round her shoulders, urging her towards the door.

"*Viens donc.*"

Then they were outside in the stormy dark, with the deeper darkness of the mountains looming ahead of them.

*   *   *

Bussac led the way round the corner of the cottage, where the track turned up past the byre towards the steep pasture behind. The worst of the storm appeared to be over, but the wind still blew strongly, in gusts, from the north, and a sparse, big rain was whirling along in its grip. It was no longer pitch-dark, for the higher clouds were breaking up, and now and again a racing rack laid bare a patch of stars. But the track was rough, and without the aid of Bussac's torch Jennifer's progress would have been painfully slow.

As they passed the buildings, two shadows detached themselves from the black gap of a door; the dogs, slinking out to investigate. Jennifer shrank, but Bussac stopped them with a curse that sent them flying back.

"Does she"— Jennifer was already gasping with exertion—"know the way, the secret way?"

"She does. I was sick once . . . years back, and she nursed me . . . she and an old lay-sister that's since dead. That's when the trouble started . . . I let out more than I should when I had the fever . . . and she, damn her soul, she listened and remembered . . . and looked around the place for proof. . . ."

"The letter?"

"Yes. Now . . . save your breath, girl. We're . . . not going to . . . catch her. . . ."

He was making up the dark and sodden pasture at a great rate, showing no sign of his wound except in the pain of his roughened breathing, and the movement of the hand which ever and again sought his side. Jennifer clambered and slithered beside him, her eyes fixed on the circle of torch-light that danced ahead of them. The track was plain enough to see, but muddy, and treacherous with smooth wet rock, and the impetuous buffeting of the wind on their backs made the going still more uncertain. Once, Bussac slipped. He recovered himself immediately, but he must have jarred his injured side, for she heard him bite off a curse, and in the meagre diffusion of the torch's light his face looked ghastly. But even as she checked in her stride and half-turned towards him with a query on her lips, he said, hoarsely: "No. Hurry. . . ."

Hurry . . . and here was the end of the pasture land and the beginning of the rock. At once the mountains were all about them, black buttresses blocking out the stars and breaking the force of the wind, devil's gullies that whistled with their own demoniac storms, great walls of cruel rock that echoed to the slam of the gale and the crackle of the big rain. And everywhere, it seemed, the roar of water . . . below, before, in every crevice and cleft of rock water hissed and clamoured, hurling its twisting white ropes in ghostly knots from every crag.

Hurry . . . now the torch, never strong, was perceptibly dimmer. She was gasping for breath, a stitch stabbed red-hot in her side, sweat ran warm on her body and tasted salt on her bitten lips. But the break-heart pace never slackened. There had been no time for doubt or hesitation; it had never occurred to her to wonder what the outcome of the chase would be. Everything—Doña Francisca, Gillian, the potential dangerousness of the man at her side—everything was blotted out by the immediate necessity for haste.

Some time ago they had left the track. Bussac had turned aside from it, and without hesitation plunged through what had appeared to Jennifer to be a wilderness of narrow, boulder-blocked gullies. Once a fallen tree lay clear across the way, and once they plunged up to the knee through an icy rush of water, but where the mule must have gone they could go too, and Bussac never faltered, leading the way steadily through the maze of windy shadows.

But as the way grew steeper and the going more difficult Jennifer realized that her companion was at last failing. It must only have been, indeed, by a miracle of endurance that he had got so far, and at such a speed. When they paused to negotiate a steep step of rock, she could see how the torch shook in his hand, and heard his breathing, now desperately hoarse and short, beside her. His free hand was pressed hard to his side, and his big body was no longer upright. But he thrust himself, somehow, after her, up and over the steep-pitched rock, and the dreadful driven scramble went on.

The path—such as it was—was leading them now through a steep gully. On their right a towering cliff pressed close, crowding them off the narrow path which clung along its face, a high track trodden between the living rock and a wall of fallen boulders which offered a welcome protection from the depths on the left whence came the steady roar of some considerable torrent. In the gully the cliffs gave protection; only as the travellers rounded a sudden corner, or struggled past a gap in the wall, a sharp buffet of wind would catch the breath and confound the feet.

But if the depths of the gully were sheltered, the upper air was still alive; the roar of the storm had risen to a high tearing scream among the peaks; it was as if the gusts of wind leaped, long-railed with rain, clear across the gully's top, steeple-chasing from crest to crest, with the whole devil's pack of the elements un-kennelled and a-yelp behind them. The electric storm had long since dissolved, but now the torrent below made its own thunder, and when the wind whipped bare a patch of the racing sky, the stars that swarmed there seemed to blaze with a fire as baleful as any lightning. Fire, air, water . . . the three elements combining in all their fury to bewilder and benumb the trespasser. . . . Jennifer found herself clinging to the cliff-face as to an anchor as she drove herself along the dizzy track. Only the earth, the solid earth, was safe. . . . *Or was it?*

The first warning she had was when the torch jerked in Bussac's hand, and he stopped dead. She heard him say, on a tearing sob: "*Sainte Vierge.* . . ."

She turned quickly: "What is it? Can't you go on?"

She saw his hand move in the starlight, lifting in a queerly final gesture towards the dark upper reaches of the gully.

And then she heard it, too.

Under the roar of the torrent, over the intermittent shrieking of the wind, she heard it—or rather, felt it, the terrible sound that was not a sound, but only a vibration filling the air, and shivering the very roots of the mountains as the sixty-four foot diapason shakes a cathedral. The last element had joined the barrage, with the very voice of chaos.

The mountain itself was moving.

For the second time that night Jennifer was pressed close in Bussac's arms, but this time she clung to him of her own volition, trembling, her head hidden in his shoulder. He was trembling too; his arms gripped her as if for his own reassurance, and his heart slammed like a piston under her cheek.

They stood, locked together, listening, while ahead of them the noise of the avalanche grew and loudened to its irresistible climax . . . and then slid away in a chain of ghostly echoes, while over it the voice of the torrent roared on, triumphantly repossessing the night.

As the sound died away to its terrible end, he said, in a voice that was unrecognizable: "Ahead of us . . . Marie. . ."

"Listen!" Jenny lifted her head, and felt him stiffen. His heart was shaking his whole body.

"What was it?"

She pulled away from him. "I heard a cry, and—there! What's that?"

Faint but unmistakable, above the deeper noises of the night, came the rattle of hoof-beats.

"The mule!" said Bussac hoarsely. His hand gripped her wrist. "Marie! You're sure there was a cry?"

"Yes. I heard someone cry out."

He swung away from her with an oath that sounded like a prayer, and flung off up the track as if he were just setting out and were uninjured. Then he seemed to falter. He stumbled, swayed, and put out a hand to the wall of rock beside him. She ran forward. He was leaning heavily against the rock; in the uncertain starlight his face was a grim effigy of pain, with a black gape of a mouth through which the breath whistled horribly. He was staring down at the hand which had been pressed to his side. It showed black.

There was nothing to say, nothing to do. Jennifer thrust a shoulder under his sound armpit, trying to hold him up. But he shook his head.

"I'm—done." It was a ragged whisper, no more. His weight seemed to slump, and he coughed, turning his head away against the wet rock.

She strove desperately to hold him up, ruthless with terror.

"You've got to help me! You can't stop! Monsieur Bussac——"

Hoofs slithered and clattered on the track above. She glanced up over her shoulder, to see a shape blocking the starlight.

"The mule!" She loosed him, careless of how he swayed and slumped down against the rock. She jumped into the middle of the track, and spread her arms wide.

The mule came down the rock-strewn path at a slithering run. Its head was up, and it looked scared, with gleaming eyeballs and flattened ears. A shod hoof struck fire. It was coming fast down the slope, filling the track, lunging heavily towards her in a rattle of broken stones.

"Stop!" said Jennifer, stupidly, in English, and stood her ground.

It was coming faster. It was almost on her. It saw her, and she heard its nostrils crack as it snorted in sudden fright. Its forefeet shot out stiffly, ripping fire from the rock, and it came to a slithering, rasping halt, with its haunches gathered under it, and its breast almost touching her shoulder.

As it began to back, veering and snorting, her hand shot out to grasp the reins. She seized them, pulled the mule's head down, and dragged it to where Bussac was. And because she had no time to be afraid of the beast, it obeyed her, and came quietly.

Bussac was as she had left him, huddled together at the foot of the cliff, his head turned to one side, his cheek against the wet rock. Jennifer knelt beside him, the mule's rein looped over one arm, and grasped at the front of his coat.

"Monsieur Bussac! Get up! Here's the mule! Can you get on, d'you think? *Monsieur Bussac!* Oh, God, make him get up!" she cried frantically.

A shiver seemed to run through the man's huddled frame. He raised his head, and a hand went up to it. He seemed to be dazed. His breathing was shallow now, and quick. He looked, it seemed vaguely, at Jennifer and then his dark gaze moved beyond her to the mule. He stared at it for a moment, then his tongue came out to wet his lips, and he said, in that same painful whisper: "The saddle. . . ."

Jenny glanced up at it. "What d'you mean? What about the saddle?"

He fetched a long rasping breath. "The girth's slack. She's put the . . . stirrups up . . . and tied the rein on . . . its·neck."

"Yes? What of it? Monsieur Bussac——"

"Don't you see? She's . . . got there. She's sent it . . . back. Corentin's mule . . . borrowed . . ." His voice was shaken away from him in a muttered curse as he coughed again.

"Yes, but——" Jennifer drew in her breath. "I *see*! You mean that Gillian—Marie—must have already reached the place? Beyond the landslide?"

He nodded, fighting for breath.

"And the mule was already on its way back when the avalanche came down. . . ." She turned her head up the valley. "The cry I heard—the cry I heard. Monsieur Bussac . . . it was this side of the avalanche, I'm certain of it . . . a cry and a clatter of hoofs, both at once."

He said thickly, "Doña Francisca. Landslide may have got her. Or else the mule . . . starting to bolt when the fall came . . . met her. Frightened her. . . ."

Jenny said, on a long breath: "*This side of the avalanche.*"

He moved a little, so that his shoulders were against the rock. "Listen." His hand came out, and gripped her arm with surprising strength. "It's a chance. You'll have to go on. I can't. That damned—hellcat. I'm done." His grip tightened convulsively, as if pain had wrenched at him, and his voice came jerkily, but hard and clear: "I think I know where the landslide'll be. There was a place—never mind. It's between here and the cascade, and it'll have blocked the way. Marie's already through. She was to wait by the cascade, and turn the mule back."

He paused. The grip on her arm was slackening, but the man's eyes held hers, hard and compelling. "The *señora*'ll have to scramble over it—or come back. Either will take time. You'll have to get there . . . first. You can, I think. There's another way."

"Tell me."

He gave a little sideways jerk of the head. His fingers dug at her arm. "At the next corner . . . on the left. A path down between two pointed rocks. It runs . . . below this, almost down to the water. Harder going, but shorter, and all right, if you can see."

"It's light enough. It goes to the cascade?"

"Yes. Listen now." He dragged himself up a little, his face thrust out of shadow into the starlight like a mask of pain and effort. "The way into Spain . . . a rock bridge across the face of the cascade. Safe enough if you take it . . . slowly. But you must . . . hurry. This storm . . . the river'll be filling up fast, and at high water the cascade . . . drowns . . . the bridge."

He drew her closer. His voice was weaker now.

"Get across with her. You'll be in time. If the water's rising, the *señora* may be too late. If not, and if you can't hide in time . . . well, it's a narrow bridge, and it's easy to . . . hold."

"Yes," said Jenny, hoarsely.

"If that murdering bitch does catch you——"

"Yes?" Her voice was a croak.

"Why, you'll have to . . . kill her . . . Snow Queen," said Bussac, and his grip went slack and fell from her sleeve.

He was still breathing, but there was nothing she could do. She let go the mule's bridle, then she searched Bussac's pocket for his knife. It was in his left-hand pocket, and her hand came out warm and sticky. Blood . . . but she hardly noticed: she had the knife.

She straightened up, gripping it, pushed past the quiescent mule, and almost ran on, up the narrow track, alone in the now strong starlight.

CHAPTER XXIV

BRIDGE PASSAGE

THE way off the track was easy to find. It plunged off to the left, winding down among the fallen scree like a dizzy natural staircase. She went down it at a break-neck speed, with a sure-footedness born of a desperation that had forgotten fear.

Here and there a sturdy sapling helped her; she would slither boldly down in a miniature avalanche of shale until she fetched up against its solid shaft, then, swinging round as by a newel-post, would plunge unhesitatingly down for the next foothold. Bruises she must have collected by the score, but she never felt them; mercifully she did not fall. She hurtled down the scarp in a series of short, zig-zag rushes, ricocheting as it were from rock and tree and back to rock again, until at length she landed with a scrambling thump on what was discernibly a track.

If anything larger and less agile than the chamois ever used the track there was no evidence of the fact. But a way could be picked through the tumble of rocks, and Jennifer, able now to see pretty clearly, managed to propel herself along it at a very fair speed. Propel—because only rarely did she dare make any move without the aid of her hands; the path was shaken, almost, by the roar of the torrent close beside it, and the air was chill and luminous with flung spray. Beyond the raging water rose the gully's further wall, black and sheer, a giant precipice. She clung closely to the rough overgrown rock on her right as she pulled herself along the almost non-existent path.

This did, indeed, vanish completely before very long.

Jennifer stopped, sobbing for breath, and looked around her in an access of panic.

Then she realized that the ground she was on was soft and friable, loose stuff in which her shoes sank ankle-deep, and where raw-looking jags of rock stuck up like fangs. She glanced round her. Above and below the same tumble of earth and rock bore witness. She was crossing the track of the landslide. She made her way cautiously across the shifting, sliding stuff, and presently regained the path.

This now began to climb, mounting the hillside rapidly, in dizzy deer-steps that pushed steeply up towards the ever-loudening thunder of the invisible cascade. She heaved herself, somehow, up the break-neck staircase, once more blind and deaf to everything but the need for haste. It seemed that she had been stumbling for ever, bruised and breathless, in this nightmare of wind and rain and darkness, through the water-haunted depths of the bare mountain.

Then suddenly, round a jut of steep rock at a bend in the staircase, she came upon the cascade.

Here the gully took a sharp turn to the west, and, down in its sheer depths, the storm-wind had no way. Nor had it a voice. The only voice was the enormous thunder of water, the only wind the wind of the torrent which, a short way ahead, poured glimmering down from some remote and undiscovered watershed hundreds of feet above.

To Jennifer, pausing and blinking against the rock-face at the bend of the gully, it seemed as if the great force were pouring out of the high night sky. Then, with one of those sudden changes of mountain-storms, a rack of cloud, lifted over the wind, laid bare a swimming and luminous moon, so that to her bemused eyes it was now as if the waterfall fell in a long white thunder, straight from the pool of the moon itself.

The gully now etched itself sharply, black and white in the moonlight. On either side towered the cliffs, stark and bare; ahead, and as stark, loomed the great barrier of rock over which the torrent poured like an arras. To right, to left, ahead, the place seemed impassable.

But above, like an arc of shadow across the torrent's face, she saw the road to Spain. A dreadful little bridge of rock, fallen from the sides of the gully, and wedged into a nightmare arch that wavered insubstantial in the starlit spray. Behind it fell the cascade in a steady thunderous sheet of white, to smash itself in fury on jutting ledge and fallen rock, then to leap, in a hundred spouts of roping and whirling water, into the bellowing black pool at the bottom of the gully.

She blinked again. Yes, there it was. Beside the cascade, at the end of that unbelievable bridge, wavered through the edge of the spray a tiny light. A lantern. It moved, swaying a little, its uncertain nimbus of yellow light dimming and shifting as spray burst and smoked in front of it.

She was there. Gillian was there. Waiting.

Jennifer ran on, with a prayer tasting bitter as the rain and sweat upon her lips.

*   *   *

She had actually begun the steep final scramble that led up to the level of the "bridge" before it occurred to her to wonder what on earth she was going to say to Gillian.

Gillian had, after all, last seen her as the victim of Bussac's anger in the cottage kitchen—an accomplice of the police, and an obstacle to their safe flight from France. How would she receive Jenny's apparent inclusion in Bussac's plans for that flight?

She paused, fighting for breath, leaning against a high step of rock which barred her way, and looked upwards. The path seemed to smooth itself out in the moonlight, a deceptively easy ladder of rock rising straight up to the cascade; Jacob's ladder, propped against the moon. . . .

She rubbed her burning face with her coat-sleeve, as if to wipe away the crowding fancies of exhaustion, and, fixing her eyes on the lantern's point of light, began the last stage of her climb.

The lantern stayed where it was, swaying a little as its bearer moved. But steady enough. Gillian was still there, safe. The Spanish woman could not have reached her yet. So far, so good. . . . But how in the wide world was Jennifer going to persuade an excusably distrustful Gillian to cross the cascade with her instead of waiting for Bussac? How get her away from a danger which she obviously could not suspect?

The strain and terror through which she had passed, the actual physical exhaustion she was now fighting, had left no room or capacity for reasoned thought. It was only as she hauled herself, sobbing and almost done, up the final few feet of the climb, that the simple truth came to her, with all its implications.

Bussac would never take Gillian into Spain. The man was either dead or dying. What was certain was that, as far as Gillian was concerned, Bussac was out of the game. The issue lay, quite simply, between Jennifer and the Spaniard. All she had to do was to hide herself and Gillian from Doña Francisca until she could get her safely down to help and civilization—and England. There was no question of crossing that dreadful bridge. In the darkness, in the black gullies and crevices of the bare mountain, a troop of men could hide with perfect ease. She could spin some tale to Gillian. . . .

She dragged herself up the last steep little pitch of rock, and went forward at a stumbling run towards the lantern's light.

Gillian had put the lantern down near the edge of the

water; its yellow gleam shimmered steadily, glassed in the wet slab on which it stood. Now and again spray spurted from the torrent's edge and burst across the light in a comet's-tail of sparks. She herself was nowhere to be seen.

Jennifer ran forward, to drop on her knees by the lantern, shielding its light with her body from the way pursuit would come. Then a dark figure detached itself from the blackness of an over-hang near by, and Gillian's voice, clear above the thunder of the cascade, cried: "*Quoi donc, mam'selle?*"

Jennifer was fumbling with the lantern, gasping: "Quickly, Madame Bussac! Put this out. We've got to hide!"

"But why are you here? Pierre said——"

"Pierre's coming later. He was stopped. He sent me to warn you. I'm no enemy of yours, you know. I explained things to him after you'd gone. I want to help. Now, *put this out!*"

There was something in tone, in face, in shaking desperate hands, that gave their own command. Gillian stooped, found the screw and turned it. The warm little light ebbed and died away into the chilly *clair-obscur* of white moon and black mountain.

"Where's Pierre?" demanded Gillian.

"He can't come yet. We are to hide now, and make our way down to him later. We——"

"Is he in danger?"

"Yes," said Jenny truthfully. "We must go back." She stood up and caught her cousin's arm in an urgent grip. "Come now—straight away. We must find cover."

Gillian turned immediately towards the cleft of shadow where she had hidden before. Jenny, snatching up the dead lantern, followed, with a little sob of thankfulness at the ease with which her thin story—no story at all—had been accepted. Gillian turned again and reached out a hand.

"*Venez donc,*" she said. "We can get up here——"

She stopped and stiffened, staring beyond Jenny's shoulder. Jennifer whirled.

From somewhere above them, from the tumble of new rock where the landslide had been came a rattle of dislodged stones. Then across a patch of moonlight came a shadow, black, swift, shapeless, with a dark cloak blown round it.

"Here's Pierre!" cried Gillian, and ran out again into the clear moonlight.

Afterwards, Jennifer could never quite say what happened next.

She herself dropped the lantern with a crash, and jumped forward. She saw Gillian's face, lifted in the moonlight, change from expectancy to bewilderment, from bewilderment to apprehension, to fear, to terror. She saw Doña Francisca coming down the scree towards them like some great evil bat, the knife gleaming in her hand. Then at sight of Jennifer, she screamed: "You! I knew it! You!"

With a swoop like a great black bird of prey, she plunged towards them down the break-neck scree.

And Gillian turned, with a little sob of fear, and ran straight out across the face of the cascade, as if the slender arch of fallen rock were a highway bridge, and the uncertain moonlight the glare of noon. Without knowing quite what she did, Jennifer turned and followed her.

*   *   *

To the right, the great thundering wall of water, shutting off the light; to the left, the roaring drop to the black pool . . . the bridge itself was only a scramble of rocks fallen and flung by some convulsion of the mountain across the dreadful gap of waters. It seemed to shake with the roar of the fall; the tilted rocks streaming black and treacherous under the fans of intermittently flung spray.

And across this terrible bridge Gillian fled, with Jenny at

her heels. They were out in the centre now; poised, it seemed, precariously in space above a great hanging cloud of moon-tinted spray, on which the shadow of the bridge trembled like a darker rainbow. The noise was terrific. Was it only fancy, or was the torrent pressing closer and ever closer to the bridge? Every few seconds some great shining fan of water leaped out, slapping down on the slabs. Jets of foam shot down like twisting white ropes, to smash at their feet and fray off into glittering fringes that fumed down to thicken the rainbow haze. The torrent crowded closer. The rocks streamed. Gillian was two-thirds of the way over, scrambling up a tilted boulder sleek with sliding water. Jenny, clinging below her, glanced back.

Doña Francisca had reached the bridge. Had paused there, daunted, possibly, by the sight of that fearful crossing. She was shouting something inaudible, but she made no move.

Beside Jennifer came, faintly, through the bellow of the water, an echo of the cry.

She whipped round, just in time to see Gillian gain the top of the boulder, then slip, slither for a moment with frantically clutching arms flung over the streaming rock, and fall back on to the slab where Jenny stood, to lie inert and limp, her body wedged precariously between the rocks, and her head hanging helplessly over the outward drop.

Jenny went down beside her, clutching at her coat.

She heard a laugh, clear above the water's din, and turned her head.

The woman had a foot on the bridge. Her mouth was a black grin in a white face. She gripped the slack of her robes in the other hand, and stepped carefully on to the bridge.

CHAPTER XXV

APPASSIONATA

THE black scree behind her seemed to burst into life, as another, blacker shadow detached itself from the darkness and hurtled down the slope in a welter of rattling stones. There was a gasping shout. A man leaped down the last headlong yards of scree and raced forward in the moonlight. The white light caught the dark hair, the loose-knit body that, but for the limp, moved beautifully. . . . .

"*Stephen!*"

The din of the water drowned Jenny's cry. It was the same soundless, desperate little prayer, but this time the answer was already there. . . .

He shouted again. The noise volleyed sharply from rock to rock, cutting through the steady roar of the water.

Doña Francisca, who was some way out on to the bridge, checked in her careful progress, the wind of the fall tearing her black robes out from her body with such force that she swayed as she turned. Her arms went out for balance, the sleeves flapping, and the loosened skirt of her habit streamed out wet and heavy, dragging at her body. In three great strides Stephen had crossed the empty space of moonlit rock, and was at the bridge. Jenny heard him shout again:

"Come back, you fool!"

But the woman swung round once more, and, cautious no longer, sprang forward across the bridge towards the girls, knife in hand.

Stephen moved even faster. In one bound he was on the bridge and hurling himself recklessly across it. The woman looked back once, faltered, and then came on, but the thick wet robes hampered her, clinging to her legs. Two more strides, three—and then he lunged and snatched at her arm. He missed, but his hand closed on her sleeve. Somehow she tore it free, and thrust herself forward. Her flying veil whipped him across the face, making him falter and lose way. She was yelling something. She was on them. Whether the fury of revenge still drove her, or only the panic desire to escape—or whether reason had finally snapped its chain, they were never to know. Jennifer, crouched over her cousin's body, was actually wincing backwards from the sweep of that terrible knife when Stephen's arms came round the woman from behind, pinioning her in a vicious grip. His hands closed brutally on her wrists, and he dragged her backwards against him.

But her desperate impulse lent her strength. She turned on him, turned even in his arms, her wet wrists slipping in his grasp; she whipped round as an adder turns, and, like an adder, struck. Jenny saw his body flinch as the knife went home, saw his hold momentarily loosen, saw him stagger, blinded by a flapping fold of the woman's veil as she wrenched the knife high to strike again.

Then, even as she launched the stroke, her foot slipped. Her arms went wide and high, flailing the air like wings. But the momentum of that vicious stroke thrust her on, throwing her past him, tearing her clear of his desperate grasp, propelling her to the very brink of the bridge where she hung poised—it seemed interminably—leaning forward like a diver about to plunge into that dreadful abyss. Her eyes were open, her hands out before her, flailing the empty air, then, with a high, tearing scream, she lurched forward into the ghastly dive, and fell.

One moment she was there, poised like a black evil bird above the starlit spray. The next she had vanished, swallowed by the torrent, and above her, vanishing, the moon-rainbow wavered a little, and was steady.

*   *   *

He was on his knees beside Jennifer.

"Stephen—oh, Stephen!"

"Are you all right?"

"Yes. But you——"

"It's only a scratch. Later." His hands held her with comforting strength while his eyes went past her to Gillian. He raised his voice above the thunder of the cascade. "What happened to her?"

"She fell."

"Out of the way then. And hang on to that rock. The fall's filling up. It'll be over us in another ten minutes."

It was true. The rocks that made up the little bridge were all awash. It had not been fancy after all. The cascade had indeed been moving slowly nearer, as the storm-rains swelled the source above. And now the edge of the falling torrent scraped, as it were, the inner edge of the bridge, striking and bursting over it in continuous fans of spray. Now and again the frail structure shook to the crash of some wide-flung heavier load of water. The slab where Stephen and Doña Francisca had fought was already under an inch of slithering water.

Stephen braced one foot in a crack, the other against a boulder, and laid hold of Gillian. Jennifer pulled herself to her feet, clinging to the rock.

"I can get back."

"You stay where you are." His voice compelled her. "I'll be back."

And somehow, with a heave and a grunt of effort, he had got Gillian's body over his shoulder, fireman-fashion, had steadied himself by the boulder, and had turned to make his way off the bridge. Jennifer crouched close to the rock, the water pouring now past her legs and slapping down on to her shoulders, cold, cold . . . her whole body seemed to be streaming with the icy water, her hands were dead, her very brain frozen, beaten into numbness by the roar of the torrent and the snow-broth chill of its spray. Stephen had been right. She could no more have made her own way back across the torrent than she could have flown out over the rainbow in the moonlit haze.

So she clung with dead fingers to the rock, and watched with horrified, fascinated eyes as Stephen walked solidly back over the bridge with Gillian slumped across his shoulders like a sack of coal. Only once he staggered, when a jet of water struck him on the shoulder, but he recovered himself straight away and, putting his feet with heavy deliberation down on the streaming slabs of the bridge, he moved stolidly on.

He was there. He was lowering Gillian on to the moonlit rock.

She realized then for the first time that the scree was alive with men. The shadows broke apart, rushing forward and coalescing again as men ran down the scree and crowded towards the bridge. The whole thing had happened at a speed that afterwards she could never quite believe; the others could not have been much more than seventy yards behind Stephen when he reached the bridge, and now as he carried Gillian's inert body to safety, a dozen hands reached to help him. Someone took Gillian from him. Torches flashed. A lantern waved. She was borne swiftly back to a sheltered corner. Men bent over her, knelt. . . .

The others still crowded at the bridge where Stephen was fighting his way out of his sodden coat. Two of the men pushed forward, as if remonstrating with him, but he thrust his way past them, and, once more, set out across that perilous arch, making his steady way towards Jennifer.

She watched him coming. He was a quarter of the way over—half-way, and moving in a cloud, a snow-storm of spray. The stars behind him glittered like ice-crystals. The moon looked shrunken with cold. Jennifer shrank, too, a tiny huddle of shivering flesh and icy bones whose very eyeballs were fixed and aching with the cold. . . .

Then he was beside her, his unfelt touch was on her body. He had the end of a rope in his hand, and he knotted this round her, cursing under his breath as he fought the soaking cord.

He said through his teeth: "You're perfectly safe. They have the other end. Just go steadily. Look straight ahead."

Her own teeth were chattering uncontrollably. "And—you?"

"I'm all right. Get going."

It was the hardest thing she had ever done in her life, to let go of the rock and walk back across the bridge. The mere act of straightening her cramped body shook her with the new fear of her own weakness, while to assume that her strengthless legs would ever carry her forward was an act of faith of which she felt incapable. . . . But even as she hesitated, panic locking her bones, Stephen's hands, swift and brutal, tore hers from their hold, and swung her round to face the roaring space. She saw rather than felt him seize her icy hands and clamp them on the rope which stretched from her waist to the end of the bridge, its other end held fast by three men. She could see them clearly in the moonlight. One of them grinned and beckoned. Another got down on to the bridge, one hand outstretched. He was not so very far away.

Not so very far away. . . . Confidence flowed to her along the taut rope, and when, from behind, Stephen's hands impelled her, she began to walk steadily forward, towards that waiting hand. . . .

A few seconds later, she had grasped it, and was drawn at last towards the safe rock at the side of the cataract. Willing hands reached for her, strong arms took her and swung her free of the bridge. A babel of questions met her.

But she paid no heed. She twisted in their hands like a

wet fish, to watch Stephen balance his way along the dreadful bridge, till he, too, was finally gripped and pulled to safety.

And so for the third time in the story Stephen looked up and saw her running towards him with outstretched arms. And, as is the way of all stories, the third time is the right time, luck's time, winner-take-all time. . . . This was it. The barriers were down, dust in the wind. The sleeping princess was awake, the guarded bower as if it had never been. He held out his arms and she ran into them as if they two had been alone in the darkness, not out in the brilliant moonlight exposed to the grinning gaze of a dozen men. His arms accepted her, he pulled her to him fiercely. Only now, his own barriers crumbling, did he realize how deep and absolute had been his need of her; and in the very moment of fullest realization she was here and she was his; his anchor, his still centre, his searing flame, his peace. . . .

He released her, and she stood for a moment in the circle of his arms, blinking up at him. He laughed down at her, but the blaze was still there at the back of his eyes, and she could see the thudding of his heart where the soaked shirt clung to his body. He was breathing like a runner. He said: "We've an audience, darling. Do you mind?"

She blinked again, and turned her head a little dazedly. The men who had come with him were standing round the two of them, much as cattle will gather in a curious circle round any strange phenomenon that invades their pasture. And twelve pairs of dark eyes watched them steadily, without the slightest trace of embarrassment—watched them, indeed, with approval, envy, and the passionate interest of born connoisseurs.

Mrs. Silver's only daughter flushed, laughed, and turned back into Stephen's arms. "Mind? Not a bit," she said happily, and lifted her mouth to his again.

CHAPTER XXVI

FINALE: *Tranquillo*

It was cosy in the cottage kitchen. Outside, the storm had abated, and the exhausted wind scarcely moved the shutters. Jennifer, exhausted too, lay back in a chair by the blazing fire, with the warmth of Doctor Lebrun's brandy lapping through her veins.

The memory of her arrival at Bussac's cottage was as hazy as the dreams that now invaded her. She had a vague recollection of having her soaked outer things torn off her, of being wrapped warmly in dry blankets, deposited in the big chair beside the fire and plied with hot coffee liberally laced with brandy.

She blinked round the too-familiar little room, now decidedly overcrowded by a host of purposefully moving shadows that she took to be the police. But she was beyond worrying or even wondering what was going on. Her eyes drooped again. A sleepy warmth invaded her. Her body in its nest of blankets began to relax as the heat from the fire reached out to her, her muscles one by one slackening towards sleep. . . .

*   *   *

. . . Someone was asking questions, and Stephen's voice, quiet and very tired, was answering them. She opened her eyes again, to see him just beside her, sitting on the floor with his shoulders against the front of her chair and his dark head near her knee. His legs, lamentably clad in crumpled, newly dried flannels, were a-sprawl across the front of the fire.

He was smoking, talking with a sort of controlled weariness to Jules Médoc, the Superintendent from Luz, who, perched on a small stool facing the fire, yet managed to give the impression of presiding in a court of some administrative importance. His black eyes were eager and alive, his gestures sharp and in startling contrast to the heavy, even reluctant movement of Stephen's hand as he lifted the cigarette to his mouth.

He drew on the cigarette almost fiercely, and expelled the smoke like a long sigh.

"So there you have it." With a dismissive gesture he flicked the butt into the fire. "I've told you all I know. Most of it was guess-work, but according to what Bussac told you tonight, it was substantially correct. The only thing I couldn't make out was why a man like Bussac should submit to being blackmailed over such a long period. It wasn't in character. But from what you say she had more or less cut herself in as a partner."

Jules Médoc nodded. "That's so. It appears that she really did enter the business innocently in the first place. She's used Bussac once or twice, many years ago, to help her own friends out of Spain. For all I know it was Bussac who originally helped her own escape. Then she discovered just how much he was making out of the traffic during the Occupation, and conceived the idea of helping him with that and taking her cut. She was in a position, through her Spanish connections, to help him out on the other side. . . . I mean, if he could hand his 'passengers' over to guaranteed help in Spain he could count on more 'trade' and in fact charge more. I honestly believe she started the business in good enough faith, and fooled herself for a time that she could touch pitch and not be soiled."

"And when she discovered what had happened to Isaac Lenormand she was too far in to pull out?"

"Perhaps. But I don't think so. I gathered from what Bussac said to us that he'd have been glad if she had. But once she had something 'on' him she was in a position to demand more. And did."

"And condoned Lenormand's murder in the process?"

Jules Médoc said: "One can't guess how by this time she managed to justify herself to her conscience. I think the greed for money and power had gradually tightened its grip till in the end she couldn't stop. It happens. Demand begets demand. She must still have tried to persuade herself that the end justified the means. Perhaps she was successful, but I don't think so."

"You mean that conscience catches up in the end?"

Jules Médoc said very soberly: "I mean that she must have lived on the edge of hell for a very long time. One cannot violate oneself and not become a place of torment."

There was a little silence, through which the old clock ticked solemnly.

One can say that sort of thing in French, thought Jennifer sleepily, and it doesn't even sound odd. It's true, too. She blinked at M. Médoc with drowsy respect.

Stephen said: "An ugly and reluctant partnership. It was bound to smash itself—and them with it—in the end. And now it only remains for you to take that triptych apart." He smiled. "With great care, of course."

"Care of the most delicate," promised M. Médoc. "This has been a great night's work for me, monsieur, and I shan't lightly forget what I owe to you and mademoiselle." And he sketched a little bow towards Jennifer.

Stephen turned his head. "Awake, Jenny? How are you?"

She put a hand out of the welter of blankets, and his own closed over it. "Lovely and warm." Her eyes sought the couch on the other side of the fire, where a burly, thickset man, who appeared to be the doctor, was still bending over Gillian. Memory stabbed at last through the mists of sleep and weariness, and brought her awake with a jerk.

"How is she, Stephen?"

The doctor had turned at the sound of her voice. He said, before Stephen could reply: "How is she? Lucky. That's what, lucky. All three of you luckier than you deserve."

He moved aside to reveal Gillian, cocoon-like in her wrapping of blankets. She looked very pale in the flickering shadows, but her breathing was even, and her eyes were open. She turned her head, and the firelight gleamed on the fair hair. The grey eyes were wide and puzzled. They hesitated over the doctor, groped past Jules Médoc and Stephen, paused over Jennifer. . . .

Then they widened. They were smiling.

Gillian said weakly, in English: "Why, it's never Jenny?"

*   *   *

After that, things seemed to resolve themselves very quickly. Two of Jules Médoc's men, gruffly supervised by the doctor, carried Gillian in her wrappings to the police jeep which was waiting outside, and the doctor, following them, paused to look down at Jennifer.

"Better get you to bed too, that's what. And your young man." Then, as Jennifer made a startled movement of recollection, he put up a hand the size of a small ham and waved her back into her chair. "Nothing the matter with him," he said fiercely. "Knife hardly touched him. Merest scratch. If he tells you otherwise he's malingering." He glowered down at them both. "Lucky, that's what."

Jennifer was holding tightly to Stephen's hand. "*Lucky!* That and more besides, Doctor! If he hadn't found us . . . Stephen, how *did* you find the way up to the cascade?"

"Darling, we followed your torch." He laughed as she stared at him. "It isn't as mad as it sounds. We weren't very far behind you, you know, and in those places you can see a light for miles. We saw it dodging up the gullies, and then, when we thought we'd lost it, we came on Bussac, and he told us the way."

"Simple, when you know how," said the doctor. He peered down over his glinting spectacles. "Here! What you crying for?"

She wiped her eyes. "I'm not."

He snorted. "Women! Told you she'll be all right. Meant it. Remembers up to that accident. No more."

She struggled to assess this. "The accident? The car smash?"

"That's it. Thinks that's how she was hurt. Told me so." The blue eyes were kind under the fierce white brows. "Retrograde amnesia," said the doctor gruffly, making it clear. "Gap. Complete gap."

"You mean," said Stephen, "that she thinks she's just come round after the car accident? She won't remember the time between?"

"Just told you," said the doctor impatiently. "Gap, that's what. Won't remember any of this. . . ." A gesture took in the cottage kitchen, hesitated oddly over the now-shut bedroom door. . . . "Him," said the doctor.

Jennifer stiffened in her blankets, looking at the door.

"May remember later on," said the doctor, "but won't matter so much then. Stronger. But all for the best now." He opened the door, and nodded brusquely at her. "Lucky, that's what."

The door slammed behind him. But Jennifer did not hear it. She looked across the little silence and met Jules Médoc's eyes.

"Pierre Bussac?"

Stephen said gently: "He died Jenny. He lived long enough to tell the story, then he died. They brought him down while you were asleep."

"I—see." She turned her head away.

Jules Médoc said, in simple wonder. "You would weep for that one?"

Jenny looked at him. "I'm sorry he died like that, monsieur. I—I'd have liked him to get away. I suppose that's wrong, but whatever else he did, he did save Gillian. Once, when Lally Dupré robbed her and left her in the storm, and again tonight. He may have been a murderer, but he loved her in his own way, and I for one, shall always remember him kindly."

Stephen's hand tightened over hers. "Then so shall I," he said.

Something moved in the corner beyond the couch, a singularly shapeless shadow which turned out, on inspection, to be Father Anselm. He, too, looked tired, but his little black eyes were bright, and he regarded Jennifer and Stephen with great kindness.

"God is very merciful," was all he said, and Jennifer knew that he, too, was talking about Pierre Bussac. Nobody had mentioned the other—that other whose body must be even now washed up, gaunt and black, like a drowned crow asprawl on a rock in mid-stream.

She said suddenly: "Does the Reverend Mother know?"

Father Anselm nodded soberly. "I have been to the convent. In fact, I was already on my way when the police caught me up. The girl, Celeste——"

Jennifer sat up sharply, then grabbed at her blankets as they slipped, and gripped them to her, staring with shocked eyes at the little priest.

"Celeste!" she cried. "How dreadful! I'd forgotten all about her! Oh, dear! I'm sure she was running away to Luis, and——"

"So she was," said Father Anselm, "so she was. And the boy brought her straight to me. 'You will look after her for me,' says he, solemn and proud, 'she is to be my wife, and I will have no talk in the village. So I leave her with you.'

Alors, there she is, asleep at my house, and today she goes back to the Reverend Mother's care while she prepares for her wedding. You, my child"—he was looking down at Jennifer and now there was the ghost of a twinkle—"have slept a long time. Look."

He went past her to the window, and, reaching up, pulled open the shutters. The pale light of early morning filled the room, killing the small glow of the oil-lamp, and picking out with chilly clarity the evidence of last night's terrible little story. There was the clutter of broken china and scraps of food where Jennifer had torn the cloth from the table; there the charred fragments of a rag soaked with blood and brandy; there on the floor by the table-leg a dark irregular stain. . . .

Stephen exchanged a swift look with Médoc and got, albeit stiffly, to his feet. He stood between Jenny and the tell-tale disorder of the room.

"And we," he said cheerfully, "haven't been to sleep at all. And here's the jeep coming back." He looked down at her and spoke soberly in his own language. "It's over, Jenny. Whatever's happened, it *is* over, my darling, and the best thing we can do is to go away and go to sleep. That's not callousness, it's common sense. For us, it's over. Tragedy always has a dreary aftermath, but we don't have to wait. You and I and Gillian—we move on."

"Yes," said Jennifer. They smiled at each other.

The jeep roared up the hill outside, changed gear, and rattled to a halt on the cobbles. Jules Médoc got up, stretched, and grinned at them both. "You're lucky, that's what," he said.

*   *   *

They sat in a coign of rock, high above the valley, where the smooth turf washed up to their feet like a small sea, afoam with tiny flowers. Below them the convent lay, white-walled in the sun. Nothing moved in the valley but the stream that glittered over sun-drenched boulders, and, tiny in the distance, a chestnut horse that gently carried his rider across the grass into the shadow of the convent wall.

Once again, chill and silver through the hot blue air, the convent bell began to ring. Jennifer, without turning her head, put a hand out, and, instantly, Stephen's met it. For a few minutes more they sat there, gazing down the empty valley. . . .

There came from behind them the sound of voices, of boots on rock, of voices polite in academic altercation. . . .

Round the bluff they came, sturdy, solemn, untiring, with rucksacks on their backs and hammers in their hands; Miss Shell-Pratt and Miss Moon. Their eyes were bent on the ground as they passed, their tongues were going busily. Their rucksacks were full to the brim, no doubt, with little pieces of rock that they were prepared to cart back at enormous trouble to Cambridge, there to put them away in compartments labelled Paragneiss or Ultrametamorphic Orthogneiss or even—this was a counsel of despair— No.99. S.E., V. des O.: Pyr.: (?).

They approached, talking vigorously.

"The schistosity," said Miss Shell-Pratt, "plane or linear . . ." A green lizard flashed across the rock and was gone. A great black-velvet butterfly alighted on a wild lupin. . . . "Plane linear," insisted Miss Shell-Pratt, peering at the rock, "as Gotterhammer explains in his notes to *Grund-komplex des südöstlichen Pyreneengebietes*. . . ." Here her eye ran absently across Jennifer and Stephen, and she paused, to identify them almost immediately with a subdued air of triumph. "Ah! Miss Silver! Mr. Bridges!"

"Masefield," said Stephen, who had risen.

"Ah, quite so." Miss Shell-Pratt had the air of one who takes lesser cultures in her stride. She gestured largely. "An interesting area, don't you think?"

"Oh, decidedly."

"A lot to do," said Miss Moon from behind her companion. And indeed her gaze had already moved on beyond the group towards the next rib of exposed rock, to pass on, with what was perhaps a shade of dismay, to the towering shapes of the ridges beyond. "A *lot* to do," she repeated, and looked down uncertainly at the very small hammer in her hand.

But Miss Shell-Pratt was made of sterner stuff. She became brisk. "Yes, indeed! Plenty of work there! *Most* interesting! We must be getting along. Come on, Moon."

They strode down the slope.

Stephen put down a hand, and pulled Jennifer to her feet. He put an arm round her, and they stood for a while, looking down from the shoulder of the bare mountain at the green and golden valley below.

"The enchanted valley," said Jennifer softly. "Paradise. . . ."

The small flowers stirred at their feet. The lizard slid back to lie on his stone, a crescent of living jade. The butterfly swayed on the yellow lupin beside them. Faint, but clear, Miss Shell-Pratt's voice floated back to them. "The felspars," she was saying firmly, "are allotriomorphic towards the biotite, augite, and hornblende. . . ."

The lizard vanished. The butterfly flew away. Cambridge, after all, had had the last word.